LOVE MAGNET

ALLIE MCDERMID

Copyright © 2022 by Allie McDermid

All rights reserved.

The right of Allie McDermid to be identified as the author of this work has been asserted by her in accordance with the Copyright, Designs and Patents Act 1988.

No part of this book may be reproduced in any form or by any electronic or mechanical means, including information storage and retrieval systems, without written permission from the author, except for the use of brief quotations in a book review.

All characters and events in the publication are fictitious and any resemblance to real persons, living or dead, is purely coincidental.

ALSO BY ALLIE MCDERMID

Love Charade

Love Detour

Love Magnet

Long Time Coming

1

Steph Campbell placed another vodka and Coke on the bar. She'd lost count of how many she'd made tonight.

Cal's was busier than she'd even seen. Even with a full set of staff behind the bar, she was still struggling to keep up.

It was brilliant.

Tonight was the annual Lovefest opening event in the Glaswegian suburb of Shawlands. Since its conception three years ago, Lovefest always kicked off in Cal's, a pub at the very centre of the action on Shawlands' main road. The month-long event ran for the entirety of August and focused on all things love and everything couple-y.

Romantic notions didn't entirely float with Steph and she'd done her best to avoid anything Lovefest since it began, but there was no escaping work. So sometimes, in fact more often than not, she found herself in the thick of the festival.

The opener was the same every year: a couple's event, kind of like speed dating with a twist, intended to break the ice and start the month with a bang.

Regardless of its motive, the event brought with it an ever-increasing crowd and, more importantly, a bulging till.

'Yo, what can I get for you?' Steph asked the next guy in line. He was a bull-necked, rugby-player-looking chap and he didn't hide the quick once-over he gave her, his eyes trailing the length of her with judgemental precision.

She was used to it. With her short blonde hair, baggy clothes, and tattoos, she didn't exactly scream *guy magnet*. Men either hated her look or took it as a challenge.

She'd bet good money this guy was jumping on the latter.

'A pint of Stella, please.'

'That all?' she shouted over the music and crowd.

He nodded and she got to work. Pint down and money exchanged, she was ready to move on when he leaned closer. As she was only four foot eleven, he towered over her, and he really had to angle to get near. She held steady, making him do the legwork.

'Are the staff involved in tonight's event or are you off limits?'

Steph pulled at the corner of her bottom lip with her teeth, hiding the cringe her face so badly wanted to pull. A room full of eligible women wasn't enough; he still wanted a challenge. 'Married, sorry.'

'I don't see a ring.'

'I don't wear it so I can enjoy awkward conversations like this. Hey, what can I get for you?' she asked the next person in the queue. Rugger boy was soon jostled out of the way, despite not looking convinced.

Which was fair enough. She'd been single for the last four years, but he didn't need to know.

Her next punter could ask all she wanted, though.

Brown hair, green eyes, a nice smile. Steph's eyes darted to her name badge: *Hannah*, with a yellow top.

That was the thing about the Lovefest event. There was no hiding your team. Green-topped badge: you were seeking a guy. Orange-topped badge: you were here for either. Yellow-topped badge: you were after a woman.

If only life was always this easy.

She poured a Pinot Grigio and a rum and Coke. Hannah had obviously struck up conversation with someone already.

God, it was hot. Steph skirted around her colleague, Novak, as she replaced the wine bottle in the fridge. She held it open and relished the blast of cold air for a second. Right, back to work.

Hannah flashed a killer smile as she took her drinks. Whoever had snared her was lucky.

In a moment of weakness, Steph had briefly considered joining the event. She'd never set out to be single: work and life had just got in the way. Well. Mainly work. Before she knew it a huge chunk of time had passed and thirty-five was a distant memory; she was on the slow decline to forty.

Thirty-seven, single, and only assistant manager. She'd expected to be ticking a few more boxes by now.

But the bar needed her. It was their busiest night of the year, bar Hogmanay, so there was no chance she could be on the other side and avoid serving. Her best chance was clicking with a customer, but at the rate they were having to serve, there was no opportunity for chat.

This was the thick of it. An hour since it opened. Peak drinking, prime mingling. Another hour and they'd be at the tip of the rollercoaster, finally ready to start the descent. Steph would be home by one o'clock, if everything went to plan.

A few couples were already clear. Most people were still working the room. Nerves needed quashed and bravery heightened. Alcohol was the easiest solution.

That was another reason not to attend these stupid things: Steph was utterly shite at talking to women. Conversation, yeah, that was okay. She could hold her own. But flirting? *Nada*. She'd never had game. Her tattoos did a lot of the legwork for her, but she could never coast on that alone.

'Stevie,' she called to the pink-haired woman on shift tonight. 'We need more shot glasses when you're done with replen.'

'On it.'

Steph scanned the length of the bar. No sign of bar manager Donnie. That inconsiderate prick had done his usual disappearing act, and earlier than usual by the look of it. For months now he'd got into a routine of coming in at eight in the morning and leaving at five. Nothing needed done at eight a.m. in a fucking bar. Not to mention they didn't even open until ten. She'd called him out more than once, to be told it was paperwork and other duties. Bullshit. The guy was a skiver and work-shy. If Steph didn't pick up the pieces, Cal's would be a disaster. Sometimes she wished she had the balls to walk away, but she loved this place as if it was her own and the team were too good to muck about. She had no choice but to sort Donnie's messes and keep her mouth shut.

The latter was getting harder by the day.

To be fair, she'd probably had a stick up her arse about Donnie since he'd got the manager's promotion and she didn't. Even when they were both assistant managers he was playing silly beggars.

It was no wonder she had no time to herself outside these walls.

'What can I get you?' Steph asked the next punter.

'Vodka Coke,' the guy answered, his voice unsure. 'And your nose is bleeding.'

Fuck. Not again.

2

Gemma Anderson navigated the crowd. She hadn't expected this event to be so busy. It was tough to see people's name badges when they were packed like sardines.

She kept to the perimeter, enjoying the breathing space that came with it.

Cal's was bigger than she remembered. She'd only been once since she moved south from Glasgow's West end, and that was a lifetime ago. Even then, she'd only been in its cocktail bar at the front. To its rear was a pub and burger joint. Today she was in its centre: the club and event space. It was a mammoth venue, and tonight it was packed to the rafters.

Her hands were still sweaty; her heart thrumming against her ribs despite the calming effect of her third Sauvignon Blanc.

She'd chatted to a few ladies tonight, all equally nice in their own special ways, but none gave that elusive spark. No change there.

Since ending her marriage to Logan and coming out as a

lesbian, she'd done her fair share of dating. Still, connection eluded her.

On the upside, there were some truly stunning women here tonight, so at least she knew there was no mistake there. Women were an absolute marvel. Why it had taken her nearly thirty years to figure that out was beyond her.

Gemma looked at her card again. *1000 words*. She guessed she was on the hunt for *A picture is worth*.

Every attendee received one half of a well-known idiom on entry. The challenge was to find its partner by the end of the night, and hopefully do the same for yourself in the process. It was a great icebreaker. The whole working-the-room biz was taking her in directions she'd never considered.

She'd just spent twenty minutes talking to a lovely butch lady called Caroline. Gemma was no stranger to dating apps and people like Caroline would usually have been a hard pass, but maybe it was time she went beyond looks and stepped out from the status quo.

Yes, she preferred women like herself – feminine, dare she think it, straight-passing, tall-ish and slim – but look how well that had worked out so far. The spark wasn't there with Caroline, but maybe it would be with someone else.

Gemma scanned the room, looking for another lady to speak to. She was used to networking events, holding her own in male-dominated work environments and carrying on tedious small talk, but walking up to women and starting conversation was proving harder as the night went on. Incomplete catchphrase or not.

She'd had high hopes for the Lovefest opener. Especially after the results of the last one. Every year, five new couples from this event went on to compete, having a date a week paid for by the local business group for the whole of August.

Eventually, the public chose a winning couple, and they were awarded five grand. A lesbian couple had won last year and rumour had it they were still absolutely smitten with each other.

She didn't care about the money, but meeting someone and sharing the spectacle of the competition with them would be fun. A great story to tell the grandkids.

'Having a good evening?' a guy with short brown hair and glasses asked, sidling up to her spot on the edge of the crowd.

'Yeah, it's been fun so far,' she replied with a half-smile.

'Aaron,' he said, extending a hand as he looked at her name badge. 'Nice to meet you, Gemma.' His eyes narrowed in contemplation. 'Is your badge right?'

She studied the sticker on the left boob with a tilt of her head. 'Yep. My name is definitely Gemma.'

He smiled, masking an awkward chuckle. 'No, I meant the colour.'

'Oh,' she said, as if she didn't know exactly what he was on about in the first place. 'That's also correct.'

If she'd been a bit braver she would have made a joke. Called herself a full-on raging lesbo, or something. But she wasn't quite there yet. In terms of how comfortable she was with her own sexuality, she was still paddling in the training pool, nowhere near graduating to the deep end. It would come in time. Hopefully.

Her family had been wonderful. Shocked at first, naturally. But Mum and Dad just wanted her to be happy. Granny had been a worry. She was nearing ninety and Gemma didn't want to put any unnecessary strain on the poor woman. She was her best friend, by all accounts, and it wasn't worth the risk. She could stay in the closet a while longer if it protected her. But Mum knew best, as she often did, and Granny was as cool as a cucumber about it. In fact, she was Gemma's number one cheerleader when it came to getting a girlfriend. Given how adept Granny was getting on her iPad, Gemma often worried she'd set up a dating profile and have a bash at getting a date for her granddaughter herself. Although she was forever posting stuff she shouldn't, or messaging the wrong people by accident. Gemma could only imagine what trouble a dating profile would get her into.

Aaron pulled a face between embarrassed and apologetic and made his way back to the throng. Even in Cal's dim lighting she could see he was now a lovely shade of red.

No harm done. This was an event for talking. He'd attempted conversation, which was more than could be said for Gemma.

Everyone who looked like they might have yellow or orange badges was engaged in conversation so, without leering at every passing woman's tits, she was out of possible matches.

Tonight was heading for a bust. Which was a shame: she'd all but run out of steam on dating apps. It was so very droll having to message. She'd much rather connect face to face.

If only she had an LGBTQ+ friend, they could at least go to gay bars together. She'd still not been to a pub or a club with a rainbow flag at the front door. The friends she'd retained from her marriage and the dwindling unmarried or un-child-burdened university friends she had were all very much straight, and none were close enough to be a wingman. She didn't have the courage to go on her own, get a seat at the bar, and see what happened. She'd fantasised about it enough. But to actually do it? Her heart rate was rising just at the thought.

A part of her felt robbed, which was an absurd notion to say the least, but if she'd only done herself a favour and figured things out a little sooner, she could have a gay posse. Instead she'd firmly cemented herself in cis-het hell and been carried away by the tide of weddings, mortgages, and babies. She was just lucky she'd not quite got around to the whole baby thing just yet. Logan hated her enough as it was. Throw a child into the mix and it would be unbearable.

She finished her wine and ambled round to the end of the bar, leaving her empty glass and debating grabbing another.

There was no harm in going home. She didn't live far away. Ten minutes and she could be in the comfort of her living room, enjoying a glass of cold wine from the fridge while in her PJs.

'You okay?' asked a voice from behind.

Gemma turned to find a short blonde woman covered in tattoos. What looked like an intricate moth poked out from beneath the edge of her wavy bob, skilfully tucked behind her ears, as if to reveal only enough to draw you in. A detailed pattern bloomed over her throat, and without thinking Gemma turned her head to inspect it further.

'Do you want a drink?' the woman asked, confused by Gemma's lack of response.

She kicked back into gear. 'Debating it.' It was only then Gemma noticed the two wads of blue roll tissue up each of the woman's nostrils. 'Are you okay?'

The woman waved a dismissive hand between them. 'Just a little nosebleed. No biggie.'

She stepped further behind the bar. 'We don't usually

serve this far down, but I can grab you a drink if you want to order? I'm on my way back.'

Gemma scrunched up her face. 'Hmm. I think I'm just going to head home.'

'Really? Trust me, this my third year working the Lovefest event and most matches happen in the next hour or so. Just because you've not met anyone yet, doesn't mean you won't. Patience is key.'

Gemma considered it. Perhaps she *was* being too hasty.

The blonde woman took her silence as objection and leapt into action, grabbing two shot glasses. 'Look, let's both do a shot. I'll pay. Then do one more turn of the room for me. If you still aren't feeling it, fair enough.'

'Are you secretly Cupid or something?' Gemma asked with a chuckle.

'I just like to know everyone's having a good time.' She topped each glass up with Sourz.

It had been a long time since Gemma had done shots, but she was off tomorrow. Why not? She held out a hand, indicating she was on board. 'Okay. One shot won't hurt.'

'That's the spirit!' She held her glass up, proposing a toast. 'To love.'

'To love.'

They downed their shots and the blonde's face broke into a smile. 'Sorry, that was super corny.'

It was, but Gemma didn't mind. 'Are you sure you should be working?' she asked, unable to take her eyes off the blood blooming down the tissue.

'No choice: I'm the assistant manager and it's busy.'

'Well, where's your manager? You need to sit down or something.'

'Ach, nah, it's fine. They never last long.'

'You get them a lot?'

'You a doctor?' Her tone was meant to be friendly but Gemma could tell she was over the inquisition.

'Just a concerned citizen. Can't have Cupid dropping dead.'

She smiled. 'Well, do me a favour: go find a match and then it at least won't have been in vain.'

Gemma saluted, instantly regretting such a bizarre move, but she was committed now. 'I'll do my best.'

3

That weekend, Steph sat in the pub, laptop open and paperwork strewn over the table. She pinched the bridge of her nose between finger and thumb.

These accounts were impossible to unravel. Why the hell did Cal let Donnie do them? Nothing added up.

She stared at the numbers, hoping they would magically regroup and make sense.

Stevie appeared by the table. 'How you getting on?'

'It's absolutely fucked.'

'Will I get in trouble?'

Steph's face softened. Stevie was only twenty-one and was juggling here with her uni work; she couldn't afford to lose this job.

'Of course not. We all know it's Donnie's fault. I just need to figure out where he went wrong and fix it. But, do me a favour, will you?'

'Yeah?'

'Get me another Coke, please?'

Stevie left with a smile, happy Steph was on the case. The issue had started at the close of the Lovefest opener.

The safe float was down a hundred pounds. Stevie had seen Donnie pay the DJ in cash earlier in the evening, which wasn't their usual protocol. But she counted the float, so she was responsible for the missing dosh.

That would be bad enough, but it had led Steph to an absolute shit show of accounts for last month. It was a complete work of fiction. Even down to how much the staff were paid.

Either he couldn't do maths to save himself, or he was fiddling the books.

Steph knew which one she believed.

He was off today, or she would confront him about it. She was in the mood for taking him on. Funny how she was only ever like this when he wasn't about.

She leaned back, stretching her arms out as she arched her back. It was busy for late afternoon in the pub, but Lovefest had that effect. Especially now they'd taken on board the daytime deal she'd suggested. One large pizza and two drinks, perfect for luring dates before the inevitable evening rush. You had to capitalise on Lovefest while it lasted. No sense in wasting a golden goose.

Couples filled the tables; some established, some new. Her eyes drifted to the pretty blonde in the middle booth. Gemma from the opening event. Looked like she'd taken Steph's advice and found a date, as she was in the company of an equally hot brunette.

It was a shame. Gemma was totally Steph's type. Physically, anyway. Pretty, feminine, and a good few inches taller. Looked like Gemma had similar taste, though. A petite tattooed scruff like herself wasn't going to cut it.

Steph clicked up the inventory files for last month and wasn't surprised to find they were a shambles too.

She held in a groan as Stevie placed her Coke down with

a silent nod of support. The anger swelled in her chest, like an untamed beast fighting to be free. Why him? Why let Donnie run the bar when she was far more capable?

Sometimes she wondered if he had something on Cal. It was the only explanation that made sense.

She took a sip of Coke as she pondered the numbers.

Usually she would do this in the office, but she needed to have eyes on the bar today. Donnie had changed the rota last minute and now they didn't have enough staff. Soon she'd have to vacate the table for punters and get back to serving. But she was no nearer to solving the puzzle.

It looked like they had a lot more stock than they actually did. The question was: did she go to Cal and tell him, or just order more and hope that her decision wasn't challenged when Cal did her annual review next month? There was no way she'd waste profits holding stock they didn't actually need.

She stuffed her hand into the pocket of her jeans and manoeuvred slightly to free two paracetamol she'd snuck out earlier. She popped them, washing them down with a big glug of juice.

Her head was throbbing.

This she could cope with, but the nosebleeds? They were fast becoming a nuisance. You couldn't hide a nosebleed.

The doctor wasn't any help and served as a stark reminder of why she never bloody visited them. Stress. That's all it was. *Take some time off work; relax.* She'd soon sleep, lose the sore heads and aching muscles.

Time. Off.

The doctor should be doing stand-up, not practising medicine.

Steph jotted down the names of a few suppliers, ones

she knew would do her a favour and confirm how much they'd actually received last month without reporting her questions back to Cal.

She prided herself on having great comms with their wholesalers. Her favourites were local breweries – you got to go out and meet them face to face. Actually strike up friendships. That couldn't be beaten in the world of business. It meant that more often than not, Cal's was the launch place of new brews, sometimes weeks before other pubs.

It kept their menu exciting and the punters coming back.

You couldn't ask for more.

'Nose better today?'

Steph's heart leapt from her chest and she visibly jumped.

Gemma.

Standing at her table.

Looking gorgeous.

Steph's mouth went dry, all moisture flooding to her palms.

She gulped: it was like swallowing sand.

'So far, so good,' she finally managed.

Gemma's lips pulled into an amused smile. 'Glad to hear it. Nosebleeds can be nasty.' She leaned over the table, looking at the guddle of paperwork surrounding the laptop. 'I see even Cupid has admin. Glad it's not just me.'

Steph's cheeks burned hot. 'My plan worked, then. You got a match?' she asked, tipping her head towards the brunette currently scrolling on her phone.

Gemma stole a glance at her date. 'Unfortunately not; this is the work of Tinder. But thank you for trying. I did have a good time.'

'You never know. I've heard things often happen after the opener. It's the magic of Lovefest.'

Gemma shook her head, that amused look still lingering. 'Well, I hope you brought your bow and arrow. I could do with some help.'

'Date not going well?' It looked like it was; lots of smiling and conversation. How much more could you want on a first date?

Gemma shrugged. 'On the fence. Speaking of which, I'd better nip to the loo before she thinks I've done a runner. See you around, Cupid.'

She turned back as she neared the toilets and Steph mimed shooting an arrow her way. Silly, but it got a fresh smile.

It warmed Steph's heart to see people making connections at the Lovefest events. The name was ridiculous but then maybe love was meant to be corny. Find the right person and you were a lovesick teenager again.

Last year's winners, Ashley and Hazel, were often in the pub and things seemed to be going from strength to strength for them.

And they weren't the only ones. There were a few regulars who'd successfully paired up *à la* Lovefest.

It would seem everyone was romancing but Steph.

She rolled her neck, willing the paracetamol to work a little faster.

Maybe the doctor was right: she needed to take a step back, relax a little.

Her thoughts immediately turned to dating apps and her stomach turned. She just wasn't cut out for it. Too much meaningless chat. How else were you meant to meet women, though?

A couple of regulars sprung to mind, ones that quite

clearly fancied her. She was no egotist but sometimes you just had to admit the truth: she was a tall (or should that be small?) drink of something to a select few. Just a shame none were her type.

Perhaps the real kicker was that she was still good mates with her ex, Maisie. That in itself wasn't a problem. However, Maisie getting married soon was an issue. It was a glaring red flag that Steph had done precisely zero to change her ways, while Maisie had moved on, dated, found her soulmate, and got engaged.

Steph remained a workaholic who put the pub first and herself second.

Maisie's words. Not hers. Could be, though. They were true.

What was the point, though? Remove work and there was a sinkhole bigger than Steph could fathom – how the heck are you meant to fill that and not drive yourself insane?

She had no need for a hobby.

And who the fuck does stuff on their own, anyway?

As if she was going to go hiking or mountain biking by herself.

No. If she got work sorted she would be fine, content as could be without a partner.

She growled under the breath as the numbers on screen jumbled further. She didn't need painkillers; she needed whisky or a pint. Something to silence the voice in her head and help her see sense.

Donnie needed to go. It was just a question of how.

4

Gemma nodded, trying to look interested in the story Gianna was telling. She kept finding herself zoning out, though. *Oops.*

She was lovely. On paper this should be a fantastic date: physically, she ticked all the right boxes. She worked in HR, so knew the pressures of corporate life. And, she was the same age as Gemma. Tick, tick, tick.

But in person? *Whomp whomp.*

No ticks: time to tear up the score sheet and shove it in the bin.

There was just no click. No spark. No *je ne sais quoi* to reel her in and leave her wanting more.

Such a pity, because their messages on Tinder had been promising.

And damn, she was smoking hot. A kiss would have been nice. No point if she wasn't the full shebang, though.

'Do you think?'

'Huh?' *Shit.* She'd zoned out again.

'Do you think I was wrong to report them or would you have done the same?'

A work question. *Double shit.* This sounded like it required back story.

Gemma pulled her best thinking-it-over face. 'Hmm, tough one. Always best to go with your gut. If that means going by the book, you have to.' Protocol. Everyone loves it, right?

'See, I thought that, but now I feel bad.'

Phew. 'Don't feel bad – you did what you had to do.'

Gianna reached over and placed a hand on Gemma's before giving it a squeeze. Nothing. Aren't you meant to feel fireworks or something when your partner touches you?

She'd felt it when Kimberly Lincoln had kissed her at guide camp during a game of truth or dare. And she definitely felt it when she'd get drunk with her friend at university and make out.

Nothing with Logan, but she'd convinced herself she just wasn't into sex by that point and that it was perfectly normal. Yes, Logan was okay-looking, and kissing could incite feelings below the belt if she really put her mind to it, but on the whole, it was a spark-free zone.

Holy shit, she was doing it again. She zoned back to Gianna.

'—but I guess that's just the issue with having a job like mine. You have to accept the fall out.'

'Definitely. Although, I can't say I get much with mine.'

'No?'

'Well, I mean, I get the occasional pissed-off client, but on the whole it's a game of patience and negotiation, and we nearly always get what we need. Being a commercial solicitor isn't the most dramatic of jobs.'

'But you enjoy it?'

'I love it.' No word of a lie. Tell people you're a solicitor and most roll their eyes, but Gemma really did love it.

Structure. Law. A strict code of conduct. What wasn't to enjoy?

'That's good. So many people hate what they do these days.'

'Do you?'

'Sometimes.'

'That's a shame. Would you never change?'

Gianna shook her head, almost as if she was embarrassed Gemma had suggested something so unimaginably crazy. 'Far too old for that.'

'Thirty-three is hardly old.' It wasn't. It had felt that way in recent years, but she knew better now. She had a whole life to live yet.

'Far too stuck in my ways.' Gianna sipped her wine, her eyes wistful.

'If you could do anything, what would you do?'

Her eyes tilted to the long, winding industrial vent suspended from Cal's ceiling. It looked like a robotic snake. Gemma sipped her wine, waiting for an answer, enjoying the view of Gianna's kissable neck as she pondered.

God, she could kill for sex.

Maybe that was part of the issue.

She was positively bursting with the need for it.

Gemma had shared a few drunken kisses with women, but her bloody brain had always managed to talk her out of going further.

Perhaps a one-night stand was the answer.

Could Gianna be the one?

'I think,' she said, and Gemma almost jumped, having completely forgotten she'd asked a question in the first place. 'I would quite like to be a mortician.'

Gemma choked on her wine. That was so off the radar

that the answer had smacked her on the side of the head, leaving her dazed. 'Like, for the dead?'

Gianna laughed. 'I wouldn't be much use to the living.' Her cheeks blushed red. 'Sorry, I know that sounds morbid. It's just something I've always had an interest in.'

'No, no. Don't apologise. I just wasn't expecting it. Why don't you, then? Go back to uni, I mean?'

Her date scrunched her face up. 'Way too much time to retrain. I don't want to waste my thirties on university only to be starting my career in my forties.'

'So you'd rather stick at something you hate for the rest of time?'

'Well, when you put it like that.'

Gemma couldn't tell if she was joking or not. 'Just, I believe in following your heart. No matter how scary it is. Inconvenience is temporary. Whereas desolation can be fatal.'

'You're a glass-half-full person, by the sounds of it.'

'Try to be. Speaking of which, fancy another?' she asked, gesturing to her nearly empty wine.

'Go on then.'

'My round,' Gemma said with a wink as she slid out the booth.

The bar's assistant manager was still deep in paperwork. She'd looked ridiculously stressed earlier, and Gemma had worried it was to do with her nosebleed the other day. It was nice to see her without the plugged nostrils. She hadn't noticed the nose ring that night, but did now. She'd often wondered if she could pull one off. She smiled to herself. *Never in a million years.*

No chat on the way past this time. In fact, she didn't even look up.

She was glad she'd agreed to Gianna's idea to come to

Cal's. Daytime drinking wasn't her usual forte, but it was the Saturday of a long weekend: why not? She'd taken yesterday off, anticipating a hangover that never materialised, so had spent the day pottering in her flat instead. It was nice to do nothing.

She ordered their wines and looked back at the table. Gianna was gorgeous, no denying it. No harm in staying out and seeing where today went. Maybe she just needed more time. You couldn't expect fireworks as soon as you met.

Gemma's eyes travelled to the assistant manager. She had her hair in a messy knot today, showing off even more artwork on the back of her neck. That must have hurt. She didn't mind tats, but really wasn't cool enough to make them work herself. Her inner voice of rebellion had contemplated something small, something hidden, to mark her newfound truth, but the pain scared her. How sore was a tattoo? Suppose it was all a matter of where you got it.

Drinks paid for, she made her way back to the table.

If she did get a tattoo, what would it be? A heart? A subtle rainbow? No, far too gaudy. Maybe a butterfly. Just on her hip bone. For her eyes only. Well, and hopefully a special someone further down the line.

She was so engrossed she didn't see the arm flying her way until she was karate-chopped in the stomach.

'Oh shit, oh sorry, fuck,' the assistant manager rambled.

Gemma stood frozen, wine clutched at chest height. She surveyed the damage: nothing spilled. Just her racing heart to calm.

'I'm not straight,' the blonde continued.

'Huh?'

'I meant, I'm not thinking.' She shook her head, her cheeks burning bright. 'I wasn't thinking straight.' She hovered her hands over Gemma's midriff. 'I was stretching and should have been more aware of my surroundings. Are you okay? Did you spill anything? Can I buy you more? Fuck. I'm so sorry.'

Gianna was looking now, her face a picture of confusion. Gemma shot her a smile before turning her attention back to the bar manager.

'When I said shoot me with an arrow I didn't mean something quite so literal,' she joked.

'You're okay though?'

'Yeah, maybe a little bruised, but I didn't spill any wine. That's the main thing.'

Her shoulders relaxed, her brown eyes still pleading for mercy. 'I'm not having a good day. Sorry again.'

'Anything I can help with?' It was out before Gemma had a chance to think about what she was saying, her mind on autopilot.

'Don't suppose you're an accountant?'

'Solicitor, sorry.'

She nodded, looking as deflated as a wilting balloon. 'Worth a shot. And sorry again.'

'No harm, no foul.' Gemma lifted the glasses slightly. 'Better get back to it. Before I suffer any more attacks.'

'Next round's on me.'

'You don't need to.'

'No, really. Say Steph's getting it. Although, I'll be back on bar soon. I could serve you myself.'

Steph.

So Cupid had a name.

5

Week two of Lovefest and sales were up thirty-three % year-on-year. It was phenomenal.

'Did you get that inventory problem sorted?' Gary asked, twisting in the brewery's office chair.

Steph had escaped the confines of Cal's and Donnie's ominous presence to pick up a new brew from local boys Southside Slugs. It was a nice set-up, just big enough to keep up with demand while being a manageable size. The unit was part of an industrial park near Polmadie. It looked like a normal, red-brick-corrugated-roof, boring space, until you got inside and saw the gleaming, stainless steel brewery equipment. Metal kegs lined the far wall, ready to be shipped to Cal's in the next few days. The air was hot, hoppy, and delicious.

Steph could totally see herself owning a microbrewery. Sometimes it was all she thought about. Brewing beer had started as a hobby, but she had soon fallen down the rabbit hole and the sizeable cubby off her living room was filled with brewing paraphernalia. At any one time she usually had about three beers on the go. It was an expensive industry, though, and she definitely didn't have the funds to progress her fun and games to a real, functioning business.

'Aye, well, sort of. I think Donnie just entered the figures wrong,' she replied, trying to keep on the right side of professional.

'Man's a muppet,' Gary said, not missing a beat. He stopped writing the paperwork he was preparing. 'You know what he asked me last time he was here?'

Why was Donnie here? She was the one managing this account.

'No,' she replied, lacking the energy to ask questions.

'*Got any spare kegs going?* He would repay the favour. Meaning he would give me free stuff if I came to Cal's.'

'Oh, he did, did he?'

'Aye, transpires he was having a BARBECUE that day.'

Steph rolled her eyes. He had no shame. How was he getting away with being so blatantly awful?

'Did you tell Cal?'

'I've not spoken to Cal in ages. Just you.'

'I'll let him know. That's not on.'

Gary clicked his tongue to the roof of his mouth as he continued with the paperwork. 'So, box of promo bottles for you by the door, and we'll get these kegs to you ASAP. Sorry again for the delay.'

'No worries. I'm sure it will be worth the wait.'

They'd brought out a new brew for Lovefest – Love Slug. It would seem the festival's reputation was reaching far beyond the border of Shawlands these days. It was meant to be ready for opening, but a delay in labelling had held things back. Perfection took time. Steph was just happy her connections meant they were the only bar in Shawlands to be serving the coveted brew.

The launch was this Saturday, with a singles event planned to celebrate.

Would Gemma be there?

It had been a few days since Steph had whacked the poor woman in the stomach, but she still blushed at the memory. What an idiot.

At least she hadn't spilled her drinks. If Steph had tipped two white wines down the poor woman's top she would have had to leave her job and move to Spain.

'Lovefest going well, then?' Gary asked, tearing the paperwork away from its carbon sheet to reveal the copy underneath.

'Oh yeah, it just gets bigger every year. Cal's making a mint off it.'

'And what about you?'

'Me?'

'You going to any of these Lovefest events?'

Steph laughed. 'Is this a roundabout way of seeing if I'm single?' She looked herself up and down, taking in the shorts and baggy tee. 'I don't think we're exactly on the same page.'

Gary chuckled while turning a lovely shade of crimson. Shit: she was only joking. She didn't actually think that was why he was asking. 'Nah, not for me. My cousin's single. We were at a family thing the other day: she was moaning about getting dates, you sprung to mind, I showed her your picture . . .' he trailed off. 'Now I'm saying it out loud, it seems a bit creepy. Sorry.'

Steph leaned against the edge of Gary's desk, tongue in her cheek as she fought the grin spreading across her face. 'Is a bit, yeah.'

'Not interested, then?'

She shook her head. 'Not super keen on blind dates.'

'Not a blind date if I show you her picture,' he said, raising an eyebrow.

Steph considered it. 'Right, go on. But don't be offended if I say no.' It would do her good to go outside her comfort zone, find a little peace outside of work. Just what the doctor ordered. Literally.

He pulled out his phone and brought up Facebook. 'Zara,' he said, turning the phone to face Steph.

She was bonnie enough. Long brown hair, dark eyes, friendly smile. 'What does she do?' Steph asked as she flipped through the photos.

'She's a recruitment agent.'

'So she works in a call centre?' Steph said with a quiet laugh and handed the phone back.

'Alright, smart arse. Yes. I guess you could call it that,' he retorted with a smile. 'So?'

'I'm busy with Lovefest stuff, but yeah, I'm sure I could squeeze in a date.'

The mere thought made her stomach flip, but seeing all these fledgling couples had got Steph's brain working overtime. Could be a great way to meet someone.

Gary beamed. 'Awesome. What's your number? I'll get her to text you.'

～

STEPH WADDLED THROUGH THE BAR, the box of booze resting on her hip. She was surprised to see Donnie at the end of the bar, the epitome of casual as he leaned against its edge, talking to Stevie.

An alarm bell sounded at the back of her mind.

She hit the snooze button and powered on to the stockroom.

'What's that?' Novak asked as she hefted it onto the chest freezer with a thud.

'Samples from the Slugs. Not for resale.'

Novak inspected a bottle, admiring the funky label featuring their signature slug character surrounded by love hearts. 'Looks good. Gary doing fine?'

'Aye, yeah. And I think I might have scored a date.'

'With Gary?'

'Aye, with Gary. No, you eejit. He's set me up with his cousin or something.'

'A date for Steph. Very nice. When is it?' He was still looking at the bottle. Probably pondering how to ask to open one mid-shift.

'Not sure yet – she's going to text me.' She leaned closer while checking over her shoulder that the coast was clear. 'What's the deal with Donnie?'

'What do you mean?'

'Why's he still here?'

'Oh.'

'*Oh* means I won't like it.'

'It means I don't want any trouble.'

'Novak. Spill.'

He peered over her. All clear. 'I think he was chatting to Stevie about the missing money.'

'Oh, really?' she said, pulling a *would-you-believe-it* face.

'He tried getting her alone at the weekend but it was too busy. I heard him mention the safe when I was refilling the glasses.'

Steph pursed her lips. She'd heard enough. There was nothing that could be done, but the thought of him dragging Stevie into his mess added a whole new layer of anger to Steph's cynicism.

'Don't tell him I told you,' Novak pleaded, his eyes wide as he put the beer bottle back in its box.

'No, no. Course not. I'm not going to say anything to him. Not without talking to Stevie first.'

Novak sighed with relief. 'You know I hate working with him anyway.'

'I know. I promise. No choppy waters from me. Well, not about this, anyway.' She left before he could protest.

Donnie was still talking to Stevie and conversation promptly ended when Steph came to halt by their side.

He had over a foot in height on her, but she didn't care. He was a slimy sleazeball with slicked-back hair and a penchant for ill-fitting shirts. He was the kind of guy that liked to talk loud at parties and demand attention, even if he had no clue about the subject. He would argue the sky was green if someone like Steph said it was blue.

To put it simply: he was an arsehole.

'Donnie,' she said, forcing a smile. 'You're working late.'

'Had a few things to catch up on in the office.'

Ah, yes. The office. Where Donnie spent most of his shift. 'Nice,' she replied, with a bob of her head. 'Can I chat to you for a second?'

She could feel Novak's eyes on her from the opposite end of the bar as he checked the garnishes. He needn't worry: this wasn't about Stevie and the safe.

Stevie stepped away and Donnie remained silent, waiting for Steph to talk. Not even a hint of recognition that she'd requested his attention.

'So,' she started, her face already deadpan. 'Gary said you were angling for a free keg.'

'So?'

'So, that's not on.'

He smirked. 'Says who? I'm the manager. You really having a go at me for this?'

'You might be the manager, but that doesn't mean you can be cheeky to the suppliers or scam Cal.'

'Excuse me?'

'You heard.'

It was a battle to keep her voice low. Donnie's body language hadn't changed from speaking to Stevie. He was still lolled over the end of the bar, a foot on the rung of a stool.

Steph crossed her arms.

'It's no biggie, Steph. It's called doing someone a favour.'

'Does Cal know?'

'Why would that matter?'

'I'm sure he'd love to know you were out and about bargaining his profits away.'

Donnie chuckled under his breath. 'Hardly. Listen, this has nothing to do with you. I suggest you stick to your job, and I'll stick to being manager.'

'I'm watching you,' Steph said and wished she was tall enough to stare him out or at least have an ounce of menace. Right now, she felt like a yappy Chihuahua having a go at a Great Dane.

Donnie rolled his eyes, knowing full well that silence wound Steph up more than a snappy comeback. He pushed away from the bar and wandered back to the office.

There was no point telling Cal, and Donnie knew it.

No. She would hold onto this. Her time would come.

6

Another week, another date. Tonight it was Heather's turn.

She was nice. Her styled auburn hair flowed around her face and down her shoulders, adding to the summery look of her floral dress.

Gemma had gone for a cute vest and jeans. It was bloody boiling today. Thank God for the cool beer Cal's was serving.

She'd enjoyed her date with Gianna last week, spark withstanding, so it was a pleasant surprise to see another Lovefest event being held this weekend. Nothing like charging in with an arsenal of conversation starters.

There was a new Lovefest beer in town, so the ladies were being treated to a tasting board of brews.

Gemma wasn't usually one for beer, but given the weather conditions, a nice crisp glass was exactly what she needed.

She swiped at the condensation on her glass as she listened to Heather talk.

'Which is how I came to Glasgow,' Heather said, completing her story.

'Do you miss York?'

'Sometimes. But Glasgow is good. Of course, my family is still down there, so it's not like I won't be back.'

The accent had thrown Gemma. She knew, somewhere at the back of her mind, that Heather was from York, but her brain hadn't quite pieced things together. A hazard of talking to so many women at once. 'Still, production manager at the BBC – that's exciting.'

'It's amazing, I won't lie. I always wanted to work in TV; it's a dream come true.'

'Meet many celebs?' Gemma had seen a presenter from STV once, ordering a porridge in a coffee shop up from the office. She seemed quite snippy. She imagined most celebrities probably were.

'Sadly, I deal with more stuff behind the scenes; all the boring stuff, I guess.'

Silence fell and Gemma searched for more questions. Suddenly her mind was a leaking bucket, words spilling out the holes, never to return. She sipped her beer.

'Nice day, isn't it?' she finally settled on. Jesus, that was pathetic.

'Yeah, hot.'

To be fair, Heather wasn't giving her much to work with in return: her attention had suddenly wandered.

'Can't beat a good beer when it's hot. Is that your usual tipple, or . . .?'

'Yeah, it's not bad.'

Gemma got the distinct feeling that Heather wasn't really listening. She sipped her beer again, searching her date's face for clues. She followed her line of sight, subtly twisting to see what had caught her attention. A pretty blonde girl in a low-cut top.

Fantastic.

~

'It was awful,' Gemma said, flopping onto Granny's sofa. She'd accidentally posted a photo album to Facebook of badly angled selfies, her gladioli, a Scotch egg, and a rather creepy photo of the view from the living room. Now that was deleted, they were free to discuss more pressing matters.

'Hold up, hold up,' Granny called from the kitchen as she checked her roast chicken. 'I can't hear you.'

Sundays were for family roasts. Everyone piled round to Granny's: Mum, Dad, Archie, Sonia, and the kids.

Gemma always went early. Well, pre- and post-Logan. This was prime gossip time.

She rubbed at her eyes, only peeking out from behind her fingers when she heard the shuffle of Granny's feet.

A hand connected with her leg on the way past. 'Sit up, I can't hear you when you mumble.'

Gemma didn't dare argue. 'It was horrible, Granny,' she moped, sitting up straight.

'She sounds a right rotter.'

Gemma pouted before righting her face as she noticed a very important missing element to their Sunday morning chat. 'Gin?'

'Oh, sugar.' Granny rose on shaking legs but Gemma leapt to her feet, stopping further movement.

'You sit. I'll grab them.'

She padded through to the kitchen, straightening her sweatshirt as she went. It was bad enough that Granny insisted on cooking a roast dinner every Sunday, never mind having her run about playing hostess with drinks. She'd broken her hip two years ago and it still gave her gyp. The more rest she got, the better.

Gemma grabbed two crystal glasses from the cupboard and poured each a generous measure. She stalled, pondering if she'd been *too* generous. Wouldn't be good if they were pie-eyed when everyone else arrived.

Stuff it.

Yesterday's date was a disaster. She deserved to be a little reckless.

Granny was sitting deep in thought, rolling her pearl necklace between finger and thumb. She flinched when Gemma sat her drink on the coaster by her side. 'Goodness, I didn't even see you come back.'

'What were you thinking about?'

Granny took a sip of gin, her lips curling and her eyes twinkling with delight at the strength. 'I was thinking, *How could some woman look at another when this beauty is giving her attention?*'

'Obviously, I wasn't enough.'

Granny waved her away. 'No taste, some people. So, who's next?'

'Granny!' Gemma scolded with a snigger. 'You make it sound like I have a conveyor belt on the go.'

'This Tinder,' she said, the word sounding like she was grappling with a foreign language. 'That's what it feels like. You lot get complacent. You see lady after lady. You think it's never-ending. In my day you had your neighbour, your work folks, and maybe friends' friends if you were lucky.'

'I think that would be easier,' Gemma replied, wincing as the alcohol warmed her throat. 'I think I might give it a rest for a while, if I'm honest.'

Granny's face grew serious. 'Now, now. I didn't think you were a quitter.'

'It's not quitting,' Gemma retorted, defiant. 'It's just a breather. It's all going south a bit.'

'And what about this Love Festival?'

'Lovefest?'

'That's the one. No pretty girls there?'

'Nada.'

'That's a shame.'

'No harm in a breather.'

'No. But I was hoping to go to a gay wedding before I die.'

Gemma swiped at Granny's knee, narrowly missing. 'Granny. A: you're going nowhere. And B: don't you dare put that pressure on me,' she joked.

Granny ignored her. 'You know Charlotte, from cardio?'

'Yes.' Gemma already knew where this was going. Granny went to a cardio group every Tuesday. Their tongues got the biggest workout: the amount of gossiping they did would put *Loose Women* to shame.

'Her granddaughter is still a lesbian.'

'Still! Crazy. Still a lesbian from the other nine million times you've mentioned her.'

Granny put on her best doe eyes. 'You don't think one little date might be nice?'

She'd shown Gemma Corrin's picture a while back. She was on the wrong side of masculine for her, with cropped dark hair and boyish clothes. There was no doubt she was likely a lovely woman, but in terms of looks she just wasn't Gemma's type.

'I'm okay, thank you.'

'She's a paediatrician,' Granny offered, as if it was Corrin's CV that might be putting her off.

'Let me have a rest from dating and I'll have a think.'

That pleased Granny. 'Okay, but not for long. I'm still counting on great-grandchildren from you.'

'A wedding *and* children? You're really not cutting me any slack,' Gemma laughed.

'No point in beating about the bush at my age.'

'Speaking of weddings,' Gemma said, only pausing to take another drink. 'I'm in two minds about Julie's.' Her best friend's wedding was slowly nearing and the closer it got, the less Gemma wanted to go.

'What do you mean?'

'Archie told you Logan's got a new girlfriend, yeah?'

'Of course, but that was months ago. What does she have to do with anything?'

'I just kind of thought I might have someone by now. Going alone feels like a right kick in the teeth.'

'Ah. Well, no one else you can take?'

Gemma shrugged. 'Nobody.'

Granny narrowed her eyes while taking a slow draw of her gin. 'I sense hesitation.'

Nothing got past her grandmother. 'I guess friends are kind of thin on the ground these days.' Gemma scrunched her face up, her gaze firmly fixed on the carriage clock adorning Granny's mantelpiece.

'You guess? Guessing is how you play Botticelli. Do you have friends or not?' Granny asked with a smirk.

'I do, but they're still in Logan's circles. I need some of my own. Really, I want someone more likeminded.'

Granny looked even more sceptical at that revelation. 'You mean a lesbian friend?' Granny took a sip of gin, a fresh question springing to mind. 'Is that not just dating?'

Gemma blew out her cheeks. 'No, you can have gay

friends and not be attracted to each other. Just like men and women can be friends.'

Granny opened her mouth as the front door flew open, saving Gemma from further questions. Two seconds later the twins appeared, closely followed by Archie and Sonia.

To describe the five-year-olds as a whirlwind would be putting it lightly.

Leo rushed to Granny, pawing to be picked up, and Gemma grabbed Noah on the way past, scooping him onto her lap for a cuddle.

She growled into his neck. 'Hello, little monster.'

He giggled and gave her a squeeze.

'You guys are early,' she said to Archie, who was lingering in the doorway. They usually arrived not long after Mum and Dad at twelve.

'Meltdown central this morning, sis.' he said, twirling a toy rabbit in his hands. 'Thought you guys could help defuse it.'

Gemma looked at Sonia, who was ducking under her brother's arm, aiming for the kitchen. 'Archie or the twins, Sonia?'

The silence and a roll of her eyes told Gemma all she needed.

Archie took a seat in the armchair as Noah clambered down, grabbed his brother, and went full speed to the kitchen.

'Gemma,' Archie said, her name a painful whine.

'Yes?' Her face was sullen, knowing this wasn't going to be something she wanted to hear. She tipped her gin back, finishing it in a one-er.

'I just want you to know, Logan and I are going out next week.'

'Great. Congratulations.'

He was still fiddling with that bloody teddy. She wanted to grab it and chuck it across the room.

'Just thought you should know. Joanne won't be there. It's just the lads.'

Joanne, Logan's newish girlfriend. *Right*. 'Amazing. And you know, I wouldn't care if she was there. I left him. He's allowed to move on.'

'I know, it's just, I don't want it being weird.'

Wouldn't be weird if he didn't make it bloody weird. 'I get that, yeah. Thanks for letting me know.' She scratched her collarbone, suddenly feeling too hot.

'You let him know Gemma's been on lots of dates,' Granny piped up.

'Granny!' Gemma yelped. She turned back to Archie. 'Please don't.'

Sonia appeared, the boys pushing past her like excited dogs, each clutching a biscuit as if it were a sacred treasure.

He mimed sealing his lips. 'As long as you're okay with everything.'

'Of course. Why wouldn't I be?' Strange thing to say. Okay, as in okay she was dating women, or that Logan was?

'You're okay with it, then?' Sonia asked, taking a seat beside Gemma.

'Yeah, of course.' What the heck?

The look Archie threw Sonia could cut glass. She missed it, Gemma didn't.

'I can't believe they're having a baby,' she said, sinking into the sofa.

'A baby? Who? What now?' Gemma stuttered.

Sonia looked like she'd just spilled war secrets.

'I hadn't quite got to that,' Archie groaned.

Gemma sat up straight. 'Logan's having a baby? With

Joanne?' Why did her stomach feel like someone was wringing it out?

'I was going to tell you,' Archie said half out of the corner of his mouth, looking sheepish.

'Sorry,' Sonia said, taking one of Granny's big cushions and hiding behind it.

'How long have you known?' Gemma asked.

'Not long: a few weeks,' Archie replied.

'So he's got her knocked up,' Granny said. 'An accident, I presume?'

'Yeah, not planned,' Archie said.

Granny nodded, her lips pulled thin. It wasn't often she was rendered speechless.

'I, erm, I'd better check on the chicken,' Gemma said, getting to her feet. The wind had been taken out of her. The trip to the kitchen felt like a marathon.

She opened the back door and relished the cool air as she stepped outside.

A baby. It wasn't like they'd been in any rush to start a family: she'd been pretty vocal about her career coming first. But still, it was a shock.

What a shitty, shitty week.

7

Steph gave herself another once-over in the mirror. She looked good. Ish.

Zara had been surprisingly easy to talk to, and over the course of the week they'd exchanged more than a few flirty messages.

Tonight, they were off to a couple's evening in The Reading Lounge, a pub not far from Cal's. Although, it could have been further. She didn't want to go anywhere near work today.

She was surprisingly chill about this evening.

Maybe it was the complete lack of expectation. The weight was on Gary's shoulders, not hers. She would meet Zara, see where it went. If their texts were anything to go by, conversation wouldn't be a problem.

Still, she'd tried on what felt like nine thousand outfits before settling on this one. Clothes were her passion; she loved putting together outfits. But tonight? Nothing felt right.

It had been an age since she'd been on a first date. Not

only had her style changed, but her body had, too. *Thirty-seven. Fucking hell.* Last time she was standing in front of a mirror like this she was firmly in her twenties.

In the end, she went for a light denim shirt, similar shorts, her white Nikes, and white socks. It was a good combo: classic, strong.

The evenings were still balmy and hot so it gave breathing space for the inevitable sauna-like atmosphere of the pub.

Tonight was Couple's Truth or Drink in the pub which, despite sounding ominous, Steph was looking forward to. Nothing like an icebreaker to start the evening – they could go somewhere quieter after.

A knot formed in her stomach and she couldn't place if it was nerves or anticipation.

Maybe a wee beer would settle things. She did have thirty minutes to kill while she tidied the clothes strewn across her bedroom.

She padded through to the small open-plan kitchen and grabbed a beer. She was settled on the sofa, about to pop the cap, when she spied her phone on the coffee table. The lock screen lit up with a fresh message, highlighting the thirteen missed calls from the last hour.

Fuck.

She already knew what this would be about.

This is what she got for trying to be clever.

Steph's hands clutched the bottle and opener, suspended mid-air as if frozen.

This was a crossroads.

Either she said *fuck it*, not her problem, opened the beer and got on with her night, leaving the team in the shit. Or, she called them back, found out how bad it was, and went from there.

Steph looked at the beer, then to the phone, and back to the beer.

Indecision fizzed in her muscles and her chest tightened.

She really wanted to go on this date.

Still could. Probably.

But the thought of starting the evening dealing with fallout wasn't ideal.

'Fuck,' she growled, slamming the beer and bottle opener onto the table.

This was her own fault. She should have stuck to what she knew: damage control and keeping the peace.

But no. She had to get smart, thinking she could land Donnie in the shit.

Steph shook her head and leaned into her sofa's cushions, wishing they would swallow her up. She should have known. As soon as she swapped shifts to get tonight off, she should have known.

She looked at her phone and ignored the messages: she knew what they would say. Instead, she looked at the missed calls and weighed up which one to return.

She opted for the general bar number and pleaded with the universe to let it go unanswered. At least she could say she tried, then.

No such luck.

'Hello, Cal's,' a female voice greeted. Sounded like Kara. Even in those two words, Steph could detect stress.

'Hey, Kara, is that you?'

'Steph?'

'Yeah.'

'Christ on a bike, thank God.'

'What's wrong?'

She knew what was wrong but she wanted to hear it, just

to be sure. She couldn't admit to having a hand in this fuck-up.

The truth was, when she'd seen Donnie's mess of an inventory she'd debated ordering in 'extra', but she'd done the maths. If they kept going at the volume they were, it would last until Sunday. One day of angry punters. A quiet day at that. Then a new delivery would arrive on Monday.

Only, they'd obviously been a lot busier than anticipated.

Now, well, now they were a pub with no spirits. Well, affordable ones at least. No one was going to be happy if forced to pay £12 for a single vodka and Coke.

'We've basically no spirits.'

'No spirits?'

'Yep. I know.'

'How can you have none? Inventory said there were loads.'

'Well, it must be wrong,' Kara snapped.

Anyone with eyes could have seen the stock was depleting in storage. Why did it always fall on her shoulders?

'Where's Donnie?' He was scheduled to be on bar until six; he would have known it was going to run out well before that.

'Done his usual.'

'You're fucking kidding me.'

'No. And he's not answering his phone.'

The sound of the bar made hearing Kara hard – it was busy. Nothing would hold Donnie back from clocking off early, though.

'What can I do?' Steph sighed so loudly, her neighbours probably heard.

'I know you have your date tonight.'

'Just tell me.'

There was pause. Steph closed her eyes and chewed on her top lip.

'Can you nip to the cash and carry for us?'

Tears threatened, a ball of frustration lodging itself in her throat. She wanted to scream and stamp her feet, smash something, punch something, do anything to release the agitation swelling in her chest.

To drive, it was only fifteen minutes, but plus the return journey, getting the stuff, unloading the stuff, doing the paperwork for the expenses, and all the other fuckery that went with it—she was looking at more than an hour.

Not that she would be in the mood to go on a date after this.

'Right. Yeah. Okay. Text me what you need.'

Goodbyes said, she flopped the phone onto the sofa and let out a cry a grizzly bear would be proud of.

If Donnie had pulled this shit, he would have got away with it. The universe always seemed to favour guys like him. People like Steph? It went the extra mile to fuck things up should she fancy levelling the playing field.

She was meant to be going on a date.

Why not let them run out later, when she was so drunk it would mean nothing to turn her phone off and deal with things tomorrow?

Sex.

She was, probably, going to have sex.

Not any more.

Now she'd only be getting hot and sweaty lugging heavy boxes.

She retrieved her phone. Text or call?

Probably best to cancel with a call. That seemed the proper thing to do.

The phone rang for an impossible amount of time and Steph prayed for voicemail. Her guardian angel was definitely taking the piss tonight, because as she thought that, Zara picked up.

'Hello?'

'Hey, Zara – it's me, Steph.'

She chuckled. 'I know – my phone told me who was calling. What's up?' It suddenly occurred to Steph they'd never actually *spoken* before. Zara had a much stronger Glasgow twang than Steph had imagined. Her tone was friendly and mellow, a voice Steph could get used to hearing. For a second she considered blowing Cal's off after all.

She took a deep breath. 'I have a work issue.'

'Ah.'

'Yep. I think it would be better for us both if I cancelled. Saves me mucking you about. It could take an hour to sort, it could take two.'

'Nothing I can help with?' *Oh, you sweet angel.*

'No, honestly. It's a massive fuck-up and I'm best to just get in and sort it myself. I'm sorry.'

Silence hung on the line and Steph strained to listen to the background noise. Was she in a pub? She could hear chatter in the background.

'Okay,' Zara finally replied, disappointment clear. 'Well, I'm with some friends now, so if things change just give me a call.'

'I promise I will.'

All wasn't lost: she just needed to snap out of this foul mood.

STEPH LEANED against the racking in the stockroom. She was hot, sweaty, had a thumping headache, and her stinking mood still reigned supreme.

She'd completed the paperwork and discovered a strange wad of cash in the safe. What the hell was that earmarked for?

The stuffy office felt like it had no air, so she'd come back here to contemplate Zara.

It was an hour and forty-five minutes after they were meant to meet. She probably could still see her.

Only problem was, Steph really wasn't in the mood. And why start things off when you're not on top form?

The sweat pooling along her spine really wasn't helping matters.

Better to wait and reschedule.

It was a vicious cycle, though. Thinking about it put her in a worse mood, which made her want to meet Zara and drink her problems away. Release her tension with a night of drunken sex.

That was a terrible idea, though.

She blew her cheeks out.

Time to brave the bar.

She creaked the store door open and the noise of the bar hit her in the face. The club wasn't even in full swing yet. Today was going to be beyond busy. If this had been her shift, she probably would have stayed late to help out. Not clock off early like Arsehole Donnie.

Her blood boiled.

She took a deep breath.

No point getting worked up.

What was done was done.

She slinked behind the bar and poured herself a pint.

'You look nice,' Novak said, as he ducked into the fridge for a bottle of tonic water.

'Aye, well, don't get used to it.' Her tone was clipped and she felt bad being short with them, but her mood was set. It was either this or silence.

She stood at the end of the bar and downed half her pint, the cold brew softening her temperament.

'You still going out?' Kara asked.

She shook her head. 'Nah, not tonight.'

Kara shot her a weak smile. 'Sorry.'

'Not your fault.'

'What you going to do with your night, then?'

Steph shrugged and polished off the rest of her beer.

The red mist lessened and she scanned the crowd: it really was packed. 'You guys going to be okay if I go?'

'We'll do our best,' Kara said.

'That's not what I asked,' Steph replied with a smile.

'Honestly, you've done enough. And sorry again. I know this was my shift but I couldn't leave these guys and get to the cash and carry. It's just too busy.'

'I know. It's cool. It's Donnie's fault.'

'I'll make sure Cal knows you saved the day.'

'Won't make any difference.' Steph's eyes settled on a table of one, not far from the door.

Gemma.

One glass.

She looked bloody bored.

'Is she on her own?'

Kara leaned closer, attempting to get level with Steph's line of sight. 'Ah, your hottie. Yeah, she's been here nearly an hour. Not met anyone yet.'

Interesting. Steph's mood perked up, the vitriol in her bloodstream suddenly diluted.

This would never go anywhere, but she was at a loose end. Why not?

'Kara, get me a Sauvignon Blanc and a fresh beer, please.'

8

Not even a text.

Gemma had never been stood up in her life. Until now. Her stomach twisted, caught somewhere between embarrassment and anger.

To add insult to injury, she was being ghosted.

She looked at the message typed on her phone – a scathing, fury-driven reprimand – but had second thoughts and quickly deleted the whole thing.

What had she done wrong?

Aileen. Thirty. Originally from Dumfries. She was a doctor's receptionist.

She didn't seem the type to flake.

Oh God, what if she was dead? Guilt clenched Gemma's insides.

An hour had passed: she'd given her time enough to make an appearance. If she was dead, no point wasting the evening here.

Gemma felt a little bad at her internal monologue's flippancy.

She smiled in spite of herself.

It was only then she clocked someone standing at the table.

Steph.

'Hey, can I take a seat?' she asked, a drink in either hand.

'Yeah, of course, go ahead,' Gemma replied, straightening her posture as she put her phone away. Her heart tapped against her ribs, surprised by the sudden shift in events.

Steph placed the wine in front of Gemma. 'I got you a fresh one.'

'Thank you. On a break?'

She shook her head. 'Nah. I was meant to be off, but duty called.'

'I thought you were looking fancier than usual.' Gemma's cheeks flushed, although she wasn't quite sure why.

'I was meant to be on a date. I'm guessing you're having as much luck as me tonight?'

'That obvious, huh?'

'Just a lucky guess.'

'How come you're not going out?'

'I can't be bothered after being here. Not in the mood.'

'So you thought you'd bother me instead?' The corners of her mouth turned up; she was amused at her own joke.

'I can go if you want,' Steph replied, her face falling.

'No, no,' Gemma replied, waving a hand over the table. 'I'm kidding. Company would be nice. I'm feeling a bit sorry for myself, truth be known.'

Steph raised her glass, proposing a toast. 'To turning things around.' They clinked glasses and took a sip while holding eye contact. 'I'm Steph, by the way,' she said, replacing her glass on the table.

'I know – you told me after savagely attacking me the other week.'

Steph smiled. The kind that twinkled in her eyes more than showing on her lips. 'I don't think *savagely* is the right word, but yes, still embarrassed about that. Sorry.'

'It's fine, honestly. The doctor says my ribs should be fully healed in a few weeks.'

Steph's eyes dropped to her pint as she shook her head, fighting a smile. 'So, still not found Mrs Right?'

'Nope. I think I might jack the search in. This week has been brutal.'

'With dates?'

'With everything.'

Steph's face grew concerned. 'Any—no,' she said, slicing the air with her palm. 'You don't need to tell me if you don't want.'

No harm in sharing. In fact, it might be good to have a moan. 'My ex-husband is having a baby with his new girlfriend.'

'Ex-husband? They're—' she searched for the right word. 'Unusual.'

'In our line of work, anyway.'

'So, you *are* gay? It's just your label at Lovefest said you were...'

Gemma sighed. Everyone always wanted to know her history. Here come the questions! She should go out armed with an FAQ sheet. 'Yes. I just figured it out a little later than most.'

'You got there in the end. That's what matters. You're happier now?'

That was a new one. 'Yeah. Lots.'

'Good. So, him having a baby is good or bad?'

Was that it? Where were the fifty thousand questions

wondering how she never knew she was gay? 'Erm, both, I guess.'

Steph nodded, as if she was a dab hand at having baby-bound ex-husbands. 'Must be weird. I guess if he was a woman you'd still be married and you'd be the one having the baby. Or at least, that's what I'd be thinking.'

She'd hit it on the head. Maybe she did have an ex-husband. Who was Gemma to judge on looks?

'Are you a mind reader as well as Cupid?'

'Just putting myself in your shoes.'

Gemma took a sip of wine, re-evaluating the woman before her. 'Do you want kids?'

'We've only just met.'

Gemma swung a foot out, intent on a playful whack to the shin, but missed. 'You know what I mean.'

Steph smiled coyly. 'I did, yeah. I thought me and my ex would have them. Getting a bit old now.'

'Always such an emphasis on age.'

'Meaning?'

'All these self-imposed time limits. Why does no one just *live*?'

'Easier said than done with babies. At this rate I'll be geriatric before I even get a date.'

'Don't tell me Cupid has trouble dating, too? There's no hope left in the world.'

'So busy helping other people I forget about myself.'

'Well, we'll need to sort that.' Gemma scanned the room. 'No one here that's your type?'

Steph gulped, her eyes trailing the tables surrounding them. 'It was a lot easier when you all had name badges on.'

'It was a bit, wasn't it? So, you like girls you wouldn't necessarily know were gay?'

'I guess that's one way to describe it. Basically, I think you and I have the same taste.'

'Good thing we look so different or we might be competing.'

'I wouldn't fancy my chances there.' Steph took a swig of beer and Gemma admired the mandala pattern on her hand. So intricate. 'So, Gemma, what's your story? What could I expect to see on your Tinder bio?'

'Ooft, right.' Gemma took a good glug of wine, gearing herself up. 'Gemma. Thirty-three. I live in Shawlands but I'm originally from Bearsden. I'm a commercial solicitor and I like watching romantic comedies and going for walks in the woods, and I've always wanted to give painting a go but never got round to it.'

'Wow. Lot to take in. Let me unpack that,' Steph said and took a sip of beer. 'Commercial solicitor: what's that entail?'

Gemma scrunched up her face. 'I think I'd need to buy you a few more beers before you manage to feign much interest in that. Leases, trade agreements, negotiations. Boring stuff like that.'

'Nah, don't play it off. You obviously enjoy it, so it must be exciting to you.'

'I do, actually. Do you like your job?'

'Not tonight. And romantic comedies? So you're a big softy at heart?' Steph said, quickly changing the subject.

'Can't beat a happy ending. What about you?'

'Me?'

'What would your bio say?'

'Good question. I've never written one. Erm, let me think.'

'Probably best to start with your name.'

'Thank you. Yes. Let's go with that. So, Steph, never

Stephanie,' she said, holding a finger in the air. 'Call me that and I'll kill you. Thirty-seven—'

'You're never thirty-seven.'

'—people always think I'm younger cause of my height. I got IDed for a lotto ticket the other day,' she snorted. 'Live in Shawlands but originally from Portsoy.'

'Where's that?'

'Near Banff.'

'Which is?'

'Near Elgin. Aberdeen? That neck of the woods.'

'Ah, so north. Thought I detected a hint of something else.'

'I don't have much of an accent now. Been in Glasgow for twenty years.'

'Go home much?'

Steph pulled a face. 'Never. Parents weren't exactly down with the whole gay thing.'

Shit. 'Sorry.'

'Doesn't matter. I got over it a long time ago.'

Gemma didn't know what to say. The thought of losing her family was unimaginable. She wanted to ask questions, but now wasn't the time or the place. *Shit.*

Steph filled the gap, saving Gemma from putting her foot in her mouth. 'Erm, and I like horror films and books. And tattoos, in case you didn't notice. I, erm . . . I dunno what else. I just work, really. Honestly, work is pretty much all I do.'

'Do you think that's why you're single?'

Steph snorted into her beer, so much she had to pull at her nose before answering. 'You sure you're a solicitor and not a lawyer?' she jibed. 'I feel like I'm on the stand.'

Gemma leaned forward. 'So I'm right?'

'It has been mentioned before, yes. What about you? Why are you single?'

'Well, it's not for not trying. I think I'm too picky.'

'Oh, really? What's on the list?'

'Must be about the same age as me. Feminine. Not too bothered about hair colour—'

'How very laid-back of you.'

'—must have a good job, be self-sufficient, no baggage, easy to talk to. Oh, taller than me; that's sexy. Erm, funny – I like someone with a sense of humour. Similar interests. I don't know, I feel I'll know it when I see it. I'm still searching for a spark.'

'A spark? So you believe in love at first sight?'

'I'd like to think so.'

Steph rolled her eyes.

'What?' Gemma whined.

'You've been watching too many romcoms.'

'Hardly. Problem is, now I'm swearing off dating apps I don't know where to go. This is all so new to me.'

'I dunno how much help I can give. I'm not exactly a hotbed of local lesbian knowledge.'

'I'm going to have to rethink your nickname.'

Steph thought for a moment. 'You busy tonight?'

She shook her head. 'Nope. I thought I was going on a date, remember?'

'Fancy going somewhere else?'

9

'She's never gay,' Gemma hissed into Steph's ear.

Now they were standing, the height difference was obvious. Just a shame Gemma's preference ran in the opposite direction. Still, Steph was having a good time. She couldn't remember the last time she'd had an impromptu night out.

'I swear, she keeps looking over.' She'd agreed to be Gemma's wingman. Whatever that was. So far, she'd brought them to a different bar and that was it.

They'd left Cal's and gone to Johnny Whu's, which was a strange little bar in the centre of Shawlands. Steph had never actually been before but had heard great things, so it was a good opportunity to try it out. The place had more of a college bar theme than she'd anticipated, but it was packed and had a nice atmosphere, so she was more than happy to stay.

'So what happens now?' Gemma asked, her breath hot on Steph's ear.

'You should go talk to her.'

'And you?'

'I'll be here, silently cheering you on.'

'Hmm.'

'What?'

'Aren't wingmen meant to be the ones doing the preliminary checks? Bigging the other person up?'

'Huh?'

'Aren't – can you hear me?'

Steph shook her head and Gemma leaned closer, her hand now firmly on Steph's waist.

'I said, shouldn't you be the one talking to her, bigging me up?'

All Steph could register was the feeling of closeness and the smell of Gemma's perfume.

That wasn't why she was here, though.

'I guess, yeah,' she shouted.

'On you go then. Plus, I still don't think she's gay.' Gemma straightened herself, looking smug.

How the heck was she meant to do this? Just walk up to the woman? She *had* been looking over a lot.

Steph focused on her drink, taking a long draw as she psyched herself up. Talk to a random woman, discover her orientation, and if she was into Gemma. Easy stuff. As if. Suddenly being a wingman wasn't so fun. She'd thought it would be a good excuse to hang out with Gemma; now she was in the firing line.

'You chicken?' Gemma asked, looking like she was enjoying this a little too much.

They must have looked like an odd pair. Gemma's long blonde hair was styled in a ponytail, and in contrast to Steph's laid-back denim ensemble she'd gone for tailored trousers, a chiffon vest, and a contrasting suit jacket. Her high heels made Steph's insides resemble melted butter.

Add in her sparkling blue eyes and she was damn near perfect.

This would be an easy sell.

Steph just had to break the ice.

'Not chicken, just deciding on my first words. I've never done this before.'

'Well, how do you usually chat women up?'

'Eh, I don't.'

Confusion fogged Gemma's features. 'I really should have checked your CV before heading into this.'

Maisie had approached her. She'd been with friends, enjoying endless sun and beer at West Brewery, near the centre of Glasgow. They'd snagged each other's gaze a few times and before Steph knew it, a gorgeous woman with fiery red hair was taking a seat on the grass next to her. Conversation barely stopped in the years that followed. Why th—

'You okay?' Gemma asked, dangerously close again. 'You looked a bit sad.'

'Just thinking. You promise not to laugh when this goes wrong?'

Gemma put a hand over her heart. 'Guide's honour.'

Steph downed her beer and put the empty bottle on the tiny wooden shelf running the length of the wall behind Gemma.

A deep breath and she was headed to the bar, smiley woman located en route.

She almost walked right past her, but Steph could feel Gemma's stare boring into the back of her head, so she slowed her pace as she passed close to the standing table. Her heart rate was insane, her palms instantly a mess.

The woman zoned out of the conversation with her two

friends and focused on Steph as she passed. This was going well.

She smiled.

The woman smiled back.

If Gemma's eyes were lasers, Steph would have no head left. She could almost feel the heat on her skin.

She stopped mid-step, still holding the woman's gaze.

'Hey, how's it going?' Good. Sounded normal. Not like her insides were in a blender.

The woman nodded, her cheeks burning red. 'Yeah, good, you okay?'

She was cute, no denying it. Smiley, green eyes, long brown hair. The slit of her maxi dress showed off a toned calf.

Her friends sized Steph up but she paid them no heed. Her eyes were locked with Gemma's crush.

'So,' Steph started, having no clue what would follow. 'I saw you looking,' she said, signalling towards Gemma. Yikes, not as smooth as she'd hoped.

'Oh, God, sorry,' the woman interrupted, her cheeks growing darker. 'Is that your girlfriend?'

This was playing out surprisingly well.

'Oh, no, no. She's just a friend.'

The woman's eyes dipped the length of Steph before trailing back to find hers. Okay. Maybe not that well. For Gemma, at least. 'Good to know.'

'I, er—' Shit, words. She needed words.

'So, you're single?' she asked, turning her body towards Steph, away from her pals.

This evening was about Gemma, not her. She couldn't agree to be her wingman and then couple up with the first woman she approached, leaving Gemma alone. She was already having a shit week; she didn't need Steph adding to it.

'I'm not, sorry. My friend is though.'

She looked at Gemma then back to Steph. 'Ah. Shame. It was you I was looking at earlier, sorry. That's embarrassing.'

'Nah, it's cool. Doesn't matter. Have a good evening.'

The woman raked her eyes over Steph a final time. 'You too.'

Jesus. One wrong move and Steph's heart would break through her ribs. When did this room lose all its air? Fuck.

The bar was quick to serve her and she gave the lady a wide berth on the way back to Gemma.

'That didn't look successful,' Gemma said, taking her fresh wine off Steph.

'You were right. Not gay,' Steph lied.

Gemma's face betrayed her scepticism, but she didn't follow it up. 'You tried, though. Thank you.'

'So, who's next?'

'I think we've both done enough for the day.'

'Dating really sucks.'

'It does. I hate it.' She gulped her wine. 'I was going to make a joke about staying married but that might be a step too far.'

'Aye, I don't think we're quite there yet. Any more matches on Tinder?'

Gemma took a wavering deep breath and pulled out her phone. A few taps and she turned it to Steph.

She'd never been on Tinder. Stevie, Novak, and most of the other bar staff had it, so, yeah, she'd seen it in passing, but never properly. It always felt like a bit of a meat market to her. Swiping and dismissing people based on a two-second look at their face.

A profile stared back at Steph. Carly. Thirty-six. Waitress. She was pretty.

'We've been chatting quite a bit,' Gemma said, looking forlorn.

'You're really over this, aren't you?' Steph asked, handing the phone back. She'd seen enough.

Gemma shrugged. 'Just gets a bit much after a while.'

'Dating should be fun. You're putting too much pressure on yourself.'

'I know, it's just . . .' she gulped her wine again. 'I was at the top of the snakes and ladders board and then *whoosh*,' she said, slicing a hand through the air. 'I'm right down the bottom again, and I think Logan and his friends, and his family, they're all looking at me like I'm a failure.'

Steph screwed her face up. 'Logan? Was that your husband?'

'Yeah.'

'Well, let them judge all they want. You're happy. You're living your truth. They can mind their own business. It's how you feel that matters. Don't let your past smother your present.'

'Very wise.'

Steph smiled, and she hoped the warmth reached Gemma. She meant every word: it wasn't some guff to lead her on. 'I know how you feel. My ex is getting married soon and I look at myself and see nothing has changed. She's marking milestones and I'm stuck in the mud.'

'Why don't you change things, then?'

'No one to change things for. Only myself. Sometimes it's easier to do nothing. No matter how miserable it makes you.'

Gemma pouted. 'That's very sad and deep.' She put her hand on Steph's shoulder. 'Cupid, we need to get you laid.'

For a brief moment Gemma's eyes lingered on Steph's, anchored steady, and the room moved slower around them. Any other planet, any other timeline, and Steph might have chanced leaning in for a kiss. But she knew it was pointless, and it had been an age since she'd made friends outside of work. It was more important to hold onto the new connection than attempt a drunken snog.

Time zipped back to normal speed and the sound of the bar flooded Steph's ears. 'God knows it's been a while,' she said with a smile as she rolled her eyes.

'At least you've done it,' Gemma joked, avoiding eye contact.

'What? Like? Huh? I thought you were married?'

'Oh, Lord,' Gemma said, flustered and flushed. 'Yeah, with guys, of course. I'm not a virgin.'

Steph couldn't help the *yip* of laughter that escaped: there was just something about the look of cute indignation Gemma had at the notion.

'What's so funny?' Gemma said, a goofy smile spreading across her face.

'I don't actually know.' Steph wasn't about to admit how cute she'd looked.

Gemma playfully punched her arm. 'Right, well, knock it off,' she said with a smile. 'My vir—'

'Oh shit,' Steph said, leaping behind Gemma and using her as a shield.

Zara had just walked into Johnny Whu's.

'The girl I was meant to be on a date with is here,' Steph hissed, on tiptoe to get near Gemma's ear. Her hands gripped her waist for support. Firm, petite, totally off limits.

'So?' Gemma replied out the corner of her mouth. 'Go say hello.'

'Eh, how would that look? I call things off for work and she finds me in a bar with another woman.'

'Fair enough. What are you going to do?'

'Down that. We need to go.'

Steph watched Zara head to the other side of the bar and take a seat, thankfully with her back to the door. She held a hand out to Gemma. 'Now.'

Gemma's fingers laced with hers and they legged it.

~

Escape successful, they'd headed to another pub, The Griffin, and drank far too much while getting to know each other better. Gemma was surprisingly laid-back with a bottle of wine in her. Steph guessed most people were.

She'd heard more about her marriage and how she missed her old friends. Steph had learned she had a brother and twin nephews. She was close to her Granny and saw them every Sunday. Their families couldn't be bigger polar opposites. It was cute how much she gushed over them. There was no gaping hole in Steph's heart, or even an ounce of jealousy. She was better off without her family, but it warmed her cockles to know other people had the support she lacked.

Before Steph knew it, hours had passed and she was standing outside Gemma's close door, saying goodnight.

'Are you sure you're going to be okay?' Gemma asked, a slight slur to her words.

'Honestly. One of us needs to go solo. I'll be fine. I'll text you when I get in.'

'You don't have my number.'

'I'll shout it out the window, then.'

'No, no, come on,' Gemma said, beckoning Steph closer. 'Gimme your phone. I need to know you're safe.'

Gemma stabbed her number in, giving herself a one-ringer to be certain it was right before she passed it back.

'There. I wouldn't sleep otherwise.'

'Appreciated. Now, get to bed.'

'Night, Cupid.'

'Night, Gemma,' she called over her shoulder as she walked down the pavement.

10

This is horrendous x

Steph's reply was almost instant:

Come on! Can't be that bad xx

She quickly followed it up with another before Gemma could reply.

I mean, don't we all have a favourite rock? X

Gemma's bit the corner of her bottom lip, stopping the smile that had broken across her face from going any further.

Personally, I do not. You can enlighten me as to yours later x

Horrendous wasn't the right word for this date. It was dire. No: worse. It was— Gemma was saved the bother of reaching for her thesaurus by the return of her date. Although, at this rate, reading that might be better entertainment.

Alice. Thirty-one. Teaching assistant.

Gemma wished she'd been stood up again.

She seemed nice enough: friendly brown eyes, dyed blonde hair, and a pleasant enough smile, but conversation wasn't so much as stilted but as non-existent. She'd had more invigorating chats in the dentist's chair.

'So,' Gemma said, searching for another topic of conversation. 'Do you do any sports?'

'Oh, no. You?'

Urgh. The only time she'd opened up was when the topic had veered towards her favourite hobby: rock collecting. It would seem Alice was somewhat of an amateur geologist. Which, in the right person's company, would be a terrific interest to bond over. Really not Gemma's realm, though. The only rocks she liked were the ones in jewellery.

'Gym, mostly,' Gemma said, sipping on her white wine. 'I like the treadmill, but I can't run outside to save myself.'

God, her brain was shutting down. Even *her* answers were getting shorter.

Gemma searched her surroundings for ideas.

They'd opted for a pub on the other side of Queen's Park, in the neighbouring suburb of Strathbungo. It was a quaint wee place with barely a dozen tables and a bar that looked like it had seen Queen Victoria come and go.

Questions. She needed questions. She'd covered siblings, pets, careers, food, holidays, hobbies. She was close to admitting defeat when inspiration struck.

'Do you have a shocking fact to share? Like, something that always surprises people? I'm missing the nail on my right big toe.'

She winced internally. Is this what it had come to? Talking about toenails (or lack thereof)?

'Erm,' Alice said, thinking. 'Not really. I can roll my tongue.'

Not exactly front-page news, but the reply was close to double digits in words so Gemma took it as a win.

She waited, sure Alice would follow it up with a

question. Maybe she just didn't care about Gemma's big toe enough to ask. She wasn't sure she even cared herself at this point.

Nada.

Time to admit defeat. Gemma drained the last of her wine. 'Alice, this has been lovely, but I really need to go.'

'Oh, really? You won't stay for another?'

She wanted to prolong this torture? Was she on the same date? 'Sorry. Have to dash. But it was lovely.'

An awkward hug goodbye and Gemma was free, the muggy August air hitting her as she left the pub. It was the perfect weather for a stroll around the park: it was just a shame she had no one to do it with.

No point wasting a good evening in her pyjamas. She power walked to Cal's.

∼

'SHE WAS MAYBE JUST NERVOUS,' Steph said, placing a Sauvignon Blanc in front of Gemma.

She'd nabbed a stool at the pub end of the bar: the place was packed tonight. More Lovefest shenanigans. She was getting sick of it all. Happy couples seemed to be everywhere, taunting her at every turn.

'I know, but it all felt so forced.' She downed a large gulp of wine, the cool alcohol like a calming blanket around her. 'She was perfectly lovely, just not for me.'

'You're really expecting instant fireworks, aren't you?' Steph asked, leaning against the bar. She had on a sleeveless T-shirt today. Its huge drop was so low that Gemma could see the tats that snaked around her torso. It was too dark, though; she couldn't quite work out what they were. She averted her eyes, aware she'd probably stared too long already.

'Not fireworks. I just want to get on with her.' She held her head in her hands. 'Why's it all so tough?'

She jumped when Steph's hand closed around her forearm and gave a reassuring squeeze.

'I thought you were jacking it all in, anyway?'

Gemma sat up straight, letting out a groan. 'I was, but then Alice messaged me. I thought, why not?'

Steph reached for a cloth under the bar and Gemma's eyes followed the gap in her T-shirt. Was it flowers? Something organic.

She flicked her eyes back to Steph's face as she wiped down her station.

'How did you and Logan meet?'

'At an awards ceremony. His firm and my firm were up against each other. There was lots of champagne. I gave him my number and the rest was history.'

Steph pursed her lips, thinking. 'Sounds decent. Much better than dating apps.'

'I can hardly count on being nominated again *and* meeting a lesbian solicitor.'

'Stranger things have happened.'

'Speaking of strange,' Gemma said, leaning closer. 'If I told you I was missing a toenail, what would you say?'

Steph's eyes grew wide, her face contorted with confusion. 'Eh – what? A toenail?'

'Yes.'

'*Okay*. How did you lose that?'

'Thank you,' Gemma said, throwing her hands up and nearly losing her balance. 'Alice didn't even flinch.'

'You were talking about toenails? I think you might have

been the banter sponge, not her. Why the hell were you talking about toenails?'

Gemma's cheeks reddened. 'I was struggling, okay? But, my point is, she didn't follow it up.'

'Fair enough. So, how did you lose it?' Steph's eyes wandered to the end of the bar and the queue that was forming for Novak. 'Quickly, I'll die of suspense if I have to dash before I find out.'

'Hockey match. Girl stamped on me. Stud turned it black. It never was the same. Doctors took it off eventually.'

Steph screwed her face up. 'Lovely. Right, I'd better serve. Don't go anywhere.'

Gemma sipped her wine. She'd tried in vain to arrange drinks with some old friends this week. It wasn't to be. Either they were child-laden, too busy, or simply left her on read.

She missed social events. She and Logan were always doing something, whether it was going out for dinner, hosting drinks at their house, or visiting friends. There was always something to do. Summers were for standing around in manicured gardens, the smell of the BARBECUE lingering around you, a cool glass of wine in hand, attending children's birthday parties that were as much for the adults as the kiddies.

This summer had been spent on her phone, attempting dull and unimaginative conversation.

How was your day?
What do you do for work?
Where do you stay?
What's your favourite food?
Blah. Blah. Blah.

She'd been so down in the dumps and focused on Logan's news that she'd even let her mind wander to the idea of being a single parent. But it wasn't just children that loomed on the horizon: she wanted someone to share the journey with. She deserved that. Only now it wasn't just a case of sticking one and one together to make two. She needed connection as well. Basically, and she knew Steph would call her out and blame romcoms, but whatever: she wanted to marry her best friend.

Just a shame she didn't have one any more.

Not that she would marry Julie anyway. Really not her type.

She shook her head, aware this internal monologue was spiralling. She knew what she meant, though. Looks weren't enough. She wanted someone to live life with. Someone who made coming home the highlight of her day. Someone she could just be herself around.

'Are you really missing a toenail?' Steph asked, appearing back at Gemma's end of the bar.

'Why's that so hard to believe?'

'It's not, it's just, I dunno. I thought you were winding me up,' she chuckled.

'Me? I would never. What about you?'

'Sporting all ten of my nails. Well, twenty if you count these bad boys,' she replied, doing her best jazz hands.

'Nooo, silly. Got an interesting fact for me?'

Steph blew her cheeks out. 'Honestly? I don't know. That's a tough one.' She rubbed her chin, deep in thought. 'Right, I don't know if this counts. It's nothing weird or wonderful about my body, but when I moved to Glasgow, I was sixteen, I had no qualifications, nothing. So I needed a job. Can you guess what I did?'

Gemma shook her head.

'I was a bingo caller.'

She grinned so hard her cheeks hurt. 'No you weren't.'

'I was. Bloody loved that job. Me and the grannies were like that,' she said, linking her pinkies together.

'I can imagine you getting on well with the older generation.'

'Especially when I was a wee naive sixteen-year-old. They watched out for me.' She took a drink of water from her glass behind the bar.

'Must have been tough, moving down here on your own when you were so young.'

Steph shrugged. 'Just did what had to be done.'

'Where did you stay? Did you have friends, at least? Apart from the grannies.'

Steph's gaze shifted from Gemma's and anchored in the distance. 'Erm, I was homeless for a bit, but I sorted that and now look at me.' Her eyes snagged Gemma's again and a smile pulled at her lips. 'Everything worked out in the end.'

It was obvious she didn't want to talk about it, so Gemma left a thousand questions to settle in her throat. 'Did you get a sparkly jacket, at least?'

'To call the bingo? No. Sadly. Just wore my regular clothes.'

'Pity.'

'I know, right? I could totally pull it off,' she said, and did a wee spin, arms held taut like she was holding onto the lapels of a suit jacket.

Gemma giggled. 'We'll need to get you one, find you an excuse to wear it.'

'Chance would be a fine thing. So, that's my past. What about your future? Where do you see yourself going?'

'Ooft. Big question.' Gemma thought, sipping her wine as she did so. 'I love my job, so I'll probably move up the ranks when I can. But mainly: have kids, settle down. God, that's so boring, isn't it?' She rested her head against the palm of her hand.

It was no wonder she couldn't get a girlfriend. She was boring and basic.

'Not boring. I think most people want that.'

Gemma wasn't convinced. It sounded very boring and privileged to her. But she couldn't help what her heart desired. 'And what about you? What does the future hold for Steph Campbell?'

'Unsure, to be honest.' She leaned on her forearms, getting close to Gemma as she dropped her voice. 'I'm getting a bit old for antisocial late nights and workplace drama. I think I want to do something different.' She held a fleeting finger to her lips, letting Gemma know it was a secret.

'What would you do?' Gemma asked, keeping her voice low.

Steph waggled her eyebrows. 'I don't want to say, in case it doesn't work out.'

'Oh, go on, please. I'm very good at keeping secrets. I mean, I kept that I was gay from myself for twenty-nine years.'

'True. Your credentials are top notch.'

She leaned close again and Gemma caught a whiff of her citrusy perfume. 'I want to brew my own beer.'

'Really?' Gemma blurted. 'That's so cool.'

Steph's brow furrowed. 'Really? You think?'

'Oh, yeah. Do you make any at home now?'

'Actually, yes.'

Gemma couldn't help but appreciate how proud Steph looked. It was cute.

'And I've even got a wine on the go too. Just for fun, that one. Should be ready in a month or so. Will probably be potent. You should come round to mine and try it, when it's ready.'

'Now there's an offer I can't say no to.'

'Queue's back – I'd better boost. Don't go anywhere.'

No chance of that.

11

'So,' Cal said, getting comfy in the seat opposite Steph a few days later.

Cal had never been anything but lovely to her, but she was still dreading today's meeting. It was crazy to think a year had passed since her last annual review. What stung was that it would be the same chat as twelve months ago: Donnie should go and she should be manager. Cal had done nothing to change the situation, and it was steadily getting worse.

'So,' Steph repeated, and waited for Cal to lead the conversation.

They were in a booth up the back, tucked away from punters and curious ears. Not that there were many on a Tuesday morning.

'How do you feel the last twelve months have gone?' It was a loaded question, and despite Cal's calm eyes, it was obvious he knew he'd pretty much just pulled the pin on a grenade and sat it on the table.

Steph held his gaze, wondering how best to start this. She'd rehearsed this a thousand times while unable to sleep last night. Now the time had come, though, the words were missing in action.

'It's been interesting.' Best to start off small, get the lay of the land.

'Interesting? How so?' Cal was a nice guy: his smile told you as much. It also warned you not to fuck with him. She'd seen him lose his temper and it wasn't pretty. Always justified, but never pretty.

The clog in her throat remained. Throwing Donnie under the bus was the right thing to do, but bursting with a torrent of his misdoings felt wrong. 'I still don't feel I'm getting the support I need from my manager.'

Cal nodded and skimmed the pad of notes at his side.

He was looking older these days. Grey streaked his once-ginger beard and the tummy he'd been cultivating over the last decade now looked like he was smuggling a beach ball when he turned to the side.

Steph hadn't fared any better. It's funny how one morning you can wake up and suddenly realise you've aged ten years. Crow's feet lined her eyes and she'd found a grey hair the other day. It was all downhill from here.

'What kind of support are you needing?' Cal asked.

She stifled a groan. He knew. He totally knew. This was him leading her up the path, wanting her to outright say what Donnie had done.

'Physically being in the venue might be a nice start.'

Cal's features creased, hinting he might not be as clued up as she thought. 'Meaning?'

Steph scanned the empty club space. She had to say it. He was the one in the wrong, how was she at fault by simply telling the truth?

She cleared her throat. 'Donnie has a new habit of starting at eight and leaving well before his shift ends.'

'Eight?'

'Yep.'

'What's there to do at eight in a pub?'

'My point exactly. He told me he's doing paperwork and stuff, but since I have to sort most of that anyway I really have no clue.' She took a deep breath, her heart beating so fast it threatened to make her voice wobble. 'It wouldn't be so bad if he stayed on shift, but he leaves early every day.'

Cal looked like she'd just hit him round the head with a keg. 'How long's that been going on?'

'Nearly a year, I'd say.'

Cal's face remained stoic. Only the slight nod of his head hinted that he'd registered her. 'Anything else I should know about?'

Jeez. Where to start? 'He's been paying cash for stuff we wouldn't usually, and not getting receipts. Plus, there's a weird stack of notes in the safe. I've looked at the accounts and I don't know what it's about.'

'Have you asked Donnie?'

'No point. We don't exactly see eye to eye.'

Cal's movements were minimal, but the red rising up his neck said that internally it was a different matter.

'And how's long's the money stuff been going on?'

Steph shrugged. 'Hard to know. I only became aware of it because Stevie said the float was down a hundred pounds the other week.'

Another gentle nod. Steph got the impression that if Cal dared to move further, it would be like flicking a tripwire.

He looked over his notes again. 'And the inventory issue – was that Donnie's fault too?'

Steph nodded and stuffed her hands between her thighs. This was like being back at school, being told off by the headmaster.

Cal lifted his gaze, his calm eyes now fogged with anger. 'And what about you?'

'Me?'

'You should have seen that the inventory was wrong, no?'

Well, he had her there. 'I, er, I—' Words were a struggle. Sickness clenched her stomach. 'I guess I should have double-checked it was right.'

'Double-checked?'

'Yes.'

'Like, when you saw the shelves were empty? When you physically went to get stock and there was only one bottle left? Do you not think that should have been a clue?' Malice nipped his tone.

'It's not just *my* responsibility.'

'No,' Cal replied, twisting the word to last a few syllables. 'But it is part of your job to make sure this place runs smoothly. If you saw Donnie made a mistake you should have helped fix it. Not set him up.'

'Set him up? *Set him up?* Are you kidding me? This was no mistake. He's at it.'

Cal put his pen down with force. 'I expected better of you, Steph.'

'How is this my fault?'

'I need you to be a team player. Sometimes that means helping out when someone mucks up. I know you don't get on with Donnie, but you need to put that aside and make sure Cal's comes first.'

Was he seriously turning this around so she was in trouble? Yes, she should have ordered in more stock, but when so much was supposedly in, how was it anyone's fault but Donnie's?

And how dare he say she didn't put Cal's first? That's all

she ever did. This job had precedence over her entire life. If she'd had a little common sense and not cared so damn much she'd still be with Maisie.

She bit down the anger. Now wasn't the time for tantrums.

She steadied herself, taking a moment to count her breaths. 'I think you and I both know Cal's always comes top of my list. My loyalty has never wavered over the years. I made a mistake. I'm sorry.'

Cal pursed his lips, his thick beard bushing out. 'Let's draw a line under this and forget about it.'

If only it were that easy.

∼

THE REST of the meeting was boring and uneventful. Numbers. Staff training. Future plans. Steph hadn't taken in most of it. Anger seethed in her veins, biting her muscles, growing more acidic as the day went on.

Late afternoon she gave in and fired off a text:

Come to mine tonight? I need to talk xx

Home alone with her thoughts, the day became a thousand times worse. It was a relief when the buzzer went.

She flicked the latch, slumped back on the sofa, closed her eyes, and waited.

It wasn't long before Maisie's footsteps filled the hall.

She dumped her bag on the armchair and Steph felt the sofa shift as she sat down.

'What's up?' Maisie asked, putting a hand on Steph's knee.

If she opened her eyes, she was going to cry. No doubt about it.

'Annual review,' Steph mumbled.

Only the gentle hum of the refrigerator filled the air.

Maisie scooted closer. 'Steph, look at me.'

She tensed her jaw. A few deep breaths and she was ready. But nope: as soon as her eyes opened, a tear escaped.

'Oh, hey, come on,' Maisie said, pulling her in close.

She hadn't changed. Same wild auburn hair, same comforting arms, and floral perfume. Same Maisie she'd fucked over for a job she now hated.

Steph wasn't a crier. She couldn't be. Her walls were so heavily fortified there was no chance for them to escape. It was different with Maisie, though. Always had been.

She focused on Maisie's breathing and rested against her chest, her ex's arms still holding her tight.

Maisie spoke into Steph's hair, 'Still got issues with Donnie?'

She nodded, her sodden cheeks dragging on Maisie's top.

'And Cal's still not helping?'

Another nod.

'Let me see you,' she said, leaning back and taking Steph in. Maisie wiped at her cheeks with her thumbs. 'Right, so, how do we fix this?'

A fresh wave of emotion welled in Steph's chest.

It was wrong to get Maisie involved, but there was no one else to turn to. She had friends, but no one close. Gemma had fleetingly crossed her mind, but she barely knew the woman: she didn't want to listen to Steph moaning about work. It was a friendship of convenience, nothing else. She didn't want to become a burden and push her away.

'Sorry,' Steph said, her voice a squeak.

'For what?'

'Getting you involved. Crying. Everything really.'

Maisie's face was a mix of empathy and pity. 'One: I chose to be here. Two: never apologise for crying. Three: yeah, you owe me.'

Steph forced a smile and pawed at her eyes, ridding them of tears. 'It just feels so unfair. I've done nothing wrong.'

Maisie repositioned herself on the couch, pulling her dress under as she brought her legs up. 'You know I think they take advantage of you.'

Steph relaxed back, her head smooshed into her sofa's soft cushion. 'I know, but Cal's a good guy. It doesn't make sense.'

'Donnie has something on him. For sure. And, yeah, he's a nice guy, but it doesn't make how he treats you right.'

Steph mirrored her position. 'Do you think I should leave?'

Maisie's eyes grew wide. 'Jesus, there's a sentence I never thought I'd hear.'

Steph chewed on her bottom lip, unsure if she wanted to share the next revelation with Maisie, of all people. But she needed to get it off her chest, and Maisie was her only option.

'There's someone I like, and—' she said, light-heartedly raising her voice to quash the smile on Maisie's face. '—even though nothing can ever, ever happen with her, it's got me thinking about us. If I'm ever going to have a relationship I need to be serious. Is it really worth the strain for a job I don't even like any more?'

Maisie was gobsmacked. 'Wow. The surprises keep on coming.' She sat up straighter, excitement pulsing through her. 'So, tell me more about this girl.'

'There's nothing to tell.'

Maisie scoffed. 'You never like anyone. She must be special.'

Steph screwed up her face. 'Honestly, nothing can happen, so it's not even worth talking about. It's just got me thinking about the bigger picture.'

'How do you know nothing can happen? Is she married? Scandal!'

Steph playfully swiped at her. 'She's divorced, actually.'

'I was joking, but wow, okay. Steph and the divorcee. Kids?'

'Nope.'

'Older? Younger?'

'You're not going to stop, are you?'

'Nope,' she said, with a wicked smile. She hopped to her feet and walked to the kitchen, grabbing two beers, just like she'd done a thousand times when they lived together. 'Place looks good, by the way,' she said, passing Steph a beer as she flopped onto the sofa.

It had changed a lot since Maisie last visited, which wasn't often. Shannon wasn't exactly on board with the whole being-friends-with-exes thing. She didn't need to worry, though. Steph would never cross any lines: she'd fucked up and it was better to have Maisie as a friend than not at all.

Maisie's taste had brought in more light, happy florals but Steph had recently taken it upon herself to paint the room's feature wall navy. A few gold industrial accessories and the place was looking more high-end than ever. She was proud of it.

'So, come on. Spill,' Maisie said, giving her knee a jiggle.

There was no use delaying the inevitable. 'Her name's Gemma. She's a customer. We've kind of started hanging out in the last month. Blonde hair. Blue eyes. Tall. Killer smile. Funny. Easy to talk to. The usual.'

'The usual!' Maisie said with a laugh. 'And she's totally off limits because? Straight?'

'Nah. She also likes tall, feminine women. And at last check, I was neither of those.'

Maisie took a swig of beer. 'Fair enough, but you're sure she doesn't like you? Like, one hundred per cent?'

'No doubt in my mind.'

Maisie pumped her eyebrows, a smile masked by her beer bottle.

'What's that look about?' Steph asked with a dubious chuckle.

'You are straight-up terrible at knowing when someone is flirting with you.'

'Am not.'

'Are so. You told me you weren't even sure if our first date was a date.'

'Right, well. Okay. Sometimes I'm not as in tune as I could be.' *How were you meant to know without sounding big-headed? And what if they just wanted to be friends? If you asked, it sounded like you fancied them and wanted a date. It was a twisted minefield.*

'I was more than a little flirty when we met *and* I gave you my number. Do you think I give random women my number in all the pubs I go to, hoping to make new pals?' Maisie said, playfully shoving Steph's knee.

'Well, it still worked out in the end, didn't it?' *Kind of.*

'Does she know you like her?'

Steph snorted with laughter. 'Why would I say that?'

'Well, you never know.'

'Nah, look, right,' Steph said, flapping a hand in the space between them. She was feeling better already, her shoulders looser, her chest lighter, like she'd been holding her breath for the last month and finally gasped for air. 'Gemma isn't the point. The point is: what do I do about work?'

'You really think you might leave?'

'If I had something else to do, then yeah.'

Maisie let out a low whistle. 'Nothing on the horizon?'

Steph shook her head. 'I could get a job in another pub, but I don't think that solves my problems.'

'And this?' Maisie said, holding up her bottle. Steph's own, a spicy pale ale.

'If you've got a spare quarter of a mil hanging around, I'm sorted.'

'What? That much?'

'Microbreweries are expensive.'

Maisie studied the bottle, as if the answers to all of Steph's problems might be at the bottom of it. 'Okay. That's out, then.'

Steph pouted. 'Thanks for listening.'

'Any time. I just wish I could help.'

'You've done enough.'

'I'm glad I did something. And I got a free beer.' A cheeky glint sparkled in her eyes. 'So, when do I get to meet Gemma?'

Steph rolled her eyes. 'Never in a million years.'

'Oh, come on. Sounds like we might get on.'

Steph shot daggers. 'You're getting married soon, missus.'

'I didn't mean to date, I just meant as a pal.'

'Speaking of dates,' Steph said, feeling nearly herself again. 'I almost went on one.'

The bottle slipped from Maisie's hand but she recovered

it at the last second. 'You, went on a date? With Gemma? I don't understand.'

Steph waved a hand between them, unable to fight the grin on her face. 'No, no. Not Gemma. A woman called Zara. And *almost* went on one. Didn't actually make it.'

Maisie looked like she'd just been asked to explain quantum physics. Her brow was so knitted her eyebrows nearly touched. 'Wait. You like someone *and* you almost went on a date with someone else?' Maisie made a show of looking around, her arms outstretched like she was feeling her surroundings. 'Have I entered the Twilight Zone? Did I fall and hit my head on the way over here? Am I dreaming?'

'Hoi! I can do dates.'

Maisie scoffed. 'Aye, but you never do. So, spill! Who is she? How did you meet? Why didn't you go out?'

'So, you remember Southside Slugs, yeah? She's Gary's cousin. He set us up and work stuff happened. Which is another huge reason why I'm thinking about all this.'

'Ah, makes sense. So, you going to see her another time?'

Steph shook her head. She'd had such a good time with Gemma that the more she thought about it, the less she wanted to go out with Zara. Her heart just wasn't in it. If she was going to date, she would hold out for someone who gave her butterflies. That might not be Gemma, but who knew who was on the horizon? 'Nah. It was a blind date set-up. I think I'll wait until I meet someone properly.'

Maisie shook her head, still dumbfounded. 'This is wild.'

'You'd think I was a nun or something.'

Maisie took a long swig from her bottle. 'Come on, you must be able to see how massive this is, Steph? You want to leave work, you have feelings for someone, and you nearly went on a date? One of those things alone would be a milestone.'

She had a point, but Steph wasn't about to admit that. 'Been a busy month.'

'I'll say.' Maisie's face oozed approval. 'Good to see you smiling again.'

'I knew you were the woman for the job.'

'Any time. But actually, I should go soon, if you're okay? I told Shannon I was meeting Stacy from work.'

'No you did not.' Steph hated it when Maisie lied to her fiancée. It made her an accomplice to a crime she was ignorant of committing.

'It's cool; all in good faith. But listen. Let's meet up for a coffee or something soon, yeah? Have a proper chat? Just try and tone the pace down or something. Next thing you'll be married. I can at least meet your future wife first, yeah? Speaking of which: Gemma?'

'You're not meeting Gemma.'

'Bye, Steph,' Maisie said, trying and failing to hide a smile. She kissed her on the cheek. 'Oh, wait,' she said as she grabbed her bag. 'What's her last name?'

'No Facebook.'

'Spoilsport.'

12

The stars had aligned, the wind blown in the right direction, and the tides turned the correct way: today had actually been a success.

Gemma was practically skipping to Cal's, excited to tell Steph about the unexpected turn of events.

She'd found a Lovefest LGBTQ+ event in a local pub: The Stables. It was nothing as grand as Cal's had put on but it was good nonetheless.

After a little bit of mingling she'd hit it off with a lady called Izzy. Thirty-four. Accountant. Ridiculously pretty.

They'd exchanged numbers and called it a night. Izzy had a big work thing tomorrow and couldn't stay out.

Cal's wasn't that busy tonight, but Gemma still plumped for a seat at the bar. It was easier to talk to Steph then.

'Don't you look like the cat that got the cream,' Steph said, already reaching for a wine glass.

Gemma held her chin in her hand, a dreamy look on her face. 'It's finally happened.'

'Huh?'

'I've met someone.'

'Really?' Steph asked, her tone a little sceptical.

'No, really. That matchmaking event in The Stables – it was great. I told you you should have come.'

'And miss working here? Never! So, tell me more.' Steph leaned against the bar.

'Her name's Izzy. She's an accountant. She likes romcoms and cats. Originally from St Andrews but has lived here since university.' Gemma punctuated the info dump with a content sigh.

'Wow. You really have fallen tonight, huh?'

'Early days,' Gemma replied, taking a sip from her freshly poured wine. 'You been busy tonight?'

Steph shrugged.

'You seem down. What's up?'

Her raised eyebrows and darting eyes signalled work stuff. 'Nothing.'

'Ah.' She'd not seemed herself recently. Not that Gemma knew exactly what that was but it didn't take a rocket scientist to know this wasn't Steph at her best.

Steph's eyes trailed the length of the bar. They were pretty much alone; none of the occupied tables were close enough to hear. 'Can I ask you a personal question?'

'Within reason.'

She dropped her voice. 'Before you left your husband, how did you know it was the right decision? Well, like, obviously it was the right decision. But you know what I mean. It was a big, life-changing thing. How did you know it was the right *time*?'

Gemma made a noise like a deflating tyre. 'Good question.'

'Sorry, it's a lot, I know.'

'No, no. Let me think.' She sipped her wine. 'It took me a long time. First I confessed to a friend that I thought I might be bi.' She looked over her shoulders, making sure she absolutely was out of earshot of other customers. 'But then, I think admitting it to myself was the hardest part, you know? Then maybe a year before I told Logan.'

'A year?' Steph blurted.

'Yep. I was terrified. I thought I could just stick it out, but in the end I decided to stop worrying about other people and do something for myself. I couldn't have stayed. It would have killed me.'

Steph nodded, her eyes full of understanding. 'Slow and steady wins the race, huh?'

'Not necessarily. But it took me a while to get the courage.'

'It must have been really tough. But seeing how happy you are now gives me courage. Especially now Izzy is on the scene,' Steph said with a waggle of her head.

'Like I said, early days. So, what's going on? Why the question?'

'Just have a lot to think about just now.'

'Don't want to talk about it?'

'I do. Just not here,' she said with a wink.

'Anything I can help with?'

'If you see any breweries come up for sale, then let me know. I'll buy a lotto ticket.'

'Speaking of which, is this wine nearly ready?'

'Close. Still a few weeks, I reckon.'

'Shame. I'm dying to try some of your spoils.'

'If you ever fancy beer, I have plenty of that.'

Gemma scrunched her face. 'Not a huge beer fan unless it's fruity. Sorry, I know that's sacrilege to your ears.'

'You never know. Try something new and I might be the one to convert you.'

'Has she texted yet?' Steph asked.

'Steph, it's the wee small hours of the morning. Do you really think she'll be up?'

'Oops. I forget my clock's different to normal people's.'

She hadn't meant to stay out this late, but the longer she stayed in the Cal's the more fun she had, and when Steph invited her back to sample some beers she'd seen no harm. She was meeting Granny at eleven tomorrow morning, so should probably sleep soon, but the high from her success with Izzy still coursed adrenaline through her veins. There was no way she'd be nodding off soon.

Staying out and feeding off Steph's energy had only made it worse. She'd even let Gemma stay in Cal's to witness the deep clean, which was super odd. With the lights on and no music it was like a whole new place.

'Welcome to my palace,' Steph said, opening her flat door and stepping aside.

Gemma wasn't sure what she'd been expecting but it wasn't this. The hall was light and airy, a stylish console table greeting you on entry.

'You can put your coat here,' Steph said, hanging her own denim jacket on the designer coat hooks near the door. Gemma had admired the marble and brass hooks online while shopping herself. Steph had good taste.

'What's up?' Steph asked, taking off her backwards baseball cap and smoothing her hair back. The way she repositioned the hat made Gemma's tummy flip and she fought the urge to linger her gaze on Steph's hands for too long.

'Nothing, just in my own wee world.' She shucked off her camel trench coat and hung it beside Steph's.

'Toilet's in here,' Steph said, throwing a thumb towards the nearest door, 'My bedroom, and here's the living room-kitchen. Sorry it's nothing fancy.'

'Nothing fancy? Your place is gorgeous.'

Steph's cheeks flushed red. 'Thank you.'

The kitchen was equally lovely, with grey cabinets and a walnut worktop. 'You have really nice taste.' Gemma said, sinking into Steph's sofa. The place was immaculate.

'You sound surprised,' she teased with a smile.

'No, not surprised, just appreciative.'

'Beer then?' she asked, leaning against her breakfast bar. Gemma much preferred Steph in this setting; she was more relaxed.

'I'm willing to try anything once.'

Gemma liked the way Steph battled a lopsided smile at that comment before ducking behind the counter. The clink of bottles followed shortly.

It was definitely the alcohol, but Steph looked decidedly cute in her own domain. Maybe it was the way the colours complemented her, or the fact that her surroundings oozed Steph, not a punter-filled bar, but she was radiant.

'Right,' Steph said, popping back up. She padded through to the living room, a beer in each hand, a bottle opener hanging off her pinky. 'I think you'll like this one. Not quite as fruity as a Sauvignon Blanc, but a similar flavour profile.' She popped the cap off with a satisfying hiss. 'Made with Cascade hops: this is a nice light lager for you.'

Gemma accepted the bottle and gave it a sniff. Nice. For a beer. A thought occurred. 'Where did you get these from, if that's your fridge?' she asked, pointing the neck of the bottle towards the fridge freezer at the edge of the kitchen.

Steph looked equal parts sheepish and proud. 'I have a beer fridge.'

'Of course you do,' Gemma said with a chuckle. She took a tentative swig. *Ooft.* It was good.

'So you should be getting floral, citrus, hint of grapefruit,' Steph said, rolling her hands around with each word. They didn't need the side lamps on: the way Steph's face was coming alive could light up the whole room. She clearly loved what she did. It was adorable.

'That's amazing,' Gemma said, and really meant it. She'd never been a beer drinker unless it was a cherry or raspberry brew, but this was next level. She could picture herself having a nice cold pint of it in the garden on a summer's day.

'You think?'

'If all beer was this good, I would never drink wine. So what do you have?'

Steph picked up her bottle. 'This wee beauty is made with crystal hops. She's a gorgeous IPA. I don't think you'll like her, though.'

'No?'

'No. She's more woody and spicy but she does have floral notes. I brought her out to show you my range, though. I've got all sorts of beers in between these.' She popped the cap off and handed the bottle to Gemma.

'You know a lot,' Gemma said, having a sniff. It was totally different from the first. Maybe it was Steph putting notions in her head but she could swear she smelled wood. She took a swig and her face contorted into a grimace. 'Nope, I don't like that.'

Steph laughed, taking the bottle from her. 'Didn't think you would.'

'So what got you started on brewing?'

'I've always loved beer so I got interested in how it was made. Home kits are pretty cheap, so I got one.' She took a long draw, smiling as the beer enveloped her taste buds. 'It was a hobby at first and now it's a full-blown passion. Hopefully I can get my shit together some day.'

'Work still not going well?'

Steph's face fell and Gemma worried she'd ruined the mood. 'Nah, and that's not doing my stress levels any good. My doctor wants to sign me off but I don't see the point.'

'He wants to sign you off? It must be bad.' She reached over and placed a hand on Steph's knee. 'You need to take care of yourself.'

'Easier said than done. But I guess that's what's got me thinking. I've given my whole life to work, made sacrifices I shouldn't, and I'm getting nothing in return. I think I need to make some changes soon.'

'Hence your question earlier.' Gemma retracted her hand, aware she'd held it there for an inordinately long time.

'Bingo,' Steph said and clinked their bottle necks together. 'It's big though, innit? And moving to another pub seems a waste of time. I have no idea what I'd do.'

'What about a job in a brewery? You've got lots of experience.'

Steph sighed. 'I've thought about it, but apprenticeships are really competitive. I don't even have a standard grade to my name.'

Gemma took another gulp of beer, her eyes locked with Steph's as she thought. There was so much she wanted to say, but this friendship was so new; it was impossible to know where the lines were drawn. 'It must have been really tough, coming here on your own when you were so young.'

Steph literally shrugged it off. 'Did what I had to.'

'You don't like talking about it?'

'Not really.'

'Sorry.'

Steph offered a thin-lipped smile. 'Don't apologise. It's just a time I'd rather forget, you know? I don't often tell people cause I don't want the questions.'

'I'm starting to feel that way about the whole gay thing. People seem to think I owe them a thousand answers. I get that they're inquisitive but I'd rather just forget it happened and move on.'

'You get it.'

'To a degree. It's nothing compared to what you went through.'

Steph looked at her watch. 'Will you stay here tonight? I want to enjoy these but I'm meeting a friend for coffee tomorrow, I can't be up too late. Saves me walking you home.'

'It's not far. I can walk on my own.'

'No, no, I insist. It's not safe. You can have my bed. Means we can enjoy another after this. I have a nice pale ale I think you'll like. Or,' She turned as if she might be able to see in the fridge. 'I probably have some white wine on the go if you'd prefer.'

'Okay, you've twisted my arm. Now, tell me more about these hops.'

Steph's face lit up and she pulled out her phone. She tapped the space beside her, motioning Gemma closer. 'Watch this video. It will blow your mind.'

Gemma smiled. Steph's energy was infectious.

∼

'You sure you want to sleep on the sofa?' Gemma asked. 'I feel bad kicking you out of your own bed. I promise to behave.'

Steph looked unsure as she rummaged through her drawers, looking for clothes Gemma could wear to bed.

'I'll be fine, don't worry,' she replied, finally settling on a T-shirt. 'This should fit – my trousers will look like shorts on you,' she said with a laugh, pulling open another drawer. 'What are you, a ten?'

'Yeah, just a T-shirt's fine,' Gemma replied, looking at the clothing. It was super baggy. It would preserve her dignity no bother.

'No, no, let me see what I've got.'

'You like clothes as much as you like beer, don't you?'

Steph turned, her smile on full beam. Gemma's stomach did that weird flip again, like it had with the hat.

'I love clothes,' Steph enthused. 'Always have. Might get a bit carried away sometimes, but—' She yanked a pair of black shorts out. 'Means I'm always prepared. Here, try these on for size.'

'Please stay through here, or I'll join you on the couch.'

'Is that a promise or a threat?'

'Both. Give it a go? For me?'

'Fine, I'm just going to nip to the loo and get changed.'

Alone, Gemma placed the clothes on the bed. She was a bit sloshed, to be totally honest. That was strong beer.

She wrestled her top off and put the T-shirt on. Not bad. Time to tackle her jeans. She had to close one eye to locate the button. Uh-oh. Freed, she almost stumbled as she stepped out of them.

Now. Pants on or off?

Why did this suddenly feel like an issue? Steph was a friend. But she was also an attractive lesbian.

Gemma paused, her head tilted as she replayed that final thought.

A giant neon sign appeared in her head, highlighting the crucial word.

Attractive.

Okay.

Beer was throwing up curveballs.

Interesting.

She was cute. No denying it.

Hmm.

She kept her underwear on, not wanting to leave dirty knickers at the side of the bed.

The shorts were tight but they did the job. She climbed into bed, the room shifting slightly as she lay down.

At least it was only Granny she was meeting tomorrow. She'd seen her hungover a bunch of times. In fact, she was usually the cause of them.

Steph chapped on the wall and called through the door. 'You decent?'

'Of course – in you come.'

There was the flip again.

Steph had on a vest and pyjama shorts. God, did she look cute.

Gemma swallowed, aware she'd been staring, and rolled on to her side, averting her eyes to the bed.

'You sure about this?' Steph asked.

'Of course. Why? What's the worst that can happen? You accidentally spoon me?'

'You never know,' Steph said, climbing into bed.

'God, I miss spooning,' Gemma whined as she rolled onto her back. She really did. Even with a stinky guy who would poke his willy into her back. She sat up on her forearm, facing Steph. No crime in spooning, was there? How to initiate this...

Steph snagged her gaze, a playful smile spreading across her lips. 'Well, you'd better hope Izzy likes to spoon then.'

Izzy! She'd forgotten about her. She slumped back into the pillow with a grin.

Steph leaned over and clicked the bedside lamp off.

'Night, Gemma.'

13

Maisie took a seat opposite Steph in Calm, a new café on Skirving Street. 'So?'

'So?' Steph asked. 'Actually, this is official, isn't it? I'm not going to have to watch for Shannon this entire time?'

Maisie blushed. 'She knows, don't worry.'

'Right. Good. I hate when you do that.'

The look she shot Steph could have killed. 'Anyway,' she said, drawing the word out. 'Any further forward with things?'

The waiter brought over their coffees and Steph waited for him to leave before answering. 'Nope. I've done nothing.'

'Steph, you can't go on like this.'

'I know, I know.' She sipped her latte: it wasn't bad. 'I had a cracker of a headache yesterday too.'

'I didn't think you looked right.'

'Thanks,' Steph replied with a chuckle.

'You know what I mean. Still not sleeping either?'

Steph waggled her head. If she gave Maisie this bone she was going to run with it forever. Screw it. 'I didn't get to bed until super early this morning.'

'No?'

'No. Gemma stayed over.'

Maisie choked on her coffee.

'Are you okay, dear?' the elderly woman at the table beside them asked.

'Yeah, yeah, sorry,' Maisie replied through coughs, a hand to her chest. She ran a finger under each eye, drying them.

Steph waited for her to settle before speaking. 'Not like that. Just in a friendly, *I don't want you walking home alone* way.'

Maisie wasn't convinced. 'Aye, right.'

'Whatever. Anyway, she's met someone else.'

'Really?'

'Yep. Going on a date next week.'

'Shit. She was cute, too.'

'Maisie, what have you been up to?'

She held her hands up in mock surrender, her eyes still streaming slightly. 'You only have one Gemma on your Facebook. It wasn't hard to play detective.'

Steph tutted. 'I should have seen that one coming. But anyway, she's seeing someone, so that's that.'

'Did you tell her how you feel?'

'Maisie,' Steph growled.

'What? I just want you to be happy.'

'Not the time or the place.'

'For you to be happy?' She hid a smile behind her cappuccino mug.

'For this conversation.'

'Right, okay. Lots of single lesbians at my wedding. Maybe I can get you a match there.'

'I don't need help.'

'Okay, okay. Yeesh. You're grumpy today.'

'Not grumpy. Just fed up.' Steph sipped her coffee. 'Sorry.'

'Apology noted. So, Gemma is a no. What about work?'

Steph shook her head. 'Nothing major on the horizon. Gemma thinks I should get an apprenticeship in a brewery.'

'I like her more and more every day.'

'Yeah, like, I get her thinking, but I can't see it happening.'

'The funk is real. What about a holiday? Why not book some time off, go somewhere?'

Steph was flat. It wasn't Maisie's fault. It was just that when you were in a rut, it was hard not to let defeat weigh you down. 'I don't think I can be bothered.'

Maisie stuck out her bottom lip. 'I hate seeing you like this. Want to come on my honeymoon with us?'

A quiet chuckle escaped. 'I'm sure Shannon would love that.'

'You never know. Might be the solution to all your problems: a *throuple*.' She gave her shoulders a shimmy, emphasising the absurdity of the idea.

'If she knew you even joked about this stuff, she'd kill you.'

'True. I should be careful. You never know who you're sitting next to.'

'So, enough about me. What's new with you?'

'Nothing. My life is wedding-central just now. I eat, breathe, and sleep it.'

'Not long. You excited?'

'Getting nervous, if I'm honest.'

'You, nervous? First time for everything.'

'I dunno. Just the thought of standing in front of everyone, saying my vows.' Maisie shivered. 'But, it will be fine, I can't wait to marry Shannon. Anything for her.'

Steph smiled. Their break-up hadn't exactly been clear-cut and blurred lines soon became their default, but seeing how happy Shannon made Maisie was more than worth the heartache. She could never provide that.

'You'll be fine. You probably deliver lectures to more people than will be at your wedding.'

'Hardly the same though, is it? I don't think my guests will appreciate a quick PowerPoint on Design in Principle.'

'You never know. Might add a little excitement.'

'Oi,' Maisie retorted, and swung a foot Steph's way.

'You know I'm joking; it's going to be a great day.'

'Aye, well, it better be. It's caused enough strife recently. So, how come Gemma stayed over?'

Steph groaned: she thought she'd avoided an inquisition. 'She came back to mine to try some beers.'

'After your shift?' Maisie asked, wiggling her eyebrows.

'What's that look for?'

Maisie pursed her lips before answering. 'I just think, if a girl hangs around for you to finish work *and* comes back to yours, it's a sure-fire sign she's into you.'

'Nonsense.'

'You think she does that for all her pals?'

'She was on a high from getting a date. All she spoke about was Izzy.'

'Mhm,' Maisie said, pursing her lips again.

'Look, I know you want this to be something, but it really isn't.'

'Why not bring her to the wedding? As a friend.'

'Ah.'

'What do you mean, *ah*?'

Steph swirled the coffee left in her cup. 'That's what this is about?'

'Huh?'

'If I bring a date to your wedding it takes the pressure off you and Shannon.'

Maisie looked like she was sucking on a lemon. She fixed her eyes on her cup. 'I guess,' she started, her voice slower than usual. 'That is true. In part. You know she wasn't keen about you coming. It would probably put her mind at rest.'

Steph pushed down the anger rising in her chest. This wasn't Maisie's fault. If she was Shannon she wouldn't have invited Steph in the first place. 'I don't need to come, you know.'

'I want you there. And if Shannon really trusted me she wouldn't have reason for you not to be there.'

'What does she think's going to happen? I stop the wedding?'

'Something like that.'

There really weren't many people she could take who would convince Shannon she'd moved on. Most of her and Maisie's friends overlapped, so they'd already be there.

'Okay. Listen, I'll ask Gemma. But I don't want you to make a big deal about it. It doesn't mean anything.'

Maisie grinned. 'Thank you. You have no idea how much easier that makes my life. However—'

Steph groaned. 'What?'

'If you could act a little couple-y it wouldn't go amiss.'

'Nope. Never. No way.'

'Okay, okay. It's asking a lot. Sorry.'

'I'm going to the toilet.'

Steph slipped between the tables and into the loos at the back of the café. She didn't actually need to go, but she sorely needed a breather from Maisie. Her head throbbed. The usual mix of co-codamol and ibuprofen was doing nothing to touch the edges.

She gripped the sink, the cool ceramic a welcome relief. If only she could press her face against it, it might ease the pain a little.

Lack of sleep wouldn't have helped. She felt rotten.

Steph locked eyes with herself in the mirror and fixed her beanie, straightening it. She really didn't want to go to this wedding.

It was going to be a day of pitiful looks and hushed conversation, she could already tell.

Maybe having Gemma there for moral support wouldn't be a bad idea.

The notion of cancelling last minute had crossed her mind more than once, but it meant a lot to Maisie. She had to go. Would it be weird to ask Gemma, though? Did that cross a line? Izzy might find it weird.

Jesus. Why was she always left on the bench? Last choice, no matter what she did.

Steph's chest ached. She rubbed a hand over her ribs, trying to soothe the racing jackhammer beneath.

She was tired and probably hadn't eaten enough today. She needed to go home, get some rest. Then maybe the room would stop spinning.

She gripped the sink again, focusing on her breathing. *In and out. In and out.* It was an age before oxygen actually stayed in her lungs.

Finally, she felt semi-normal again.

Maybe the doctor was right: she should take some time off. Get her head in order.

Another stuttering deep breath and she let go of the sink. It was like taking the training wheels off a bike and she needed a moment to compose herself, confirm she was balanced.

Time to go home.

She opened the door to the bathroom and slinked back to the table.

The look on Maisie's face said something was up.

Had she been gone ages?

She'd half-opened her mouth to say her goodbyes and spill excuses, when a familiar voice piped up from the neighbouring table.

'Steph?'

'Gemma?'

14

'What are you doing here?' Steph blurted.

Gemma choked back a laugh. 'Same as you, I'm guessing. Here for a coffee with my granny.'

Steph looked at the woman sitting beside her.

'Your granny?'

'Yep. Granny, this is my friend Steph; Steph, this is my Granny. Or Margaret to her pals.'

Granny gave a little wave. 'Pleasure to meet you, Steph.'

Steph was as white as a sheet and, truth be told, looking a little clammy.

Gemma wasn't too chipper herself. Lack of sleep and too much booze was wreaking havoc with her insides. Her stomach thought she was on a boat. Nothing some food wouldn't sort.

'Are you guys staying, or just heading off?' Gemma asked, looking at the duo's empty cups.

'Heading off.' Steph had her jacket half-on when realisation hit her square between the eyes. That and the swift kick Gemma saw under the table. 'Shit.' She turned to

Granny, flustered. 'Sorry. Shit. I mean, urgh.' She held a hand to her temple. 'I mean, this is Maisie.'

Maisie extended a hand. 'Pleasure to meet you, Gemma.'

The name sounded familiar but Gemma couldn't quite remember the connection. 'And you too.'

A strange silence floated over the tables. It was verging on awkward.

'So, best be off,' Steph said, standing so quickly her thighs connected with the table. The crockery rattled.

'I've not even finished my cappuccino,' Maisie whined.

'Well, you stay,' Steph said, already shimmying between the tables. 'Nice to meet you, Margaret.' She sucked on her lips for a second, standing by Gemma's chair. 'Gemma,' she said with a little nod.

With that, she was off.

Maisie downed the remainder of her cappuccino. 'Don't worry, this is my fault. I've asked her to do something I probably shouldn't have.'

Intriguing. What are you meant to say to that?

Maisie didn't even bother to put her jacket on, draping it over her arm instead. 'Looks like I'm paying. Bye, guys.'

Gemma checked Maisie was a safe distance away before leaning closer to Granny, still keeping her voice low, just in case. 'Was it just me or was that really weird?'

Granny pursed her lips. 'Hmm.'

'Spill.'

'Now, now,' Granny said, sipping her tea.

The waiter appeared and Gemma had to fob him off. She'd not even had a second to think about what she wanted. Maisie was long gone, the coast now clear. 'Come on, what was that about?'

'You know I'm not one to gossip.' The sparkle in Granny's eyes called lies.

'But?'

A rueful smile played on Granny's lips. 'Maisie wants Steph to take you to her wedding: there's some sort of history there, if I heard correctly.'

That did ring a bell. 'Eavesdropping. Really?' Gemma joked.

'Don't pretend you're not pleased I did. So Steph's to blame for your hangover this morning, too?'

Gemma chuckled. 'You just sat and listened this whole time, didn't you?'

'What else is a woman meant to do when her granddaughter is twenty minutes late?'

At least she'd stayed off social media. She'd been known to accidentally go live in the past.

'Sorry again. Head's not feeling too good this morning. Shower was a bit of a chore.' Gemma picked up a sugar packet from the bowl in the middle of the table, intent on fiddling with it. 'So, how's Zumba been this week? Any more goss about Jean?'

Granny stilled Gemma's hands with one of her own. 'No, no. You're going to tell me more about Steph.'

'Really?'

The waiter appeared and Gemma didn't have the heart to tell him to leave again. She went for the first thing her eyes settled on: eggs Benedict. She wasn't quite sure if her stomach could handle it, but she was committed now.

'So?' Granny said, not even waiting for the waiter to leave.

'There's nothing to tell.'

'But you stayed at hers last night?'

'It sounds like you already know what happened.' Gemma kept her tone light but her hungover head was lacking the capacity for games.

'Do you like her?'

'Granny!'

'It's a simple question.'

The waiter sat down Gemma's Irn Bru and latte. She made short work of the fizzy drink and instantly regretted it when a sharp pain gripped her chest, the carbonated air wedged in her pipes.

She took a deep breath, ignoring Granny's stare boring into her.

'Okay. So I guess I kind of do have some fledgling feelings.'

'And what about this date you've organised?'

Gemma put her head in her hands and let out a bark of laughter. 'Did they just sit and talk about me the whole time?'

Granny smiled. 'Steph was just filling Maisie in. She wants you at her wedding, after all.'

Gemma tutted, unsure how much she believed that. Something felt off but her mind was too fuzzy to do the maths. 'So, date, yes. Going out with a woman called Izzy next week.'

'Nice girl?'

'Very. We hit it off straight away – we've got a lot in common.'

'Sounds promising. But what about Steph? Does she know how you feel?'

Gemma's cheeks burned. 'It's very new. I'm not sure if it's booze-induced or not.'

'I don't understand,' Granny said and sipped her tea again.

'I've only ever felt things when I've been drunk. You know booze does funny stuff to your head.'

'All too well. I've told you the story of Mitchell Doig, yes? You nearly had a completely different grandfather.'

Gemma opened her mouth to sidetrack Granny and one of her stories. but was cut off.

'Well, how did you feel now, when you saw her?'

'Sick. But that was definitely the hangover.'

'And you prefer this Izzy girl?'

So many questions. 'Physically she's more my type, yes.' A new couple were seated beside them so Gemma dropped her voice. 'But I guess I find Steph easier to talk to. It's early days with Izzy, though. It's just a familiarity thing.'

'Why not take Steph on a date? See what happens.'

Gemma rolled the idea about her head. 'No. I'm actually really enjoying our friendship. I wouldn't want to ruin that over something that might be nothing.'

Granny nodded. 'I understand. Still no word from Julie?'

'Nope,' Gemma replied, her muscles relaxing now the topic of Steph was over. 'She'll be busy with wedding stuff, like I said.'

Granny rolled her eyes. 'That excuse only stretches so far. What does Steph think about it all?'

'Huh?'

'She's your new gal pal; have you not told her the situation, got her advice?'

'I've not mentioned it, really. Well, maybe in passing. I don't want her to think I don't have any friends.'

'She'll find out the truth sooner or later,' Granny said with a smile.

Granny was saved a throttling by the arrival of their food. Gemma's stomach wavered between lurching and excitement. She poked at the poached egg, breaking it open for a satisfying yolky ooze. 'This is why I can't risk losing Steph. I need her as a friend more than anything else.'

THE EVENING COULDN'T COME QUICK ENOUGH. Whatever was in those beers was lingering, stuck to the walls of her stomach and her skull. Or maybe she was just getting older. She had been out an extraordinary amount recently. This dating business wasn't for the weak.

Gemma got comfy on her sofa, stretched the length of the three-seater with enough cushions to accommodate a small army.

TV was rubbish on a Saturday.

Had it ever actually been good, or was she just easier to please as a child? Saturdays were spent around the dinner table with her family, watching *Dad's Army* or *The Generation Game*. Maybe it was the company that made it better.

Now she was on her own, debating if getting a Chinese takeaway delivered was too extravagant a gesture for one person.

Gemma flopped an arm out to one side and grabbed her phone off the coffee table.

Nothing.

She'd hoped for a text from Steph, at least.

Now her inner thoughts were out in the real world and in the hands of Granny, her feelings for Steph were more foreign than ever.

She was just so *different* to who she imagined herself being with.

It had taken so long to get her head around the image of her settled with a woman anyway: the thought of shifting the goalposts again was spin-inducing.

Then the memory of Steph's smile floated to the surface and it didn't seem so bad.

But was she the type of woman she could bring to

Sunday dinners? There was no getting her head around that. The thought of Steph sitting on Granny's patterned two-seater, a doily framing her head, was outlandish.

You just didn't get many people like Steph in Bearsden.

Plus, she wasn't lying to Granny: their friendship was paramount. It had been a long, long time since she'd made a new friend. It wasn't worth throwing everything away over some misguided curiosity.

Speaking of friends: Gemma stabbed Julie's name into Messenger. Her last message had been read, but still no reply a fortnight later.

The weeks were ticking by, though. Soon it would be Julie's wedding: they'd need to catch up before then, surely?

She fired off a quick *hey, how are you? X*, laid the phone on her chest, and stared at the ceiling.

She'd considered texting Logan to say congratulations. Was that weird, though? He'd given Archie the okay to share the news, so he obviously knew she knew. Was he expecting interaction? Or was it a mere courtesy?

She'd ask Archie what to do tomorrow.

It felt like only a moment had passed, but the next thing Gemma knew her phone was vibrating and she was startled awake. It took her a second to get her bearings.

With one eye shut and the other decidedly bleary, she looked at her lock screen. She'd missed a call from Julie.

Strange.

She cleared her throat and called back.

'Gemma!' Julie exclaimed like it was the biggest treat in the world to hear from her despite the fact she'd pretty much ghosted her for the last month.

'Julie, hey, how are you?'

'Bit tipsy, if I'm honest. Been at a barbecue at Tiff's. Do you remember her? One of Logan's friends' girlfriends. She was the one that hired the miniature ponies for that fourth birthday party in the Mearns, do you remember?'

Gemma vaguely remembered it. There was a weird period in her life that involved a lot of miniature animals at parties. Including a snake she'd never forget. 'I think so, yeah. Any livestock this time around?'

'Sadly not. Kids are too old. This was for George's fortieth. Lots of booze. Thankfully no miniature measures.'

Julie sounded more than a little tipsy and the party sounded raucous: chatter enveloped every word, almost drowning her out. Gemma half-wished she hadn't called her back; their energy levels were poles apart. 'Sounds like a good night,' Gemma replied, urging herself to sound chipper. She sat up straighter, hoping the change in position might wake her up.

'Listen, Gem, I can tell you anything, yeah?'

'Of course. What's up?'

Julie dropped her voice, the sound of the party dimming in the background like she'd gone inside. 'I have a teeny problem regarding my hen party.'

'Oh, right. How can I help?'

Silence on the line. Only the occasional burst of faraway laughter hinted Julie was still there. 'You see, Gem—'

This didn't sound like it was going somewhere good.

'—Logan and Paul are best friends, so naturally, we've been spending loads of time together, and I've gotten really close to Joanne.'

'Okay.'

'And, I just feel it might be a bit weird, given the whole baby thing. You know about that, yeah?'

What a way to find out if she didn't. Gemma swallowed the frustration and anger balling in her throat. 'Yeah, I know.'

'Phew. Well, you see, it makes most sense for Joanne to come to the hen do and I don't want it to be awkward. You okay to sit it out and we'll do something together another time?'

'Are you asking me or telling me?' It came out more snippy than intended, but whatever. Her supposed best friend was choosing her ex's new squeeze over her. And a pregnant partner at that. How much fun would she be on a booze-filled weekend in the Perthshire hills?

Gemma had been looking forward to the cottage.

Too late to cancel holiday dates from work, too. Maybe she could go away somewhere by herself.

Jeez. If she hadn't felt depressed before, she did now.

'Gem, don't be like that. I'm just trying to look out for everyone,' Julie whined.

'I know. Look, it's fine. I understand.' It wasn't, but it was pointless arguing.

'I knew you'd understand. You're a sweetheart.' A screeching whoop filled the line. 'Look, I'd better go. I think Innes has gone in the hot tub.'

Gemma barely had time to say her goodbyes before Julie hung up.

She groaned, a low guttural noise that shook her bones.

Tears rimmed her eyes. She sunk low into the cushions again, the realisation that her friendship with Julie was dead in the water filling her chest like an expanding balloon, ready to pop any moment.

It wasn't that she was particularly pressed about missing out, rather that the social circle was closing and she was being left on the outside. Had their friendship been situational from the start? She'd always got on with Julie: surely it wasn't purely from convenience?

She sighed.

Still no messages from Steph. Why did that feel like a massive gaping hole as well? Did Steph actually like hanging out with her? She *was* always the one going to Steph's work and initiating their time together.

God. Gemma clenched her jaw, willing the tears to stay put.

Maybe that was why she didn't want to ask Gemma to go to this wedding with her.

She was spiralling. She shook her head, wanting to break the thought process.

There was no point dwelling. Time to order some food and book a cottage, just for her. It would be the perfect time to reset and get her head in order.

But why did it feel like having Steph there would make it a thousand times better?

15

Steph was in no mood for work today. She'd made her excuses to Maisie and managed to slip in a nap before her five o'clock shift, but her headache remained. At least it was pretty much guaranteed to be busy, which would make it go quickly.

She dumped her bag and jacket in the staff room and trundled downstairs, willing her happy mask not to slip tonight. She was off tomorrow. She could stay in bed and space out on painkillers all she wanted after this shift.

It didn't take long to spot Donnie at the end of the bar. Weird. He was usually long gone before she appeared.

She could feel his bad mood at ten paces, it was like walking off the plane to a wall of heat. She was about to turn on her heel when he called her name.

'Steph, office, now.'

She stopped, her heart already rumbling her rib cage, and raised her eyebrows at him. 'What's up?'

'Office.'

Stevie shot her a look that said *good luck*.

This didn't feel good.

She dragged her feet to the office to find Donnie leaning against the desk. He'd not even bothered to sit down.

'Close the door,' he said, arms crossed, tone flat.

'Tell me what this is about first.'

The muscles in his jaw flexed but he said nothing.

'I'm waiting,' she said, still in the doorway.

He was standing to be a dick, hoping to intimidate her. It wasn't going to work. Did he really think she'd get to thirty-seven without encountering a few arsehole men intent on one-upping her? He could fuck off.

'Cal was in this morning,' he said, his eyes burning with rage.

'And?'

'Close the door.'

'I'm going to keep it open, thanks.' The table nearest the door was empty, but there was no way she was confining them to the tiny room. There was no knowing what he was capable of, or planning. She wanted witnesses if possible, and if she needed a quick exit she was keeping her options open.

She stepped closer, hoping the compromise would be enough. Only a few feet stood between them.

He was seething, the rise and fall of his chest like a bull's, ready to charge. 'He wanted to know why I've been leaving early.'

'Good. Did you tell him? We've all been wondering for months.'

He ignored her. 'And he's been looking over the accounts.'

'Naturally.' Her knees were threatening to shake, her stomach tying itself in knots.

'Any idea why he might have thought these things were an issue?'

'Because they are?' Steph replied, her brow furrowing.

His jaw clenched again, the vein on the side of his temple popping out. 'You told him, didn't you?'

'Cal's a clever man. He would be able to see it all for himself.'

He stood straight, relieving the desk of his weight. 'Stephanie. I'm the manager. You're the assistant manager. You don't need to worry your pretty little head about how I run things.' He closed the gap between them. 'There are certain things above your pay grade. You leave the important stuff to me, yeah?'

'What? Like going to the cash and carry to sort your messes out?'

'That was your fault.'

'How?'

'You should have ordered more inventory if you saw it was wrong.'

'And why was it wrong? Why was it so out?'

'You must have miscounted.'

Steph couldn't stop the laugh that cracked the air. 'Me? Me? You did it.'

'I think you're mistaken.'

She shook her head. 'You're not going to gaslight me, Donnie.'

'Gaslight? I think you'll find it's the other way around.'

'Now you've really lost it.' Steph turned to leave.

'Whoa, this conversation isn't over.'

She paused, swivelling on her heel but making it clear this was only a temporary break to her stride. 'Come on, then.'

'You ever, and I mean ever,' he said, raising his voice so fiercely that a little spit escaped. 'Go to Cal again and I'll make sure you regret it. I run this place. You answer to me.

You have a problem, you come to me. You want to make changes, you come to me. You have the slightest, daftest, wee thought in your stupid thick skull, you come to me.'

Steph nodded, biding her time. Why was everything getting fuzzy? She swallowed, steadying herself. 'Noted. So, the Lovefest closing event next week? Probably best you take that over. Tell me what you need me to do and I'll do it.'

'That's better. It's called delegation, Steph. You'd understand if you ever became a manager.'

'You're right. I'm sorry. I've overstepped.' He wanted this event, he could have it. She'd organised the whole thing from top to bottom. He didn't even have a scooby what act she'd contacted for the club and she wasn't about to share. 'I won't do anything else without your blessing.' Her chest tightened, her hands now clammy. She needed out of here, fast.

'Much better.'

If she was taller, stronger, and a heck of a lot braver, she would have wiped the smug look right off his face.

Instead, she left without another word.

She had a new worry to focus on as the edges of her vision continued to cloud. There was no way she would make it upstairs to the toilets. Vaguely aware Stevie was watching her from the bar, she fixed her vision dead ahead and crossed the seating area to the rear exit, ignoring any concerned looks.

Out of sight, she took a second to steady herself, a hand on the wall as she looked up the stairs. They waved, undulating like she was looking in a fairground mirror. *Nope.* Stairs weren't an option. She slipped through the curtain and into the display room.

She'd been meaning to clear this space out for ages and cursed herself for not having got round to it. You could hardly move for props and haphazardly stacked units. Some were ancient—publicity banners and displays sent years ago for beers or wines they no longer stocked.

Steph slipped between a box of Christmas decorations and a set of wooden shelves and leaned against the box they usually put on stage for drag artists to dance on.

Her shoulders slumped, her muscles sagging after the exertion of keeping it together.

She pinched the bridge of her nose between finger and thumb while screwing her eyes tight.

Her heart was stumbling over itself in a bid to regain a normal rhythm.

Breathe.

Easier said than done. The first inhalation was like breathing under water, but another attempt and she soon found solid ground.

She gripped her knees and bowed her head, counting her breaths.

Eventually, they evened out and she was confident enough to open her eyes.

Normality.

Just.

She needed a distraction, otherwise her brain was threatening to swerve back to Donnie and boost her back into overdrive.

Steph pulled her phone from her back pocket.

She didn't want to text Maisie. She was too involved already, and Shannon was sure to get shirty if she got in touch too much.

Was it too late to text Gemma? Was it weird to text Gemma?

Steph shrugged. She was in no mood to battle her inner voice.

Hey, hope coffee with your granny went well x she fired off, hoping it sounded off-hand and not because she was having a minor meltdown.

The reply was almost instant. Steph smiled.

It did. Although I still feel a bit rough from your beer last night. X

Sorry about that. If it's an consolation I'm having a shit shift at work so karma's already sorted me out x

Oh really? How come? X

She could already feel her head clearing, the thud of her heartbeat subsiding from her bones. Steph set to work on composing her reply.

∽

STEPH WOKE WITH A START, stiff from falling asleep on the sofa. She grabbed her phone. Six o'clock on a Sunday. Who was buzzing her at this time? Had she arranged to meet someone and forgot?

Probably just someone wanting in the close.

She swung her feet over the edge, digging her toes into her rug as she ran a hand over her face. No more blood; good.

She'd woken up to a cracker of a nosebleed and a headache to match this morning.

The nap seemed to have done her good.

The buzzer sounded again, reminding her the pain wasn't quite gone.

She got to her feet and stretched her arms out wide as she padded through to the hall. Her shoulders cracked and popped.

'Hello?' she said into her intercom, her voice croaky.

'Hey, it's me.'

'Who's me?'

'Gemma.'

Steph's stomach swooped. She pressed the buzzer, opening the door, and flew into panic mode.

Why was Gemma here?

She scooted into the bathroom, checking her reflection in the mirror as she furiously brushed her teeth. No blood, but yesterday's make-up remained around her eyes. Toothbrush in one hand, make-up remover wipe in the other, she was like a manic octopus. A few more limbs would have been good, though. She could do with brushing her hair and putting on some fresh make-up.

No time, though.

A chap at the front door signalled Gemma's arrival.

Steph spat the foamy toothpaste into the sink and gave herself a final once-over. No time to improve.

Why did it matter anyway? Gemma didn't see her as more than a pal.

She straightened her jumper, tugged at her shorts, and mustered her best friendly smile before opening the door.

'Gemma, hey, what are you doing here?'

Gemma held up a stack of Tupperware in her hands. 'Granny had loads left over, so I thought I would pop round with some grub.'

'For me?'

'No, your neighbours.' Gemma replied with a chuckle. 'Of course you.' Steph stepped aside, letting Gemma in. She bee-lined straight for the kitchen. 'Now, it's lamb. That okay for you?'

Steph lingered on the perimeter, watching Gemma shake off her jacket and place it on the back of her armchair before returning to the kitchen and popping off Tupperware lids. Her heart swelled. It wasn't often she was looked after.

She took a step closer, not sure if she should get in Gemma's way. She was a whirlwind of activity, rolling up the sleeves of her jumper before she lined up the dishes.

'Lamb's perfect.' Steph finally managed, surprised at how timid her voice was.

'Good. Now, got some dishes I can decant these into?'

Steph nodded and hopped into action, grabbing what she had from the drawer by the cooker. 'Here, will these do?'

'Perfect,' Gemma said and flashed what might have been the world's most beautiful smile. Steph's chest flushed with heat, her heart stuttering like a stalling car. She'd almost recovered when Gemma tucked a stray strand of hair from her ponytail behind her ear. Steph's heart gave up completely and took a breather for a beat.

'Why?' was all she could manage.

'Why? Oh, why the food? Like I said, Granny had some left and I thought you could do with feeding after the day you had yesterday. If you're anything like me, food isn't top of the agenda when things are on my mind.'

Steph nodded. It looked amazing. Roast lamb, vegetables, and other trimmings filled the middle box. What looked like a portion of trifle sat in the third. And the first? Hard to tell. Salad leaves and something else.

'What's this?' Steph asked, poking at the box's contents.

Gemma bumped her hip to Steph's and her heart fluttered again. 'That, Steph, is Granny's signature pâté. I would tell you what was in it but I'd have to kill you.'

'But you know?'

'Naturally.'

Steph grabbed a chunk of bread and scooped up a lump of pâté. Gemma watched, her blue eyes fixed steady on the food. The bread crunched satisfyingly and then the buttery, smooth pâté took over her taste buds. 'Oh my

God,' Steph said, a hand covering her mouth as she chewed.

'I know, right?' Gemma replied, launching back into action. 'Right, shove the oven on. One-eighty, please. I'll get this sorted and then we can relax.'

Before Steph knew it, the lamb was in the oven and she was on the sofa, pâté box in hand. She'd planned on some toast for tea: this definitely was a welcome turn of events.

Gemma plonked herself down beside Steph and took a bite of the bread she had, hovering.

'Hey,' Steph said, playfully snatching it away and holding the food high. 'You brought this for me, no take backs.'

'Sorry. Bloody good though, isn't it?' Her smile dropped, her eyes softening. 'So, how you feeling today?'

'Shite.'

'What can I do to help?'

Steph almost laughed. 'You've done more than enough.'

'Do you want me to ask round my solicitor pals, see if any of them know a good hitman, take this Donnie fellow out?'

'I didn't realise solicitors were so well connected.'

'How do you think the mafia launders their money? Actually, no. I shouldn't joke about that; probably does happen.' Her hand gripped Steph's thigh and the tension in her muscles was undeniable, like she'd forgotten Steph had on shorts and hadn't expected contact with bare flesh. To give Gemma her dues, she kept her hand steady. 'In all seriousness, though. If I can do anything, just say.' She hopped to her feet, energy dialled to ten again. 'I need to pee.'

Steph had a mouthful of pâté and bread when Gemma appeared in the doorway to the kitchen.

'What's with all the blood? Saw it on my way past.'

SHIT. Embarrassing.

'Nosebleed. Hadn't quite got round to cleaning it up.'

Gemma's eyes grew concerned. 'Looks a bad one. Right, I'll strip the bed.' She was off before Steph could protest. Her voice carried through the walls, 'You know, if this was to do with Donnie's murder, I could totally give you an alibi. Just say the word.' She laughed.

Steph could imagine her smiling and her chest ached again. God, what had she done to deserve this woman?

16

Izzy was a pure joy. And God, she was beautiful.

'You didn't fancy the closing event tonight, then?' Gemma asked, taking a sip of her wine.

Izzy shook her head, the smile that Gemma had been drinking in all evening playing on her lips. 'Did it last year; once is enough. Actually, one of my friends won, so I feel I've had enough Lovefest to last me a lifetime.'

'They won?'

'Yep. Ashley and Hazel. Did you follow Lovefest this year? Who do you think will win?'

'Truth be told, I've been so absorbed in having my own Lovefest experience I've not really followed it as intently as last year.'

Izzy giggled. 'I'm glad I'm not the only one. Gets a bit sickening, seeing all these happy couples, doesn't it?'

'I was beginning to lose hope,' Gemma said, and instantly felt heat flush her cheeks.

'Feeling a little more optimistic now?' The smile that could melt icebergs in moments returned.

'Much.'

Izzy played with the stem of her wine glass, taking in Cal's pub. 'It's nice in here, isn't it? I usually go to the cocktail lounge. Good to be somewhere a little different.'

'Glad I could be of service,' Gemma replied. 'I'd never tried Cal's before the Lovefest opener; very pleased I did. It's my new go-to place.' She looked at her empty glass. 'You wanting another drink?'

'I'd love one.'

This evening was passing in a flash. Finally, someone she could have a conversation with! Was there a spark? Maybe a few smoking embers. No burning fires just yet.

Gemma slipped through the throng and up to the bar. The tall girl with pink in her hair was serving. Stevie, was that her name? No sign of Steph.

'Gemma, what can I get for you?'

'Two Sauvignons, please.' She swallowed, hoping her next sentence would sound off-hand. Why were her hands getting clammy? 'No Steph tonight?'

'Donnie mucked up the rotas. She's working in the cocktail lounge for a few hours; she'll be done in—' She checked her watch. '—thirty minutes.'

Gemma nodded and let Stevie get her drinks. Her heart tripped over her ribs, a ripple of excitement flushing over her chest. She'd be lying if she said she didn't know why.

Steph and Izzy couldn't be more different.

Izzy was feminine and elegant; Steph was boyish and rough around the edges. If you'd asked Gemma a month ago what her perfect woman looked like, she'd have painted a picture of Izzy and called it a day. The last two years had been spent imagining her future life, hours of daydreams constructing the perfect partner, and now she was questioning it all.

This was an absolute stonker of a date, so why did her

mind keep wandering to the tattooed barmaid who was yet to even make a damn appearance?

Gemma pushed down the sigh lodged in her throat. Just when you think everything is going to plan, the universe throws in another spanner.

'You sure you don't want a bottle, by the way?' Stevie asked, having returned with two wine glasses. 'Looks like things are going well and you'll be here for another. Saves quite a bit.'

Gemma weighed up the options. Always good to be positive. 'Yeah, sure. Why not?'

'Result.' Stevie disappeared to the far wine fridge, only to return with a nearly empty bottle and a sheepish look. 'This is all we have left for now, but there's more in the back. Sorry, things aren't exactly running to plan tonight.'

'Donnie strikes again. It's okay, we'll just skip the bottle and go with that.' A sweaty man in a tight T-shirt slipped into the space beside Gemma and she willed this transaction to hurry up. He smiled. She mustered back what she could.

Stevie bobbed her head back and forth. 'Barely enough here for the two measures. How about I give you what's left in here on the house and I'll bring you a bottle when I get a sec?'

'Sounds good to me.' Anything to get away from this guy. Personal space obviously wasn't his forte.

'Fab. Sorry again.'

'Not your fault.'

Stevie rolled her eyes. 'You know how it is.' She placed the barely filled glasses on the bar mat. 'You can pay for the bottle later,' she said with a wink.

What a good egg.

'We back on rations?' Izzy asked as Gemma sat the wine down.

'Inventory issues at the bar. I've asked for a bottle, actually – they'll bring it over in a bit. That okay?'

'Sounds fab.'

～

'So, we've agreed *Love Actually* is the ultimate Christmas movie. What about books? What's your favourite romantic novel?' Izzy asked, their meagre serving of wine long gone.

They needn't have worried, though. Before Gemma could answer, a stainless steel wine cooler was placed on the table. 'Ladies, bottle of wine for two,' Steph said with a smattering of bravado.

Gemma only just caught herself before a stuttering breath escaped.

Faced with a line-up, this was not the outfit she would have said would bring her into a tailspin—Izzy's low-cut floral maxi dress would have got that crown usually—but here she was, her insides garbled.

She resisted the urge to enjoy a second glance at Steph's shorts or sleeveless top, instead choosing to settle on the bandana tied around her head. Her cheeks were flushed red, which only added to how cute she looked.

'Warm today?' Gemma asked.

'Oh my God. Dying. Cocktail lounge is packed, too. You both having fun?'

Izzy nodded.

'Loads, thank you,' Gemma said, unsure if she'd blinked in the last minute.

Steph looked over her shoulder, towards the club area of the venue. 'You've got good seats if you stick about until later. See that two-seater over there?' she said, pointing in the direction of a small table on the precipice of Cal's unmarked dividing lines.

'Yes,' the ladies chorused.

'We've moved all the other dining tables for the club starting in forty minutes. That table usually goes too, but Donnie says it will be fine. Just watch when the music starts. There will be chaos.'

'Is he about?' Gemma asked.

'Should be. I've not actually seen him because I've been next door.'

Gemma narrowed her eyes. 'I've not seen him.'

'No? Right, well, I'm moving that chuffing table, then. Better go before he appears out of the shadows.'

With that, she was off.

'A friend?' Izzy asked, pouring them both a glass of wine.

'Kind of; she's the assistant manager here.'

Izzy nodded slowly, like she was piecing a puzzle together.

'What's that look for?' Gemma asked with an uneasy chuckle.

'Nothing,' Izzy replied, looking coy.

'Something,' Gemma said, returning the look.

'She likes you.'

'As if.'

'Darling, I'm never wrong. I know a look when I see one.'

Gemma cocked her head to the side. 'First time for everything. But is that an issue if you are right?'

Her heart caught in her throat. Was Izzy playing this off? Had her poker face slipped for a second and Izzy had seen how Gemma looked at Steph? *Shit.*

'No issue from me if it's not an issue with you.'

Gemma shook her head. 'We're just friends. We're

complete opposites. Seems like it shouldn't work, but it does.'

'Nonsense. That's what the best friendships and relationships are about. Think of it this way: if two magnets are the same, they'll repel each other. Different and they'll attract,' she said, gently clapping her hands together. 'The best couples, or friends, complement each other. It's the differences that make them stronger.'

'I've never seen it like that before.'

'When you find someone you really like it doesn't matter that you're opposites, because—' Izzy took a gulp of wine. 'When you love them it doesn't matter if you're not fully aligned with their interests. Listening to them and seeing how excited they are is enough. And the best part is: you won't even notice. It will be the most natural thing in the world.'

'Sounds like you've got this pegged.'

'Just a little food for thought.'

Indeed it was.

17

The Lovefest closing event. August's second biggest night.

Against her better judgement, Steph was letting Donnie take the wheel. He'd asked for it, after all. Still, she knew she was doing it for the wrong reasons—hoping he'd slip up and cause an irreversible mess, rather than doing it from a place of understanding. The memory of her last flirtation with this approach simmered on the surface, a constant reminder that things could blow up in her face at any time.

But, she persisted.

Maybe she wanted to be fired, have the decision made for her.

The evening's preparation was half-done when Donnie had demanded control. She'd not so much as looked at it since. Yeah, she'd thought about it nearly every waking moment, but she'd left it in Donnie's incapable hands.

Steph surveyed the bar, her breath wavering slightly.

She didn't quite know where the evening would unravel yet, but there was no way it could go off without a hitch. The rotas, inventory, and tables were small blips. Something big was looming on the horizon, like a monster in the shadows. She could feel it.

The band would arrive soon. Had Donnie sound-tested earlier? Too late now.

The biggest surprise of the evening was that he was still kicking about. Steph couldn't actually remember the last time he was here for the evening rush. Maybe he was finally stepping up and taking responsibility.

When she'd finished in the cocktail lounge she'd purposely walked the floor to see if he was about. Twenty minutes later, she'd still not seen him and she'd naturally assumed the bastard had disappeared, only for him to pop up behind the bar. He wasn't doing anything – that would be too much to ask – but he was here.

He'd been outside smoking, which was exactly where he presumably was now, just as two lads in tracksuits came through the door.

They bee-lined for Steph.

'Hey,' she said, one eye on the bar and no idea where this encounter was going.

'Hey,' the smaller of the two said. He was a skinny lad with a shaved head and a diamond earring. He had on the green version of his pal's red tracksuit. If The Beastie Boys came from a council estate in Govan, here they were.

'Can I help you?'

They guy's face knotted with confusion. 'We're the talent, love.' His thick accent cut through the air like a sharp knife.

Steph only just caught the nervous laughter from spilling out. 'The talent? For what?'

He nodded, his stare unblinking. 'Tonight. We're Possil Posse.' He paused. 'You did book us, right?'

This was who Donnie had booked to perform tonight? Jesus. They couldn't be further from what this crowd expected. 'Ah, no, I didn't. Donnie did.'

'Donnie,' he repeated with a curt nod.

'Aye, yeah, so you'd better go find him. He's outside in the smoking area.'

'Can you not get him?' His voice was a whine as his bandmate hovered at his shoulder.

'Not really. I need to work the bar,' she lied. The less she was involved in this the better. This crowd liked folk music, indie rock or, at a push, a little pop. Unless these guys were going to whip out an acoustic guitar from their tracksuit pockets, Steph could bet this was going to end badly.

He pulled a face. 'Awright. Come on, Tony. Thanks for nothing.'

Charming.

Steph stole a quick look at Gemma's table as she watched the lads weave their way to the back door.

She'd barely stopped smiling. It was good to see Gemma happy, but Steph couldn't help the sour feeling in her gut at not being the one seated opposite her.

There was no way she could compete, though. Izzy was in a league of her own. Legs for days, perfect skin, a smile that could charm the pants off anyone and everyone. Next to Izzy, Steph might as well be invisible.

She wracked her brain for an excuse to go to Gemma's table. She should know better than to tease herself, but it was no use: the pull was too strong. At least she finished soon. Once she was home there would be no more temptation.

Although then her mind would be fixed on what they were up to after the date.

Steph had no business letting it bother her, but the mere thought felt like a punch in the gut.

The queue to the bar was three deep: time to work and stop torturing herself. She couldn't resist a final look at Gemma as she slid behind the bar. She sighed. Nothing left to do but move on.

∾

'HAVING A GOOD TIME?' Steph asked as she squatted by Gemma's table. No harm in a quick goodbye, especially since Gemma was currently solo.

'Yeah, I think so.'

It was hard to hear her over the live music but her eyes looked sullen.

'That didn't sound overly enthusiastic.'

Gemma snapped back to life. 'Sorry, yes. Just tired from talking and work's been busy this week. Anyway, I thought you finished half an hour ago?'

Steph pulled a face. 'Guilty. But I wanted to see what happened with the music.'

'It's, erm, interesting.'

Steph pulled a face. 'That's one word for it.' The duo had lived up to Steph's expectations and were dropping bars no one was picking up. Slowly but steadily they were clearing the place out. They sounded terrible.

Gemma leaned closer, hoping to win the battle against the music. 'I think we're going to head somewhere else now. Too loud to chat.'

'I don't blame you.'

'What?'

Steph laughed. 'I said, I don't blame you.'

Something fizzled in the air between them, and it wasn't Steph's imagination: Gemma's locked gaze, inches from her own, said she was thinking something too. Probably not even in the same ballpark as Steph's wandering mind, though.

The feeling of someone hovering behind her made Steph turn. Izzy. The fizzle died, the air returning to normal charge.

'Hey,' she said, giving Steph a little wave.

She stood straight. Damn, Izzy was tall. 'Hey. Finished my shift, just saying bye,' she shouted, her stomach tightening like she'd been caught with her hand in the cookie jar.

Izzy leaned closer, a hand on Steph's side. 'We're heading off too. Want to join us?'

'Me?'

'Why not?' she asked with a laugh. 'You busy?'

Something felt off. Why would they want her on their date? Izzy was obviously just being polite.

'You don't want a third wheel. It's been a long shift anyway,' she shouted into Izzy's ear. She damn well needed a ladder: the poor woman was having to stoop to Steph's level. 'I want to get home to my bed.'

'Fair enough,' Izzy replied, straightening herself.

Gemma slid out of the booth, draping her jacket over her arm. 'See you, then, Steph.'

There was that moment again. Undeniable. A little pop of the unspoken.

There was a pause, and Steph could have sworn the music stopped playing and silence descended as time stood still for a millisecond.

Why did she have the urge to hug Gemma goodbye?

She stood her ground, her hands shoved firmly in her pockets.

'Bye,' Izzy said, taking Gemma by the arm and toppling the false reality that Steph had constructed in her head.

She watched them leave, well aware she probably looked odd.

A group of lads swarmed around her, taking over the empty booth. They were the first new punters she'd seen since the music started.

'Sorry, were you waiting?' one asked, sliding into the space Gemma had vacated.

'Nah, don't worry. I work here,' she replied and slinked back to the bar.

'Why are you still here?' Stevie asked with a smile.

'Who could leave when these guys are performing?' Steph retorted, leaning her forearms on the bar as she watched the duo stomp about the stage. It was painful to watch, never mind listen to, but she couldn't take her eyes off them.

'Absolutely dire, eh?'

'And then some.'

Novak shattered the mood, appearing at Stevie's side with a grave face. 'Have you seen Donnie?'

Steph shook her head. 'My guess is he's gone. Kara will lead the shift now if you need anything.'

Novak nodded, a slow gesture like his head weighed a tonne. 'I'm done anyway. But I just went to get my bag and my bank card's missing.'

Steph's stomach dropped. 'Eh?'

'It was in my wallet and now it's not.'

'You're sure?' It wasn't that she didn't believe him: only, they stored their bags in the office and it was always locked or attended. The most logical assumption was that he thought he'd brought it to work but actually hadn't.

'I'm certain. I used it to get the bus this morning.'

Steph chewed on her bottom lip. 'Only people with keys are me and Donnie.'

Stevie swallowed, her eyes on the stage. 'Donnie let them prep in the office earlier.'

Ah. Well. That certainly changed things. 'Oh, really?' Would make sense if he hadn't done their paperwork prior to today: they'd need to go over everything out of view of the public.

It was a big accusation, though.

If only she'd gone home when she was meant to. She'd be well clear of this mess.

She watched the lads bounce about the stage, styling it out like they were international rap stars.

At least half the tables were empty now. So much for Lovefest being a money-spinner: the place would be dead soon enough.

'Let me go to the office, have a think about this,' Steph said to Novak. She needed peace to decide her next move.

Novak simply nodded, his face still as white as a sheet.

She plodded round to the office, the sickness in her stomach growing with every step, and gently closed the door behind her. It was quieter, but the din of the Possil Posse still permeated her skull.

She took a seat and tilted her head back, rubbing at her temples.

This was a tough call.

She kept her own bank card in her pocket. She patted it down, just to check. Still there. Along with her phone. She placed it on the desk and reached down for her rucksack.

It looked normal; untampered with.

She unzipped it, relieved to see her headphones and umbrella. Her heart sank when she checked the front pocket. She'd definitely had a tenner. Now only her house keys remained.

Fuck.

She didn't care about the money. It was the conflict she dreaded.

Steph dropped her bag to the floor and jumped when her phone rumbled against the desk.

Gemma. *You okay? Hope you're home now? X*

What was she doing texting Steph when she was on a date? Steph smiled as she replied, unable to hide the elation that Gemma provided, even when her heart was racing a mile a minute with panic.

Not yet. Have a new problem. Looks like the band have been stealing from the staff. X

The reply was instant. *What?! No! What did they take? X*

So far a bank card and some cash. Haven't checked other bags yet. X

That's shocking x

Should I confront them? X

Steph stared at the screen, willing a reply to come. Not even the magical three dots signalled Gemma was typing. Their quick-fire conversation was suddenly stalled.

Her breath caught as the dots appeared. Her eyes followed as they danced, eventually being replaced with a message.

I don't think you should. It's not safe. Tell Cal. Donnie will have their booking details. There must be CCTV? You don't know how they'll react and you don't have back up. X

Another text quickly followed.

Please promise me you won't xx

Two kisses. It was a silly, minute detail but it made

Steph's heart sing. Gemma was worried. About her. As a friend. But still.

I promise I won't. I'll go home now x

Should she have done two kisses back? Steph shook her head, embarrassed to be overthinking something so trivial when her staff had just had their bags looted.

Text me when you're in? X

Deal x

She reclined in the swivel chair, the phone cradled to her chest.

Damn, how had she fallen so quickly for this woman? This wasn't Steph's usual pattern. In fact, liking someone at all was big news, never mind the supersonic rate at which Gemma had gotten under her skin.

She needed to rein this in, otherwise she was heading for heartbreak.

A knock at the door interrupted her thoughts and Stevie's voice soon followed. 'Can I come in?'

Steph shoved her phone away and opened the door. 'What's up?'

'I'm being para, but okay if I check my stuff too?'

Steph pulled a face. 'You'd better. I'm missing money.'

'What?' Stevie yelped, rushing to her bag at the back wall. She tore it open, pulling out her cardigan before raking through the contents.

Steph watched with bated breath. Her heart leapt when Stevie's shoulders slumped, a groan of frustration tumbling out as she looked in her purse.

'My bank card is here but I'm missing a fiver.'

'For fuck's sake.' Steph tilted her head to the ceiling. She couldn't let this slide. Who knew what else they'd taken? 'Tell everyone to come in here, one at a time. We need to write this down, document what's missing.'

'You going to confront them?' Stevie asked, her features as dour as Steph felt.

'Not sure yet. Something needs to be done, though.'

∼

EIGHT MEMBERS of staff and every single one had something missing. They'd had a field day. A part of Steph wondered if it really was the band, though. Could someone actually be so stupid as to think the team wouldn't notice before their set was done?

There was no other explanation, though.

Even Donnie wouldn't be so dumb.

Gemma was right, though. This wasn't something she should tackle alone.

The urge to text Gemma settled in her mind, like an itch she couldn't quite scratch.

She shouldn't, though. Not when she was on a date.

But not keeping her up to date would make a liar of Steph. She'd promised she'd go home.

She sent a quick text: *More stuff taken, this is getting out of hand. Going to confront them x* and put her phone in her back pocket.

They'd be finished in five minutes. It was now or never.

She waited for the music to stop. Her heart was beating so fast it was like it had an echo. A quiet ripple of applause filled the bar. After a fractured exhalation, she left the safety of the office.

With every step, she got a little slower. She was a stride away from walking backwards by the time she reached the wannabe rap stars.

'Guys, can I have a word?' Her voice threatened to wobble, as did her knees.

'Aye, what's up?' asked the wee one. The other guy focused on putting something in his rucksack. Convenient that it was hidden up here, behind a speaker, and not in the office. 'You not happy with the set?'

Oh, that was only the start of it. No point in moaning about that, though. 'Don't suppose you know why my staff have money and bank cards missing?'

Wee Man narrowed his eyes as his bandmate stood tall, taking position at his side. 'You better no be accusing us of theft,' he spat, his top lip curling.

'It's likely a misunderstanding,' she replied, standing her ground. 'You've not had anything taken, have you?'

Silent guy shook his head. Did he only open his mouth to rap? What an odd couple they were.

The phone in her back pocket vibrated, signalling a call. She ignored it, willing it to stop. It was only making her tremble further.

'Do you not want to check?' she prompted, hoping to peek in their bag.

'I feel like you think we stole the stuff,' Wee Man said, crossing his arms.

'Just trying to figure out where my team's stuff went. I'd appreciate your cooperation.'

They exchanged glances and shared a quiet laugh. 'Get fucked,' Wee Man said, pushing past Steph as his mate grabbed their bag and followed suit.

'Guys,' Steph snapped, unsure where the sentence was going.

Wee Man flipped her the middle finger over his shoulder and the other pushed a stool over on the way to the door. It toppled into the nearest table and sent a glass candleholder flying to the floor. Silence descended as it smashed into a thousand pieces, scattering glass across the floor.

They didn't even break their stride.

'That went well,' Steph groaned under her breath, well aware all eyes were on her.

Time to go home. This mess could be Donnie's. He deserved it.

18

On Monday, Gemma sat on the gym's wooden bench and checked her phone. She was starting to wonder why she had it. The only people to call her were Granny and her parents. Nothing exciting except a photo posted on Facebook by Granny. Of a cat. Granny didn't own a cat.

She shoved it into her bag. You weren't really meant to use it in the locker room, so even social media couldn't delay the inevitable. She knew she'd feel better after working out, but getting started was tough.

It was busy today and ladies filled nearly every available bench or mirror space. She took a deep breath. Maybe it would be better to come back another time. Skipping one workout wouldn't hurt, would it?

No. That's how things started.

She kicked off her heels. God, her feet hurt. The office had been hellish today, so many meetings. She gave her right foot a rub, digging her thumb into the pad.

When she straightened herself, she was met with an incredibly toned stomach inches from her face. Its owner was using her T-shirt to wipe sweat from her face and clearly wasn't paying attention to how close she was to people.

They stopped walking, letting the T-shirt fall into place, and Gemma's heart left her body.

'Gemma? Hey, how are you?' Steph asked, putting her backwards cap back on properly.

'Abs—' *WORDS, GEMMA.* 'Abs-olutely terrific,' she finally managed, but the voice didn't sound like her own.

Steph bit her bottom lip, hiding a smile. 'Coming or going?'

'Coming,' Gemma replied and X-rated jokes filled her head. 'You?'

Steph put her hands on her hips, and it was only then that Gemma fully clocked her ragged breathing and sweat-soaked clothing.

'Believe it or not, going,' she replied with a chuckle.

'Looks like it was a good workout. Was it busy? I really can't be arsed today.'

Steph waggled her head. 'So-so. Machines aren't too bad. Two classes have just come out, so it seems busier than it is.' She grinned. If they'd been a cartoon a light bulb would have appeared above her head. Gemma prayed she was going to suggest the pub. 'Fancy a workout partner? Could make it more fun for you?'

'I thought you were going?' No pub. *Crap.*

'I was. But I just did weights today. A bit of cardio would do me good.'

Where was the harm? 'Sure, if you don't mind.'

Steph smiled. 'Awesome, I'll get you upstairs. Treadmills okay?'

'Yeah, sure.'

'See you soon,' she said with a wink before disappearing back into the crowded room.

Gemma let out a stuttering breath. It was time to face the music and admit the whole truth and nothing but the truth to herself. Steph was hot and by God, did she fancy her. Especially after seeing that stomach. Good Lord. What did a girl have to do to trail kisses over that?

Her date with Izzy had been good but she'd spent most of it worrying about Steph. And it wasn't just her issues with thieving entertainers that made Gemma's mind wander. Her heart did a funny skip whenever she saw her. Yes, Izzy was gorgeous and good company, but the attraction was only surface deep. She didn't make Gemma feel like her heart was in free fall, or like she might be in danger of pulling a muscle from smiling too hard.

She shook herself, aware she'd zoned out with a goofy look plastered on her face and was in danger of inadvertently staring at someone's tits.

Two minutes later and Steph could have got an eyeful of hers. Which wouldn't have been a bad conversation opener.

Izzy's observation lay fresh in her mind. Did Steph like her, too? Or was Izzy just saying that because it was obvious Gemma had liked Steph? Jeez, it was a mess. Surely, as an out-and-proud lesbian, Steph would have made a move by now? She'd had plenty chances.

Gemma stuffed her clothes away and got changed into her workout gear.

If Steph was a guy it would be a no brainer. They were hanging out a lot, most of it one-on-one. He'd be into her. No questions asked. But with a girl? What was the difference between friends and lovers?

She pulled on her trainers.

Steph wasn't flirty in the slightest.

But then, neither was Gemma. The idea made her shoulders rise and her muscles tense. Past Gemma was a champion flirter. Funny how something is easy when nothing is on the line. Now, though? Terror gripped her stomach. She could try, though: maybe a few well-placed looks, a little light banter. Start small, see what happened.

Trainers tied and her bag safely in a locker, she trotted upstairs. Steph was right: it wasn't busy at all.

'Will we see who can go the longest?' Steph asked, pushing off the column she'd been leaning against. 'Or do you want to race?'

'Length seems like a good idea. You strike me as being fast – I don't want to set myself up for failure.'

Steph hopped onto the nearest treadmill. 'I dunno, with your long legs I bet you could easily beat me. But slow and steady, that suits me fine.'

Gemma clambered onto the treadmill beside her. 'So what: we just go until one of us stops?'

'That's the plan.' Steph looked at her top: the sweat was even worse than before. 'This is minging.'

Before Gemma had a chance to thank her lucky stars, Steph was peeling the top over her head and chucking it on the ground behind the treadmill.

She'd been stuck for words before; now her unconscious was rendered silent too.

Holy moly.

The tattoo she'd seen hints of before was a snake, its body weaving along the side of Steph's torso. It was an invitation, asking Gemma to trace a finger along its meandering body down to its head and the top of Steph's hip. Truth be told, she was more interested in its tail and where it started under Steph's sports top.

Gemma tensed her jaw and turned her attention to the machine's control panel.

Running wasn't going to be easy. Not with the pulse that was already thundering between her legs.

She started the machine off slow.

'Hey, no cheating,' Steph said with an already-out-of-breath laugh. 'You have to go at least five or you're walking.'

'Working up to it,' Gemma replied, and flashed Steph a smile. But really it was just an excuse to look at her again.

She was slim and toned, the outline of her stomach muscles announcing that she clearly worked out. Gemma would feel like an oaf next to her.

SHIT. The image of their naked bodies flashed in Gemma's mind before becoming a permanent fixture.

With Steph's sweaty, glistening skin within reach it really wasn't hard to picture what it might be like.

'You struggling already?' Steph asked, still breathless.

'Do I look it?' Gemma said with a short laugh.

'Bit red in the face, Anderson.'

Desire pinged in Gemma's stomach, settling in her core.

'Could say the same for you, Campbell.'

Gemma exhaled slowly, willing her heart rate to level out. Blood was going nowhere useful. She wouldn't last long at this rate.

'How long do you usually go for?' Steph panted.

'Fifteen minutes, if I'm lucky.' Time to be brave, start with something subtle. 'Hoping I can last longer for you, though.'

Did that land? Was it too obvious? Not obvious enough?

She stole a quick glance. Steph was smiling.

'In that case, I might need to slow down,' Steph said, catching Gemma's eye.

The heavy thud of Steph's trainers slowed to a nearer a walking pace.

'Hey now, that's definitely cheating.' Gemma's chest ached: running and talking was hard.

'True, but you had an unfair advantage.'

'How so?'

'I've already worked out.'

'Fair. But don't start a challenge if you're not up for it.'

'Ooft, fighting talk. Right, let's see who can go the fastest for thirty seconds, then.'

'That's hardly a workout!' Gemma blurted with a snigger.

'All or nothing. Then I'm going to have to love you and leave you. I've overestimated my stamina.'

No! This was just getting fun. Gemma refrained from pouting. 'Okay. I'm on six: you get back here, then we'll go on three.'

'What level are you going to go on?'

'Ten.'

'Ten? Jesus, Gemma. I'll die. My legs are half the length of yours.'

'Chicken?'

'If I break my neck, let Cal's know I need my shifts covered.'

'Deal. You ready? Ten for thirty seconds.'

'You're mad. Right, go!'

Level ten on the treadmill might have been optimistic. There was a strong chance she was going to lose her footing and be flung backwards. Gemma's feet banged on the treadmill, each step reverberating through her body.

Thirty seconds, though. Not long to go.

Must be about it.

She slapped the emergency stop and the belt came to a swift halt.

Steph wasn't far behind.

They stood panting, not a word between them.

Steph put her hands on her knees and Gemma couldn't help but look down the gap of her sport's top. A ravine of sweat called her in, urging her closer.

'Fuck,' Steph groaned. 'That was fast.'

Gemma straightened herself, leaning her forearms on the side of the machine. 'I think I just did my usual workout in five minutes.'

Steph stood up, blowing her cheeks out as she tipped her head back. 'That's one way to get a sweat on.'

'I can think of more enjoyable ways.' Ooft. She was proud of that.

Steph didn't take the bait. 'You going to stay? I don't think I can keep up with you.' She hopped off the treadmill.

'Yeah, prob—' Gemma's feet got tangled as she went to step off the machine. Her lace must have come undone during their race and before she knew, she was falling forward, right into the arms of Steph.

They stood motionless, Steph's strong hands around Gemma's biceps, her own palms resting on Steph's bare midriff. You could bounce coins off her: she was rock solid.

Gemma gulped.

'You okay?' Steph asked, her brown eyes looking up at Gemma. They were so close, it was ridiculous.

'Yeah, just—' She composed herself, aware people were looking. She took a step back. 'I think the universe is trying to tell me working out is a bad idea today.'

Steph scratched behind her ear. 'Want to join me for a smoothie instead?'

∼

GEMMA HAD NEVER HUNG ABOUT LONG ENOUGH to visit the smoothie bar on the bottom floor of the gym. Usually workouts were a get-in-and-get-out affair. The place was nice. Simple plastic seats and tables sat on a faux grass rug, with a serving area styled to look like a tiki bar. The smoothies spoke for themselves: she'd gone for a delicious summer berry combo and Steph a vanilla protein shake. It was amazing; she'd definitely be back.

Steph was a lot less sweaty after a quick shower but Gemma had opted to wash at home. She'd barely done a workout, plus the threat of Steph seeing something in the open-plan changing room wasn't worth the risk. Gemma was far too shy.

'So,' Steph began before sucking on her drink's straw. 'How's it going with Izzy?'

Gemma let out a long breath. 'Not sure.'

Steph's brow knitted. 'How so? I thought you really liked her?'

Divided attention was what she wanted to say, but instead Gemma replied: 'It's good, yeah. Just not sure.'

The look didn't budge from Steph's face. 'You chasing this elusive spark again?'

Gemma laughed under her breath. 'Not so much. It's just, I don't know. It's hard to explain. I think I'm emotionally fatigued.'

Steph smiled. 'Sorry, sorry.' She composed herself. 'That's a new one. Relationships take time. Just because it's not fireworks and jazz bands every time you meet, doesn't mean there isn't something there.'

'Is that what it feels like?'

'Sometimes. Other times it's just enjoying each other's company. A lazy day on the sofa. A quiet moment in the car. Little things,' she said with a shrug.

Gemma drank her smoothie before sighing. 'Sometimes I wish there was a way to at least know everything works out.'

'It will.'

She was done moping. 'So, Steph. Tell me, what's the secret to those killer abs? A few thousand sit-ups a day?'

Steph's cheeks turned red. 'Get dumped, throw yourself into work and the gym. They're kind of just a side effect.'

'Maisie, I take it?'

Steph pulled a face, raising her eyebrows. 'That's the one.'

'And now she's getting married?'

'How did you know that?'

Shit. What she'd been told and what Granny had let slip was getting blurred. 'I think you mentioned it a while ago. When I told you about Logan's girlfriend being pregnant.' She had, hadn't she?

'Ah, yeah. It's fine, though. She's happy so I'm happy.'

'But you thought she'd be happy with you?'

'She was. But I put work first and didn't give her the time she deserved. Happy, but incompatible in the end.'

Gemma relaxed back in her seat, staring at the corner of the room as she thought. 'You know, it's weird. That's how I feel about Logan. We would have been brilliant friends. Just the wrong anatomy for me to stay married.'

'You don't think you'll ever be friends?'

Gemma shook her head. 'Never. He didn't exactly take our break-up well. My best friend—' she closed her eyes, wincing at the idea. '—well, I guess my ex-best friend, is getting married soon and Logan will be there. I'm dreading it.'

'Why is she an ex, too?'

'She's replaced me with Logan's new girlfriend.'

'Fuck.'

'I know.'

'Life's really done a number on us, eh?'

'Feels that way.'

'At least we've got each other now. It's good to have a friend in the same boat.'

Shite. Suddenly her attraction to Steph was a massive neon warning sign, flashing in her head. Was Gemma going to arse up this friendship, too?

19

Tuesday, Donnie was waiting at the end of the bar when Steph arrived for work. This was becoming a new ritual. Great.

'A minute in the office, Steph?' His tone suggested it was a question but his body language confirmed it was anything but.

She shrugged and wandered through: there was no point in arguing. She didn't have the energy or the headspace for witty remarks.

He let her go first and closed the door behind him. She leaned against the desk with a sigh. She'd done a stellar job of avoiding him since the Lovefest event at the weekend. She'd spoken to Cal and promised the team that it would be sorted. The issue was out of her hands, though, and shouting at Donnie wouldn't help anyone. She knew herself well enough that keeping things professional with him was slowly becoming impossible.

'Cal was here this morning,' he said, taking a seat.

She nodded, still not caring enough to talk.

'Hello?' he groaned.

'Right, yes, Cal was here. Fantastic.'

'A few manners wouldn't go amiss.' He huffed. 'He was asking about the Lovefest closer.'

'And?'

'Well, why's the blame on me? You were here.'

She blurted out a laugh. 'You told me, in this exact spot,' she said, stabbing a finger towards the ground. 'That you were taking over. That as manager, you made the big choices. You ran the show. Now, you tell me how any of that translates as me taking responsibility for something you did?'

He floundered. 'Yes, but, it's your *responsibility* to make sure it runs smoothly. You can't go around accusing people of theft.'

Steph tensed her jaw. 'I wasn't accusing anyone. They did it. Plain and simple. Have you heard from the police yet?'

He crossed his arms. 'Cal's fine with me following this up. He agreed it would make no sense to cause trouble.'

Steph fixed her eyes on the posters stuck to the wall behind Donnie's head. Cal didn't have his head screwed on these days. 'You think that's wise?'

'Excuse me?'

'You think it's wise you handle this and not the police? They didn't just steal money; it was cards too. That's fraud. Not to mention the AirPods they took from Tori. If you don't call the police, I will.'

Donnie huffed. 'You'd better be joking.'

'Why would I be joking? Do you realise how serious this is?'

'You're overreacting,' he replied, twisting the desk chair from side to side.

She waved a hand between them. ' I don't have time to argue about this. Why did you call me in?'

'I wanted an apology from you.'

Steph almost choked. 'Me? Why?'

'For how you reacted on Saturday. You should have come to me before threatening the talent. There's no way they'll be back now.'

'Good. They were shite,' Steph retorted. 'Can you hear yourself? They stole from the team, Donnie. Why are you defending them?'

He picked up the nearest pen and rolled it between his fingers and thumbs as he slouched in the chair. 'Apology. Now.'

'Get stuffed, Donnie.' She'd made it half a step when he grabbed her wrist.

'Have some respect.'

'Take your hand off me.'

His grip tightened. 'You're leading yourself into dangerous waters, Steph. You don't want me as an enemy.'

She shook her arm free, yanking it out of his reach. She swallowed down the fear that was dying to escape in the form of a whimper.

'This conversation is over.'

His eyes bored into her back as she fumbled with the handle, the Chubb lock refusing to budge. Her hands felt like claws, her chest frozen as her lungs gave up. There was no point. Her heart filled the space in her chest, slamming off her ribs at an alarming rate.

Finally, it clicked open and she was free.

Steph closed the office door, ignored Stevie and Kara at the bar, and bee-lined straight for the toilets. Why were they so bastarding far? And upstairs?!

Her chest was getting tighter with every step. It was like climbing a Munro.

The banister provided a good aid and soon she was hauling herself over the top stair.

She clutched over her heart, and would have breathed a sigh of relief when she finally reached the toilets had there been any air in her lungs.

She slammed onto the closed toilet and shut the door of the cubicle, letting her facade drop. Why wasn't any air going into her lungs? She was taking deep breaths but it was doing nothing.

She gripped the sides of the cubicle, trying to steady herself.

Deep breaths and count.

One.

Two.

Three.

Nope. It was no good. The world was fuzzy at the edges.

Steph scrunched her eyes up, trying to focus on her clammy skin instead of the fact she couldn't breathe.

The sound of her panting filled the tiny stall.

Jesus.

She couldn't die at work.

The vice around her chest tightened.

Was this a heart attack?

Weren't they meant to come with arm pain, or something?

God, this was so embarrassing.

Why at work, of all places? If she was going to die couldn't it be in the privacy of her own home?

The fuzziness closed in.

Steph fumbled for her phone and pulled up Gemma's

phone number. Should she? Wasn't this embarrassing enough? No, she needed to know she wasn't overreacting.

'Hello? I'm in a—'

'Gemma.' Her name came out as a gasp.

'Steph, you okay?'

'I think I'm dying.' Saying it out loud felt stupid, but the fact it felt like she was trying to talk underwater kinda underlined the fact.

'Huh?'

'I can't breathe.'

'Right, okay. You're fine.'

A tear rolled down Steph's cheek.

'You still there?' Gemma asked, panic clear.

'Yeah.'

Gemma must have put a hand over her phone because the voices in the background became muffled, followed by the sound of a door clicking closed. Then she spoke: 'Right, just take some deep breaths for me, okay?'

Steph wanted to make a joke but she couldn't. There wasn't enough air. 'Yep.'

'Okay, now focus on my voice. Breathe in, and out.' Gemma kept her voice low and her words long, eventually mimicking the sound of what she hoped Steph was doing. 'That's it, in and out. You're fine. You're totally fine. Do you need me to come get you? Where are you?'

'At work,' Steph managed, her breath starting to even out.

'Okay. You're doing good. You want to come to your work right now?'

'No.' Really, she did. She really, really did. But that would be far too embarrassing.

'I'm going to stay right here for a while. Make sure you're okay. I'm just going to talk. You listen to me and keep taking those deep breaths, okay?' Gemma paused, taking her own deep breath. 'You've given me a nice break from this meeting – thank you. It was looking like it would run late but I can probably make my excuses and get away early now. If I can do that, I'll come straight to your work. If I can't, it might be another hour. Either way, you're seeing me. Then you're going home. No arguing. They can't keep you there when you're having panic attacks.'

Is that what this was? Steph wasn't panicking. This wasn't a panic attack. Was it?

Gemma continued, 'Then tomorrow, you're going to the doctor and you're getting signed off. I won't take no for an answer. It won't be for long and Cal's will still be standing when you get back. So, what do you fancy tonight? Chinese or Indian food? I can pick up either. We'll watch a film. Only stipulation is: I get to pick.'

'Haven't I suffered enough?' Steph said with a weak laugh.

'That's the spirit. How you doing now?'

'A bit better. Thanks.'

'We can have a proper chat later. You want me to stay on the line?'

'For a bit. Is that okay?'

'My pleasure.'

~

SUITABLY STUFFED with chicken tikka masala and pakora, Steph was getting sleepy. It had been a shitty day. But Gemma had made it bearable. Even if that did include watching *The Proposal*. At least Sandra Bullock was hot.

'Are you only watching this for the scene when she's nude?' Steph joked.

'No. It's the impeccable script and the dazzling Betty White that does it for me,' Gemma replied with a wink.

Steph really wanted to lie down and stretch out. The question was . . . was she brave enough to do it how she wanted? Why not be ballsy? She'd been through a lot today: she could write things off as a symptom of stress.

She grabbed a cushion and put it on Gemma's lap, before resting her head and getting comfy. There were no protests. Friends provided friends with comfort, it was just what they did. Really, Steph craved being close to someone. It was days like today she really hated being single. The thought made her chest tighten so she stuffed it down, worried a repeat performance might be on the cards.

To her surprise, Gemma rested her hand at the base of Steph's ribs, like it was the most natural thing in the world. Maybe it was to her.

'Thanks again for today,' Steph said quietly.

She almost jumped when Gemma's other hand started to gently stroke her hair. There was nothing sexual about it; the move was one of pure comfort.

'It was nothing. You okay now?'

'Yeah.'

'Want to talk about why it happened?'

'I think work just got too much for me. It was like, I'd bottled things up for so long, if I wasn't going to find a way to release how I felt, my body was going to do it for me.'

'Bodies know best, no matter what we think. Has it happened before?'

'Kind of, but not as bad. Only twice. Once when I was in the café with Maisie, just before I met you.'

'I didn't think you were right that day. We'll get this sorted.'

They watched the movie in silence for a while, Gemma's hand continuing to stroke Steph's hair at sporadic intervals.

She'd never had a female friend like this. Plenty of friends over the years, but no one close. Not without them wanting something more.

She'd be a liar if she said she didn't want more from Gemma, but she wasn't a fool. Steph knew it wasn't on the table. A friend was just as good. Even if it was only temporary. If things worked out with Izzy, Gemma would probably lose touch.

Maisie would be gone soon as well. Married life and inevitable children stealing her focus. Steph could really do without the wedding next weekend. She sighed.

'What was that for?'

'What?'

'That massive sigh,' Gemma replied with a chuckle.

'Just thinking.'

'Good or bad?'

She took a deep breath. 'Things with Maisie, they didn't exactly end well. And she stupidly was honest with Shannon.'

'That's her fiancée?'

'Yep.'

'Which has made things, well, complicated.'

'Was there, how do I put this? An overlap?'

Steph smiled. 'Not so much. More Maisie being brutally honest about our messy past and how I'm the love of her life.'

'Jesus. Wow. Okay. I can see why Shannon isn't exactly keen.'

'Yep,' Steph said with a pop of her lips.

'So, how do you feel about Maisie? Would you take her back?'

'Honestly? No. In hindsight Shannon is way better for her. I'm just me. Shannon's a textile designer: she's got a swanky flat and a nice family. I've told Maisie as much.'

With a gentle pull Gemma encouraged Steph to roll onto her back, her eyes instantly finding hers and her hand resting on Steph's stomach. 'That sounds very harsh on yourself.'

'Well, there's more to it than that.'

'Yeah?'

'I work silly hours. We never saw each other. Maisie gave me an ultimatum and I chose work. I'm not qualified to do anything else. What could I do?' Steph flung her hands out in frustration.

'Given our conversation the other day about you leaving work, I'd say you've changed now. Is that right? Why not tell Maisie that?'

Steph laughed quietly. 'This isn't a conversation about getting Maisie back. I came to terms with that years ago. My brain's hardwired to see her as a friend now, even if she doesn't feel the same about me. Anyway,' she said, and paused, willing the next sentence to meander a little less. 'Shannon is not my biggest fan. Maisie really wants me at the wedding. She thinks it would be better if I brought someone.'

Gemma tried and failed to hide a smile. 'Oh, really? So who you taking? Donnie?'

Steph playfully batted her arm. 'Don't. Actually, I was rather hoping you'd do me the honour? Just as friends, of course.'

'When is it?'

'Next Saturday.'

Gemma whistled through her teeth. 'Oh, now. I think I

might be organising my tin cupboard into alphabetical order that day.'

'Can I help?'

'Only if you behave.'

'Dang. And there was me thinking I finally had an excuse not to go to this stupid wedding.'

'You really don't want to go?'

'Hell no. You must get it, though. You don't want to go to Julie's.'

'You've got me there.' She played with the toggle of Steph's hoodie between her finger and thumb. 'So, why are you going?'

'Maisie would be crushed if I didn't go.'

'She's asking a lot of you, you know that?'

'Not really. She just wants me there.'

Gemma pursed her lips. 'You're a good human, Steph.' She dropped the toggle. 'If you want me there, I'll come.'

Steph grinned.

20

'Gemma!' Granny called from the kitchen. 'Come help me with these veg.'

Gemma hung her coat up before wandering through. 'How did you know it was me?'

'Your parents are never early and since when have the boys entered anywhere like mice?'

'Fair point. What do you need me for?'

'Cut these veg, will you? Blasted hands are acting up in the damp weather.'

Gemma could see before she'd asked. Granny's poor fingers looked like gnarled tree trunks, swollen and sore around the joints. Gemma took her place at the chopping board and set to work.

'Now: disaster. I'm out of gin. Will a light rum be okay?'

Gemma stopped chopping. 'Everything okay? You never run out of gin.'

Granny waved a hand in her direction. 'I met Bethany in Waitrose and we chatted so long, I clean forgot half the things I went for.'

'How's her husband?'

'Not looking good. But when you get to our age, you enjoy the days you've had and count your blessings.'

'Granny!'

'Wheesht. Now. Rum?'

'Go on, then,' Gemma said with a cheeky smile.

Gemma cut the carrots into chunks, only stopping to quickly open a can of Diet Coke for Granny, and then started on topping and tailing the green beans.

'How are things with Izzy?' Granny asked as she set the rum by the board.

Gemma clicked her tongue against the roof of her mouth. 'I think that's run its course.'

'Oh, really?' Granny said, shuffling over to the small kitchen table and taking a seat. 'How so?'

How to say this to her grandmother? 'I just couldn't imagine it going anywhere.'

A part of Gemma had been starting to wonder if she was broken. She could see Izzy was physically attractive but trying to imagine sleeping with her was nigh on impossible. She really wanted it to work, like *really*. But it just wasn't happening. She'd all but given into the fact she might be wired wrong when her brain kicked into gear with Steph, and now it was all she could think about.

Suddenly she was like a horny teenager. Even if nothing happened, it was a relief to know she was capable.

'What do you mean?' Granny asked, taking a long sip of rum and Coke. Her face said it all: rum was no replacement for gin. Gemma would make a point of having a backup from now on. Gossiping grannies couldn't be trusted with such important matters.

Gemma focused on finishing the beans, searching her mind for the ideal way to phrase this in a granny-friendly manner. 'I just, hmm, not the right feelings, I suppose. She was lovely. Just not for me.'

Granny nodded gently. 'And Steph?'

Her cheeks went red at the thought, a smile fighting its way across her lips. Her cheeks instantly ached.

'Ah, that's why Izzy is off the table,' Granny said before Gemma got a chance.

'She doesn't know though. So don't go saying anything if you bump into her again.'

'My lips are sealed, darling!' Granny announced with a twirl of her hand.

'Thank you. Any more veg?'

'No. Just pop that on to boil, please. So, when are you going to tell Steph you like her?'

Gemma hoped the noisy faucet covered the sigh that escaped. She put the pot on the stove and took a long draw of her drink before reclining against the counter, arms crossed. 'Two things: I don't want to ruin our friendship, and can you really see us together? We're chalk and cheese. Do you think it would work? Is it worth risking what we already have?'

'Oh, darling. Come, take a seat,' Granny said, patting the chair nearest her.

Gemma brought her rum over and sat down.

Granny continued: 'I wouldn't worry about your friendship. Whatever happens, I'm sure Steph will keep you in her life. And as for the other thing.' She shrugged. 'If you're attracted to her, why not?'

'I know. It's just—' She paused, reflecting. Was she overthinking? No. 'On paper all we have in common is a shared taste in coat hooks.'

'Huh?'

Gemma waved a hand between them. 'All I'm saying is: is there enough common ground to make it work?'

'You get on, so there must be.'

'It's not just about getting on.' Gemma twisted the crystal tumbler between her palms. 'I know I shouldn't compare, but I keep thinking of my wedding photos with Logan. Can you really see me and Steph like that?'

Granny's eyes narrowed slightly, her gaze softening as she twigged what Gemma was getting at. 'I see. It sounds like you're getting ahead of yourself. And—' She placed a hand on Gemma's. 'Starting to sound a little snobby.'

Trust Granny to always say it as it was. 'She's just not who I thought I would like. I mean, can you see her at a work event with me?'

'So she has tattoos and doesn't dress like your friends do? Gemma Anderson, I thought we brought you up better than this. Do you want to be stuck caring what other people think, or do you want to be happy?'

Gemma couldn't meet her gaze. Granny was right. She was being an absolute bitch and she didn't like herself one bit. But it was playing on her mind, and no matter how much she tried to push the notion down, it wouldn't budge. 'I know. And if Steph ever heard me talk like this, she'd hate me. And rightly so. It sounds like I think I'm better than her or something. But it's not that.' She took a deep breath, tears threatening to make an appearance. 'It's just – since I came out I feel like there's all this pressure. I know fine well all my friends, well, people who used to be friends, I guess, will be talking about me, analysing me. And it's like, if I step further outside what they expect of me it will just be more ammunition for their gossiping.'

'So you'd rather focus on what a stuck up wee cow like Julie thinks than date a gorgeous woman like Steph?'

Gemma choked out a laugh, wiping away a stray tear that had escaped. 'Well, when you put it like that. I don't know when I started caring about other people's opinions so much. Am I a horrible person?'

Granny stood up. She was getting so small these days: it made Gemma's heart ache. She wrapped her arms around her granddaughter. 'You're not horrible. You've just had a lot to navigate recently. I don't know if I've ever said this out loud, but I'm really proud of you, Gemma. The last few years can't have been easy. But I love you and I always will. I just want you to be happy.'

Well, that did it: the tears couldn't be stopped now. 'Thank you,' was all she could manage.

'Don't let other people steal your light. It's too precious to give away to people who won't treat it with care, so choose wisely. People like Steph make you shine brighter, and the people you're worrying about impressing? They'll only dim you. Even the way you smiled when I said her name; that was a new Gemma I've never seen before. Hold onto that.'

Maybe they should have rum more often. Granny was getting deep. Gemma daren't speak; she didn't want to be a sobbing mess when the twins arrived. Instead, she held onto Granny tight and savoured the comforting smell of her perfume.

'You'll do the right thing. You always do,' Granny said, and stepped back before taking Gemma's face in her hands. 'Now, promise me you'll tell Steph how you feel?'

'When the time is right. She's invited me to Maisie's wedding next week.' Gemma sniffed, wiping her eyes. Hopefully Archie would be late as usual, give her time to hide the fact she'd been a weeping mess.

'Oh, really? What are you going to wear?'

'Probably just the dress I got for Julie's. Don't expect there to be much overlap. That's if I even go to Julie's.'

'If you want me to fake a heart attack to give you an excuse, just say the word.'

'Granny! Do not joke,' Gemma scolded.

Granny took a seat again. 'You know I'd do anything for you, Gemma.'

'Yes, well, tempting fate doesn't need to be on the roster.'

'This wedding, is it in Glasgow or will it be an overnight affair?' The twinkle in Granny's eyes said she was up to no good.

'Glasgow-ish. We'll have to stay over, *but* don't be buying any wedding hats just yet. Steph and I have a long way to go.'

'Hmm. We'll see about that.'

21

Steph waited for the green man, en route to Gemma's flat, feeling incredibly overdressed for Shawlands' Kilmarnock Road.

She'd settled on a wine-coloured suit with a simple black shirt. The twist was: she'd forgone using half of the buttons and opted for tape instead. Here's hoping it held, or the other guests would be getting an eyeful.

She'd taken the time to blow dry her usually unruly waves and properly styled her hair: she felt good. Ready to tackle the day and all the shit that came with it.

To avoid Gemma's constant badgering, she'd gone to the doctor's and been signed off for four weeks. She was a little uneasy at how quickly the doctor had agreed to it. Was she really that bad? Telling Cal was soul-destroying, like she'd let herself down. Gemma was right, though. If she didn't look after herself now, things would only get worse. Time away from work would do her good, plus she could always go back early. Four weeks was way too long. For now, she would use the time to recharge her batteries. Easier said than done. She'd never been one for sitting still.

The green man appeared, cutting through her thoughts with a shrill beep, and Steph made her way down Walton Street towards Gemma's flat on Camphill Avenue. Despite the fact she was only away for one night, her bag weighed a tonne. Eight bottles of beer will do that.

She heaved the bag into her other hand, giving her aching bicep a rest, and readjusted her shirt. The sooner she was there the better. It was one thing feeling your oats in the company of other LGBTQ+ people, but it was quite another navigating Deanston Drive with your boobs nearly out.

Finally, after what seemed like an age to cross Tantallon Road and the not-once-not-twice-but-triple-look from a passing cyclist, Steph was at Gemma's door.

She buzzed and Gemma let her in without even a greeting. Very trusting.

Was she nervous today? Absolutely. Was she thinking more about the wedding or the beautiful woman she was taking? The jury was still out.

Steph slipped the leg of her sunglasses into her suit jacket pocket, securing them in place, and started on the stairs. Two floors up, a door clicked open.

Why was she so clammy? She obviously needed to hit the gym for cardio more often.

Before she knew it, she was on Gemma's landing, the open door hinting at which was the right flat.

She poked her head in the hall, scared to enter in case she was wrong. 'Hello?'

'Hey,' Gemma said, appearing from a side door as she put an earring in.

Holy smokes, fucking hell. She was gorgeous.

Steph's breath caught her in throat: her heart forgot to beat, her brain failed to function.

Gemma's frozen state said she was experiencing something too. What, Steph wasn't quite sure.

But bloody hell. She'd hit the jackpot on dates. Shannon was going to be jealous, not worried.

Gemma had on a nearly floor-length sapphire dress with a plunging neckline and a slit that looked like it ran all the way to the top of her thigh.

Her hair was expertly braided in an elegant updo and Steph had never wanted to kiss a neck more than she did now.

Wow was the only word running on repeat in her mind, like an alarm bell.

Neither woman moved.

Finally, Gemma blinked, breaking the spell. 'In you come, shut the door. Come through to the kitchen,' she said, sounding flustered as she disappeared out of sight. She must have interrupted her getting ready.

Steph closed the door, holding a hand over her chest when she turned her back on the hall. This wasn't anything to do with panic: this was a desire attack. Her heart was racing, unable to control itself.

She dropped her bag in the hall with a clink and padded through to what she presumed was the kitchen, hoping to have calmed down enough to talk.

Gemma was standing at the counter, two empty wine glasses by her hand.

'You look incredible,' Steph said, unable to do anything else until the words were out. She could say it a thousand times and Gemma would never know how good she looked. It was impossible to put into words. She was a goddess, rendering Steph dumb.

'So do you,' Gemma replied, making no attempt to hide the way she was tracing her eyes over Steph's chest tattoos. It wasn't always a sexual thing: sometimes it was hard not to look. She understood that. But for a brief second she thought Gemma was reaching out to touch a button on her shirt. It wasn't to be, though: instead she smoothed out her dress. 'Now, I know you're not overly keen on today, and I don't want to encourage bad habits – it's only eleven in the morning, after all. But would you like a glass of wine before we call a taxi?'

This woman! She was perfect. 'It's like you're a mind reader,' Steph said, breathing a sigh of relief. 'I couldn't sleep last night for dreading today.'

'Nonsense. You have me. We'll make a day of it, have fun.'

Had Steph known Gemma was going to look like this she'd have been out like a light. 'I'm feeling better already about it, thank you.'

'You go through to the living room, I'll pour us some wine. Door across the landing.'

Gemma's flat was nice. Neutral but styled. A huge abstract painting hung over the sofa. Steph tilted her head: it looked like a raging sea, angry and wild. It was weirdly calming, though, like it was on its way to being tamed. She slipped off her jacket and lay it on the armchair before wandering to the window. Camphill Avenue didn't offer many views, despite its elevated position. All she could see was the trees of the park in the middle of the street.

'It's nicer in the winter,' Gemma said, appearing at her side and passing Steph a glass of wine. 'When the leaves are gone you can see more of Shawlands.'

'Better than mine, regardless. All I can see is more flats.' She raised her glass. 'To getting through today.' They clinked glasses and Steph took a sip, wincing slightly at the sour taste. Wine after having just brushed your teeth wasn't the best.

'Come, take a seat,' Gemma said, leading them to the sofa. 'So, anyone I should know about today? Keep my wits around?'

Steph pursed her lips in thought. 'Ohh, now. I don't think so. Not on Maisie's side. Our friends are a good bunch.'

Gemma nodded, taking the info in. 'Okay. And, who am I?'

'Huh?' Steph replied, her eyebrows arching in confusion. 'Does Shannon think we're dating, or . . .?' She trailed off. 'You said this was to take the pressure off Maisie and make her think you've moved on. I just want to get our stories straight.'

Yikes. She'd not considered this part of the plan. 'Erm. I hadn't really thought about it. I don't want to make you feel awkward or make things weird with Izzy.'

Gemma bit the corner of her lip between her teeth. 'Izzy and I aren't a thing any more. I mean, it's not like we really were to start with. But yeah, no more Izzy.'

'How come?' The wine was getting easier to drink now the toothpaste was being washed away.

'I just wasn't feeling what I should.'

Steph nodded. 'Sorry. I know you had high hopes for her.'

'Not fussed. It wasn't meant to be. I'm sure my perfect partner isn't far off.'

'You're very chipper today,' Steph said, her eyes narrowing.

'Just excited. My first gay wedding.'

'Speaking of which, we should probably phone a taxi soon. The bus won't wait on us.'

~

'We didn't decide on a plan,' Gemma said, her voice hushed in the back of the taxi.

'Plan for what?'

'Of who I am,' she hissed with a smile.

Shit. This was pretty much Steph's whole friend group. She'd not seen most of them for months; she could get away with anything, but to make them believe it would take a lot. Still, if she was going to put Shannon's mind at rest it would be the best plan. Fucking Maisie making her do shit like this. 'What are you comfortable with?'

'I can be the doting girlfriend for twenty-four hours, no bother. It's been a while but I'm sure I can remember how to play the part.'

She put a hand on Steph's and it was like every nerve ending came alive at once. Gemma might be able to play the part, but Steph was going to have to rein things in. Gemma was her friend; blurred lines would do no one any good.

It was too late to protest, though. The bus was in view, along with her mingling pals. Might as well go along with it.

'If you feel panicky at all, just say,' Gemma said and gave her hand a squeeze.

Steph smiled. Having Gemma with her was comfort enough.

'I'll get your door,' Steph said, when the taxi stopped. 'You get the full Dating Steph experience as well.'

She hopped out of the taxi and was at Gemma's door in record time. She extended a hand to help her date out as the taxi driver opened the boot and put their bags on the pavement.

Even with a crowd of bystanders between them, Steph

could feel the eyes of her close friends studying her every move.

Gemma extended the handle of her suitcase.

'No, no,' Steph said, waving her away. 'I carried it downstairs and I'll take it to the bus. You don't need to lift a finger this weekend. Unless it's to drink.'

A faint blush ghosted Gemma's cheeks. 'I get the sense there's no point in arguing with you.'

'Bingo. Now follow me and I'll get these loaded onto the bus, then you can meet my mates.'

It was awkward towing Gemma's case and lugging her bottle-filled abomination, but she made it work for the short distance to the bus.

'You ready for this?' Gemma asked, her voice quiet.

'I was going to ask you the same thing.'

Gemma held her hand out and Steph laced their fingers together. 'No going back now.'

'They're just over here.' Steph led them through the crowd. She recognised a few faces, but thankfully not many. There were vague recollections of Maisie's workmates, uni friends, and social circles she'd never quite penetrated. Four years had sieved the casual acquaintances from her head.

Thankfully, none of Maisie's family yet. No doubt they were already at the venue.

She had no issue with Shannon and her misguided expectations. Or Maisie and their turbulent past. Really, she was dreading seeing who she missed the most: the family that had taken her in and made her one of their own.

When Shannon came along it was too messy for her to stay, so Steph had slowly retreated to the shadows, distancing herself until their time together was only a memory.

Her chest tightened and so did her grip on Gemma's hand.

She could get through this. It was just a case of diverting her attention.

Steph's friends fell quiet as they approached; she wasn't even sure if they'd blinked.

Daniel popped his hip to the side, his hand cocked at an angle. 'Right, missy. Spill.' He punctuated the sentence with his trademark cackle.

His husband, Aiden, elbowed him in the ribs.

They hadn't changed a bit since Steph last saw them a year ago. Daniel had the same close-cut sandy blonde hair and impeccable style: today he favoured a navy blue suit and tie. He'd obviously won the war of words and convinced Aiden to have his usually scruffy beard trimmed, but that was the end of his victories: instead of a suit, his husband wore a resort shirt and tailored trousers. Aiden was the king of casual. Always would be. At least his thick black hair had seen a brush today.

'Guys,' Steph said, already feeling like a sitting duck. 'This is Gemma.'

Gemma gave a little wave with her free hand. 'Hello.'

The group exchanged glances. She was quite happy to let them negotiate the questions: all Steph could focus on was how damn awkward she felt.

'Gemma, you'll have to excuse our gaping mouths,' Daniel said with a look to Steph. 'But this coy little miss hasn't told us a thing about you.'

Gemma chuckled. 'Typical Steph, eh?'

Thea appeared at her husband Owen's side, Joey the toddler in her arms. 'What have I missed?' she clocked Gemma and their clasped hands. 'A lot, by the looks of it.' Joey battled to wriggle free.

'Don't worry, you're about as up to speed as the rest of us,' Daniel informed.

A call to board the bus boomed from the road.

'I didn't want to say anything in case she got sick of me,' Steph said, knowing Daniel wouldn't move an inch until she at least offered some information.

'But three months in, still can't get enough,' Gemma added with a smile.

That seemed to please him and the group set off towards the bus.

'Where's Connie and Luke?' Steph asked, falling into step with the men.

'Late, as usual. I told Maisie to tell them the bus was leaving ten minutes earlier than it actually was, but does she listen? Nope.'

Daniel was on good form today. Occasionally, if the wind was blowing the wrong way, he could be a moody wee cow and bring the whole day down with him.

They hung back, letting others pile on first.

Steph looked at her watch. Time was getting tight.

'You guys go on,' Aiden said to Thea. 'Get Joey settled.'

The minutes ticked away and soon they were the last to board.

'Are they always like this?' Gemma asked, dipping to Steph's shoulder so she could keep her voice to minimum.

'Always. They'll make it, though. Always do.'

As if by magic, two out-of-breath wedding guests appeared round the corner, ignoring the traffic lights and taking a chance as a gap materialised between cars. Connie looked ridiculous, her beautiful maxi dress hitched up to her knees as she sprinted. Luke nearly barrelled into her as she stopped.

'Jesus Christ,' she huffed. 'Fuck me. Train was late.'

'Likely story,' Daniel said, and got on the bus without waiting for a retort.

Connie straightened herself, pawing at her dress, and Luke passed their bags to the aggravated bus driver. She met Gemma's gaze. 'Oh, hi, sorry, Connie,' she said and extended a hand. She quickly retracted it. 'Actually, better not. Bit sweaty.' She turned to Steph. 'I've missed something, haven't I?'

'We'd better get on the bus. I'll explain later,' Steph replied, leading Gemma off by the hand.

The bus was packed, so there was no chance of getting seats as a group now. They passed the toddler wranglers, then Daniel and Aiden, before finally finding seats up the back of the bus.

It was a relief to be out of earshot. Steph's muscles relaxed as she slumped into her seat.

'You okay?' Gemma whispered, her kind eyes ducking level with Steph's.

'Yeah, you?'

'Grand.'

She was surprised when Gemma took her hand again, placing their clasped hands on Steph's lap.

In for a penny, in for a pound. Gemma was obviously giving this performance her all.

The bus set off, navigating Glasgow's city centre at a snail's pace. Finally, they were on the motorway and passing over the River Clyde at a more pleasing speed.

'So, fill me in on your friends,' Gemma said, twisting in her seat to face Steph as much as the tiny space would allow. This all felt very intimate, very quickly. When she'd agreed to this plan she'd not fully thought through how much it was going to mess with her head. As Gemma's thigh rested against her own, she struggled to keep her heart at an acceptable pace.

'Okay, so there's Daniel and Aiden.' Steph said, peering down the aisle to make sure they were at a safe distance. Although, the excited chatter happening around them would drown out any conversation no bother.

'The chatty guy and the one in the loud shirt?'

Steph smiled. 'Yes. So, they both manage coffee shops. Daniel works for Costa and Aiden works for Starbucks.'

'Ohhh, like Romeo and Juliet. Star-crossed lovers.'

'Exactly. They've been together for ages. Nearly as long as me and Maisie were.' Why did she have to bring her ex into this? Like she was some weird benchmark of time?

'Which was?'

'Huh?'

'How long were you together?'

'Just over ten years. Broken up four, so I've known her nearly half my life, I guess.'

'Yowzers. That's a tough act to follow. Good luck to me.'

'You'll be fine,' Steph assured, patting Gemma's hand. 'Thanks for doing this. You really didn't have to. I appreciate it.'

'Nonsense. This is fun. So, that's the boys. What about the baby-wielding couple?'

'That's Thea and Owen. The kid is Joey. Joseph on a Sunday. I met them through Maisie when she worked in The Gallery of Modern Art. She and Thea worked in the shop together.'

'Married?'

'Yep, about five years ago now. Which leaves Connie and Luke. Connie worked with Daniel in Costa.'

'They seem a good bunch. And what about us? How did we meet?'

'Now, there's a good question,' Steph replied. Glasgow city was thinning around them, giving way to suburbia and green spaces.

'Let's just stick to what happened. We met in the bar. No point in creating too many fibs. We're just pushing the day back in time a little.'

'Good idea. Too many lies and I'll start forgetting. I'm no good at lying.'

Gemma nodded. 'Where's this venue, then?'

'Some farmhouse just past Barrhead. I've never been.'

A whoop erupted at the front of the bus, stealing their attention for a second. Steph's muscles stiffened.

'You seem tense. What can I do to help?' Gemma asked, her thumb stroking Steph's hand. A shiver travelled up her spine, settling at the base of the neck and making every hair stand to attention.

'I'm fine. Just seeing a lot of people I haven't seen in a while and it's making me nervous.'

'If you need a quick exit, just wink at me and I'll whisk you away.'

'Are you always like this?'

'Like what?'

'Amazing?'

'Try to be. Occasionally I get sloppy and drop to extraordinary.'

Steph shook her head, a smile taking over her face.

～

'THIS MUST BE US,' Daniel said, looking between the key they'd been given on arrival and the door in front of him.

He opened the door, kicking it wide, and wandered in.

She hadn't expected to be sharing a room when she'd

signed up to staying over. This was going to be interesting, with Gemma now in the mix.

It was basic but clean. Three metal bunk beds, providing six beds, lined the room, and apart from a floor-length mirror on the far wall, that was it. Blue linoleum covered the floor of what would have once been a farm building. The only original feature was the massive window overlooking the courtyard below.

Steph peered out, managing to spot Thea and Joey in the mingling crowd. She and Owen weren't staying over: too much pressure with the wee one.

'Top or bottom?' Gemma asked, and Steph had to get her thoughts in order before answering.

'I'll go top,' Steph said, giving the ladder a test waggle. Sturdy enough.

'You shut your face. Don't even think about your lewd jokes, Aiden,' Daniel said with a hearty laugh, and slumped onto the bottom bunk.

Six guests. Six beds. Maisie had plumped on her bringing someone, hadn't she? Sneaky.

'You sound like the bins at the back of Oddbins, Steph. What you hiding?' Daniel asked, stretching his legs out and giving his brogues a wiggle.

She squatted down, unzipping the bag she'd popped on the floor by her and Gemma's bunk. 'An IPA, just for today,' she said, producing a bottle and holding it up by the neck for everyone to see. She'd had labels printed. Nothing fancy, just something she'd knocked up with an app on her phone, but it had Maisie and Shannon's names in a banner with the date displayed underneath.

'A woman of many talents,' Daniel gushed, hand over heart.

Aiden relieved Steph of her bottle, inspecting the label, his lips pursed with awe. 'Now, that's cool.'

'Can we crack them open now or do we have to wait for the brides?' Connie asked. She was a lot less red in the face now and her updo was back in place, having been fixed on the bus. Connie always pulled it out the bag, no ifs or buts.

'I think we should wait. Places like this usually do a firepit in the evening. If we can find somewhere to chill them, they'll be perfect to have then. Plenty free champers to keep us going until then,' Gemma said.

Daniel looked quite taken with her. 'I like your thinking. Go to a lot of weddings?'

'I've experienced my fair share. Still never been a bridesmaid, though.'

'Maybe Steph will upgrade you straight to bride.'

'Will we go downstairs?' Steph asked, getting to her feet. The draw of champagne was getting stronger the more the conversation centred on her.

'Hold on; we need to chill these,' Aiden said, searching the room for inspiration. His eyes settled on the window.

'We can't hang stuff out the window. They'll think we're a load of tinks,' Steph protested.

Gemma stood, a hand on Steph's back for leverage as she looked out the window. Her muscles were going to be jelly by the end of the day. 'There's plenty of catering staff on hand. I'll just ask one of them for an ice bucket later on.'

Daniel got to his feet. 'You'd better keep her, Steph,' he said with a wink.

∼

She'd felt better after quaffing a few flutes of champagne, but nothing could have prepared Steph for how she would feel seeing Maisie's mum and dad go down the aisle.

She'd braced herself for Maisie in a wedding dress: she knew that would have some odd recoil. But her mum and dad? God, her heart ached.

Gemma's eyes had grown sympathetic, probably thinking it was Maisie making her emotional, but honestly? Apart from the fleeting thought of *this could have been me*, there was little there.

Seeing Robin and Maureen, though? It was like someone had stomped on her heart. Then Maisie's niece and nephew had appeared as a flower girl and ring bearer. Steph had to tense her jaw to stop the tears.

She spent the ceremony stealing herself, knowing the day would only get worse.

Now the group stood in a circle, the sun beating down on them as they drank more champagne.

'Beautiful, wasn't it?' Connie beamed, her eyes fixed on Luke.

'You two will be next,' Daniel squawked into his booze.

Luke raised his eyebrows, which only added to Daniel's merriment.

Steph threw Gemma a look to apologise, but the smile on her face said she had nothing to be sorry about.

She was about to make a joke when a set of arms wrapped so tightly around her she was sure a rib cracked. 'Auntie Steph,' the little girl squealed into the lapel of her suit.

Fuck.

Maisie's niece, Annabelle.

She was half-hoping she wouldn't remember her. She

was six when Steph stopped visiting. Three years was a long time when you're little. Apparently not long enough.

Steph flicked an internal switch, hoping it would dam any emotion bubbling to the surface.

'Annabelle! Shut up! Is that you?' Steph boomed, turning her smile up to eleven as she stepped back to admire the young girl. She cocked her head to the side. 'You're as tall as me now. That's never you, surely?'

She grabbed Steph for another cuddle and Steph wrapped her arms around her, squeezing back with equal measure, her champagne flute safely balanced.

'It is me,' she replied, her smile a mile wide. 'I missed you.'

Steph kissed the top of her head. 'I missed you too.'

She looked up at Steph, her green eyes still as vibrant as ever. 'Will you come play? There's giant Jenga and a tepee and Auntie Maisie says there'll be a clown later.'

'A clown? Oh, wow.'

'I know, right?' She took Steph by the hand and tried to pull her away. Steph stayed rooted to the spot.

'I'd love to, smelly belly, but I need to stay here. With my friend Gemma.'

The girl eyed Gemma with great suspicion.

'Or,' Gemma said, her voice perfectly pitched for such an occasion. 'We could both come?' She looked to Steph as if for approval.

'Are you sure?'

'Yes, come on!' Annabelle answered for Gemma, dragging Steph away.

They cut through the crowd at a dizzying speed and before she knew it they were at the lawn on the far side of the courtyard. She quickly checked her chest. The tape had held. Thank fuck.

She sat her glass on a nearby picnic table and fiddled with her buttons, suddenly feeling underdressed as she was surrounded by a throng of children. She buttoned herself to the top.

Annabelle led her to the giant Jenga, and just as Steph bent to inspect the pieces, Justin spotted her. It took approximately two point one seconds for the boy to cross the lawn and barrel straight into her. He'd shot up like a beanpole in the years they'd been apart and Steph was no match for the excited eleven-year-old. They were soon a pile on the ground.

Gemma snorted with laughter.

'Auntie Steph,' Justin cried. Steph was sure there was a hint of the sniffles hidden in their embrace. She'd expected Annabelle to be the emotional one in their reunion, not stoic Justin.

She rolled on the ground, pulling him tighter, and they sat up. 'Hey, Justin.'

'You came,' he said, his bottom lip threatening to wobble.

'Course I came. Why wouldn't I?'

He shrugged. 'Dunno.'

'I wondered how long it would take for you to be kidnapped,' Maureen said, wandering over. She'd barely changed. Same red hair like Maisie, same kind eyes and welcoming smile.

'Hi Maureen,' Steph said. She wished she wasn't on the floor with Justin. She wanted to wrap her arms around her ex-mother-in-law and squeeze her until her arms hurt, tell her how much she missed her. No sense in making a scene though.

'You having fun?' Maureen asked, a hand over her eyes to shield her from the sun.

'So far.' She ruffled Justin's hair and he pretended not to like it. 'That's Gemma, by the way,' Steph said, motioning towards her pseudo-date. She was getting stuck into Jenga with Annabelle.

Maureen smiled. Had Maisie told her Gemma wasn't really her girlfriend? Or filled her in at all on what Steph was up to these days? Why would she? She was probably just a distant memory. 'Justin, don't you ruin Steph's lovely suit. Or your own.'

Justin huffed. 'Sorry, Steph.'

Steph pulled a face. 'We playing Jenga or not?'

'Annabelle and I are going to win, aren't we?' Gemma called towards them.

'Yeah, Justin! Me and Gemma versus you and Steph!'

'As if,' Justin shouted, getting to his feet and leaving Steph on the grass. 'We'll win.'

Steph snagged Gemma's gaze. Someone needed to tell Steph's heart this wasn't real life, because right now, she could swear she was falling for her.

22

Gemma was more than a little tipsy. But food was definitely helping to sober her a little. Which was a good thing, because the ceilidh band was in full swing.

She'd just finished the Canadian Barn Dance after an energetic rendition of the Military Two-Step. She'd left Steph with Annabelle to do the Gay Gordons.

Ceilidh dancing was one heck of a workout.

Gemma watched Steph on the dance floor, the little girl in fits of giggles as they danced.

Today had been incredible.

There'd been more colouring-in than she'd anticipated, but time at the kid's table was never a chore. Maisie's niece and nephew clearly adored Steph. She'd watched her date with a bursting heart as she played with them for the best part of the day. And when Maisie's dad had given his speech after dinner, Steph had gripped her hand tight. It was then Gemma had spied a look on Steph's face she'd taken the rest of the evening to place: longing. She missed them. Gemma hadn't dared to ask about their past, but she could make a good guess, having pieced together snippets of conversation and stolen glances.

She was glad she was here. Support was always good.

Gemma sipped her water, looking around the converted barn. The huge space was decorated with drapes of fairy lights crossing both the dance floor and seating area. It was beautiful.

Next time she got married she wanted something like this, something rustic. Her wedding with Logan was nice enough, but a church and formal hotel setting wouldn't do it any more. Well. Not that she could do a church wedding even if she wanted to.

'Having a good time?' asked Maisie. She'd changed from her earlier flowing dress into a more ceilidh-friendly number. She took a seat opposite Gemma.

'Today's been fantastic. Thank you.'

Maisie smiled, warmth radiating from her eyes and cheeks. Although the latter might have had champagne to blame. 'You and Steph seem happy.' Gemma didn't quite know what to say to that, but thankfully, Maisie carried on. 'I don't really know what's going on between the two of you but just be gentle with her, yeah?'

Ah, they'd already reached the good intentions part of the evening. She'd half-expected this: just not quite so soon.

'Of course. I wouldn't do anything to hurt her.'

Maisie nodded, her eyes trained on the dance floor. She opened her mouth as if to speak, but had second thoughts. 'It's been a weird day.'

'But a good one?'

Maisie's eyes finally found hers. 'Yeah. I think so.' There was a weight to her answer: drop it on the ageing timber floor and it would likely go straight through. 'I'd better carry on the rounds. Always someone who wants to talk to me. You know how it is.'

She was off.

Gemma switched her water for the remaining wine she had. The atmosphere suddenly felt loaded. It was no wonder Shannon was weird about Steph. Gemma hadn't seen the kids with her once: in fact, besides the ceremony and the speeches, she'd hardly seen Shannon at all.

The accordion let out a final breath and the music finished. Gemma watched Steph feign exhaustion, much to Annabelle's dismay. Three dances in a row were a lot. Especially in a suit.

And by God, what a suit. Gemma thought she was going to implode when Steph walked through her door this morning. She'd seen Logan in plenty of suits, so had assumed it wasn't a thing for her but, WOW. A woman in a suit apparently turned Gemma into a quivering mess. At least when the woman in question was Steph and her delectable tattoos.

She'd sneaked a few glances during the ceremony, when they were packed in the pews like sardines. A geometric floral piece ran between Steph's breasts and Gemma was thankful they weren't in a church. It hadn't taken long for her thoughts to turn X-rated.

Such a pity they had to endure bunk beds tonight.

'Hey,' Steph said, plonking herself by Gemma.

Right about now would have been the perfect time to kiss Gemma on the cheek, but Steph hadn't leaned into character quite as much. Perhaps that was because Gemma had selfish intentions with her role.

She wasn't about to give up on it now, though. She placed a hand on Steph's toned thigh. 'Quite the dancer, aren't you?'

Steph flashed her a smile. 'Amazing what a bottle of fizz can do.'

'Good Lord, I am going to be stiff tomorrow,' Daniel announced, flopping into the seat opposite with the grace of a cannonball.

Aiden mimed zipping his lips shut as he took the seat beside him.

'Where's Connie and Luke?' Gemma asked, scanning the room.

'Probably off snogging somewhere,' Steph replied, stealing the last of Gemma's water.

'Lucky them,' Gemma said. The words were out before she could think.

'Don't let us stop you,' Daniel replied, fanning himself with a napkin.

Steph was the colour of her suit.

The alcohol was making her ballsy and for a brief second Gemma calculated if she could get away with it in such a crowded room. Not worth the risk for a first kiss, especially not when they'd supposedly been together for three months. No one would buy it.

'You're not really into PDAs, are you, Steph?' Gemma said, scrambling to fill the silence and give a reason for their lack of intimacy.

'Pish! I've seen you snog Maisie a thousand times,' Daniel boomed, maybe a little too loudly as a few people from the neighbouring table turned his way.

Steph's blush deepened. 'Not the time or the place.' Her gentle smile said she was trying to be nice, but really it was a guillotine on the conversation.

'I need the loo. Want to come?' Shit, Gemma was trying to defuse the situation, not make it worse. Had she just made it sound like she was inviting Steph for a snogging sesh?

'Aye aye,' Daniel goaded with a wink.

Yep. Definitely played that badly.

Gemma stood anyway, intent on following through. She looked at Steph, who shook her head.

'I'm good. I'll get you back here.'

Shit.

∼

Darkness fell in record time and, as predicted, a firepit was erected outside, stripped tree trunks positioned around it like a traditional campfire.

A staff member brought out a basket of blankets and Gemma took her chance to ask for their ice, hoping to score some points with Steph. The bucket was no problem, so now they just needed the beer.

Steph led the way. A silence lay over them as they headed upstairs and Gemma couldn't quite place if it was comfortable or not.

She'd need to find a way to broach this, one way or another.

Finally alone in the bunk room, Gemma breathed a sigh of relief. She felt like she'd been under examination all day. At least here it was just the two of them, atmosphere or not.

She sat on the bed as Steph delved into her bag.

'Here, come sit for a second,' she said, patting the space beside her.

Steph looked reluctant but eventually put the bottles back in the bag.

'Sorry if I embarrassed you earlier,' Gemma said, fiddling with the slit in her dress.

'Me? When?'

'With the whole kissing thing.'

'Oh, that. No need to say sorry, I just didn't know what to say. It threw me a little.'

Gemma gulped, glad she hadn't upset Steph. Annoyance off the table, her courage returned.

'Good. I'm glad I didn't upset you. Do you think they're buying it or will we have a snog later just to seal the deal?' She hoped the fact she was joking was obvious.

Steph instantly blushed. 'I would say you're doing a good job of convincing them we're together.'

'That's a definite no to a snog, then?' She chuckled, but inside Gemma's heart wilted. There was no denying the tug at Steph's rebuttal.

Steph laughed nervously. 'You're making me think you want to.'

'Just playing my part of the dutiful girlfriend. If we really were dating I think it would be a struggle to keep my hands off you.' Her heart kicked into gear, notching up the pace it was already bringing to triple speed. Nothing like a day of drinking to make you brave.

The air sparked between them. Steph *had* to feel it too. If Gemma reached a finger out she'd surely get a shock.

She watched Steph swallow, her brown eyes searching Gemma's face for clarity of her intentions.

If this was going to happen it had to be down to her.

But if her heart beat any harder it was going to break a rib; it already felt like it was pushing all the air out her lungs.

She laughed under her breath, hoping to defuse the tension.

God, Steph was beautiful. She held her gaze, cradling it with her own. She looked lost, confused; but more importantly like she was also trying to figure out a way for this to happen.

Gemma put her hand on Steph's knee for leverage. 'I think we should, later, just to keep your friends happy. But we'll need to practice first, so it looks like we've done it a thousand times before,' she said, edging her face closer to Steph's.

She'd never been this nervous to kiss someone. Butterflies twirled in her stomach like they were caught in a tornado.

Steph went to speak, but this wasn't the time for conversation. Gemma silenced her with her lips.

They were cautious at first, like neither knew how far this was meant to go. But Gemma soon made her mind up and pushed harder, Steph's lips finding a natural rhythm with hers.

Gemma groaned when Steph's hand cupped her jaw, pulling her closer.

Soft, gentle kisses turned into something else as Gemma parted her lips and Steph needed no second invitation: her tongue found Gemma's, and there it was—not just her elusive spark, but the whole dang fire. It roared, bigger and better than the measly firepit outside. Any stronger and it would ignite the wooden barn; Steph's lips rivalled a bonfire on the fifth of November.

She tasted like wine and berries and Gemma was certain she could never experience either again in quite the same way.

Her knee moved over Steph's thigh. Gemma was no longer in the driver's seat of her brain; something further south had taken over the wheel.

Steph smiled, her hands moving to Gemma's hips.

Their kiss continued. She'd had no intentions of it

lasting this long, but hot damn, who could stop once they'd experienced Steph's soft lips?

The only thing putting this fire out would be an industrial strength extinguisher.

Or Daniel. Which is exactly what happened when he flew through the door. 'You—Oh, shit, sorry.' He slammed the door shut.

Steph laughed, their mouths still touching.

Gemma would have, too, but she was so out of breath the only thing she was capable of was a low pant and a smile.

She removed her knee from Steph's personal space, running a thumb across her lips.

They locked eyes.

Steph went to speak but only Daniel's voice filled the room.

'Are you decent? Can I come in?'

Steph chuckled. 'Yes, Daniel. In you come.'

He sauntered in, ramping up how sheepish he looked. 'Sorry, ladies. You were taking ages and I'm absolutely parched.'

'Patience never was your strong suit,' Steph said, already off the bed and retrieving beer.

'Sorry! But good thing I did or it could have been hours before we saw you again,' he said with a wink.

'Hardly,' Steph said, handing him two bottles.

'Pffft. I remember the cottage in Oban. Three hours you were away.' Steph shot him a look that would have rendered most people speechless. Daniel was impervious. 'You lezzers have the stamina of athletes once you get going.'

Steph stilled, the smile on her face hiding the fact she was silently seething. Only her clenched hand around the bottle of beer hinted at her internal monologue, giving the game away to Gemma. 'Daniel, do you want me to pass you these beers or chuck them at your head?' She laughed but her grip on the bottle didn't lessen.

'Alright, alright, but come on, we're all dying of thirst out there.'

They walked back to the firepit in silence. Gemma desperately wanted an excuse to touch Steph again. Or better yet, kiss her again.

Booze had stripped her of inhibition.

But not quite enough to break away from Daniel and snog Steph senseless.

Gemma wouldn't need a blanket when they got back outside; heat still radiated her cheeks and core. She imagined herself as one of those trees that had been struck by lightning: normal on the outside but a raging inferno inside. If she opened her mouth too wide a flame would surely appear.

'Is this one of your strong ones?' Daniel asked Steph as they passed through the downstairs seating area of the barn. A few other guests mingled, sprawled on the sofas, not bothered about the firepit outside.

'It should be a normal ABV,' Steph replied. 'Why? You not had enough alcohol today?'

Daniel cackled. 'Just wondering if Connie will be sober for her shift on Monday. She's pie-eyed.'

'Ach, she'll be fine. That's a day and a bit away.'

'You're not the one that has to deal with her spewing behind the cake fridge.'

Gemma had never met someone like Daniel. Sure, there were a few openly gay guys in her social circles, but never someone so flamboyant and loud. He was an absolute hoot but she got the impression if you crossed him it would be claws out at dawn.

If she'd come out earlier would everything be different? Would this be her friend group? Or were there squads of lesbians who also had to suffer posh children's parties and best friends who abandoned you at the drop of a hat?

The cold air hit when Daniel opened the bifold door and goosebumps erupted on Gemma's skin.

'Right, Maisie and Shannon, close your eyes,' Steph said, crossing the gravel yard to the couple. Shannon looked suspicious but did as she was told. 'Daniel, you get the rest in the ice bucket Gemma got.'

Maisie smiled. 'I can't wait to see what this is.'

Gemma took a seat on a free tree trunk, wrapping a wiry woollen blanket around her shoulders.

'Hands out, guys,' Steph said and gently placed the bottles in the couple's open palms.

Maisie's face lit up when she opened her eyes. 'Oh my God, babe, look!' she squealed, her eyes darting between the bottle and her wife.

Steph slinked over to where Gemma was sitting. She lifted an arm up and invited her under the huge blanket. Gemma's heart sang when she sat close, their legs touching as Steph got cosy.

What was this, now they'd kissed? A line had been crossed, but did Steph think it was real? They needed to have a chat.

Until then, she'd make her intentions known with touch.

Steph gripped her side of the blanket in place. Freeing her hand, Gemma snaked it under Steph's suit jacket and rested it on her back. She felt Steph's muscles stiffen at her touch. Was that good or bad?

Shannon didn't look that impressed with the beer. 'That's really cool, thank you,' she said, her face so neutral it was almost painful. She struck Gemma as being the type of person whose favourite colour was beige.

Maybe she was different when Steph wasn't around, but who changes their whole persona for one wedding guest? Still, Maisie seemed happy.

'Who's got a bottle opener? I want to try this right now,' Maisie said, her smile still on full beam.

Shannon was the opposite to Steph: tall and slim with short brown hair, not the whiff of a tattoo in sight. Her dark eyes locked with Steph's over the flickering flames of the fire. 'I've had wine and champagne all day. I don't really want to mix,' she said, putting the bottle down by the base of their trunk. 'I'll try it another time.'

'That's fine,' Steph said, her words quiet. Gemma felt her shoulders sag.

'It'll be worth the wait,' Gemma piped up. 'I never really drank beer before I met Steph. And I guess it was beer that brought us together, right?' She looked at Steph and smiled. 'I was a customer and she lured me back to hers to try some brews. The rest is history.'

Partly the truth.

Daniel let out a trademark hoot. 'You sly dog.'

'There's more to it than that,' Steph said, 'But yeah. I guess that's how it happened.'

Her voice was flat. Shannon had sucked the life out of her. It was a wonder the fire was still lit: the woman's icy resolve was like a blanket over the group.

Gemma wanted to march over there and shake her. Steph was trying her best. The least she could do was be polite.

'Well, come on then, spill,' Connie said, craning her neck in Steph's direction.

'I'll go find a bottle opener first,' Steph said, getting to her feet.

Gemma was going to join her when Maisie leapt up. 'I need to pee, so I'll walk in with you to the kitchen.'

Shannon's gaze was like a locked missile as she watched her new wife enter the barn with Steph. Gemma drowned out Daniel's chatter, focusing on the duo as they reached the kitchen.

The wall-to-wall windows offered little privacy and Steph's crossed arms said this wasn't a conversation she particularly wanted to have. Maisie's eyes flicked to Shannon and back to Steph. She shrugged and turned away from the bride, opening and closing drawers before locating a bottle opener.

Gemma's attention was stolen by Daniel as he ambled over to Shannon and retrieved her beer for the ice bucket. 'Dunno why I'm bothering to chill yours,' he mumbled.

'Excuse me?' Shannon snipped.

'Cut her some slack,' he replied, his tone and face sombre. Daniel could be serious, it seemed. Gemma liked him even more. His eyes narrowed and Shannon took the hint not to argue.

Steph returned, a weak smile in place. She handed the opener to Daniel. 'You can be the hostess.'

'Looking forward to these, Steph,' Aiden called.

Steph didn't say anything as she retook her place by Gemma.

∽

THE FIRE HAD FINALLY FIZZLED to nothing, and as the wee small hours crept further past midnight they'd retreated inside.

Numbers were dwindling, but Gemma didn't want the night to end. As soon she went to bed the bubble would burst: tomorrow they'd be sober and part ways. Tonight, she was Steph's girlfriend, and all bets were off: anything was possible.

Connie and Luke had long disappeared and Daniel had wandered off with Aiden. For now it was just the two of them huddled on a battered old sofa, hidden up the back of the barn.

'You okay?' Gemma asked, repositioning Steph's lapel.

'Yeah. I think so.'

'You think so?'

She shrugged.

'You've been flat since the firepit.'

'I just hate Shannon not liking me. I've done nothing wrong. And—' She took a deep breath. '—I dunno. It's been a weird day.'

'Is this to do with Maisie's family as well?'

Another shrug. 'In part.'

'And the other part?'

'We should probably talk about us kissing.'

Gemma looked around the room, just to be sure they weren't going to blow their cover. All clear. 'I—'

'It's okay. We've both had a lot to drink, I get it. Just part of the act. You don't need to worry.' She forced a half-smile.

Gemma's heart ached. She couldn't be part of the reason for Steph's deflated mood today. She leaned closer, intent on showing Steph it wasn't an act, when Daniel's booming voice carried down the barn.

He really had the worst timing.

'I think I'm going to hit the hay soon. You guys coming?'

'Actually, I was hoping Steph and I could have a chat?'

Maisie said, appearing behind Daniel, two glasses of wine in her hand.

Gemma guessed one wasn't for her. She looked at Steph, who gave her a gentle nod. 'See you upstairs,' she said, patting Gemma on the leg.

Just like that, her night with Steph was over.

23

'Your Granny could feed an army with these portions,' Steph said, relieving Gemma of Tupperware as she entered her flat.

'She gets a bit carried away; what can I say?'

Steph took the boxes through to the kitchen and laid them out.

'Beef today,' Gemma said, as if reading her mind.

'Thank you. You didn't have to, but thank you.'

Gemma turned on the oven and got a dish, acting more than a little at home now she'd visited a few times.

Steph couldn't help but look at her bum as she bent over to get stuff out of the bottom drawer.

They'd barely seen each other since the wedding. Gemma's work seemed to be full on and Steph had resorted to a midweek pit stop, bringing a coffee to her office after visiting Daniel in Costa one day. This being-off-work malarkey was boring as hell. She was looking forward to an evening of watching films.

Although, now it was just the two of them in private,

everything felt different. The universe had shifted a little to the left.

Gemma flashed a smile as she decanted the beef into a heatproof bowl, and all Steph wanted to do was take her face in her hands and kiss her.

They were friends, though. Nothing more. The wedding was an act for Shannon. Not that it had worked.

That kiss, though. It played in her mind like a showreel.

Gemma was something else.

She was also currently clicking her fingers in front of Steph's face.

'Earth to Steph,' Gemma said with a giggle. 'I said, do you want the starter now?'

'Depends – what is it?'

'Tempura prawns. They'll need the oven for a bit.'

'Aye, why not. You wanting a drink?'

'Do you know? No.' Gemma said, making a face. 'I feel I've had enough booze recently. You okay if I just have a water?'

'Sure, yeah. Course.'

As long as she wasn't abstaining from alcohol around Steph for other reasons. She'd been worried she was avoiding her this week, after The Kiss. Just being here was enough, though. Their friendship was intact.

Steph poured two waters and waited for Gemma on the sofa while she put stuff in the oven. Finally, she flopped down beside her, pulling a cushion onto her lap and hugging it.

'I am bushed: this week's been full on.'

'How come you're so busy?'

'A few new contracts have landed, a negotiation went south, plus I'm off next week. I need to play catch-up – well, whatever the future version of that is – before I go.'

'Where you off to?' Steph asked, bringing her legs up onto the sofa and fully facing Gemma. There was a pull to her, like Steph could never be close enough.

'I've rented a cottage on Loch Lochy. Figured if Julie wasn't having me on her hen weekend I'd enjoy myself regardless.'

'Loch Lochy? That's never real.'

Gemma barked with laughter. 'Course it's real.'

'Nah. You're winding me up. That's like a river being called Rivery River.'

'I swear,' she said, holding a hand over her heart.

Steph grabbed her phone off the table, scooting closer to Gemma. Her heart stuttered: the last time they were this close they'd kissed. She swallowed down ill-advised temptation and stabbed *Loch Lochy* into the search bar.

'Well, I'll be damned. It is a real place.'

'Told ya.'

She put her phone on the sofa, unwilling to relinquish the proximity she'd gained. She'd move if Gemma asked but for now there were no complaints.

Gemma played with the corner of the cushion she was hugging, her mind elsewhere. 'Can I ask your advice on something?'

'Yeah, sure, what's up?'

'How do you know if a girl likes you or if she just wants to hang out with you?' Gemma furrowed her brow. 'Lesbianism is hard.'

Steph laughed. 'Erm, you're asking the wrong person. I'm hopeless with stuff like this. But I guess, like, is she flirty? Touchy? The way she speaks to you, that sort of stuff. Anyone in particular?'

Gemma's eyes remained on the cushion. 'Just someone I know.'

Not Steph. It wasn't a surprise, but it still stung. If she could only grow a foot or two she'd happily shove on a dress if it meant kisses like that every day.

'So you like her, but you don't know if she likes you?'

'Exactly. Without asking her outright, how do I gauge it?'

Steph pursed her lips. She'd never had this problem. 'Why not ask her to hang out?'

'We do that anyway, that's the point. How do I ask her to hang out in a more romantic sense?'

'Where's your phone? Let's text her. I am your wingman, after all.'

Gemma was reluctant.

'Go on. We don't need to send anything you're not ready to, but we can draft it at least.'

She'd miss hanging out with Gemma. It was inevitable, though: she'd pair up soon enough and Steph would be forgotten.

Gemma pulled her phone from the side of the sofa and opened her notes app before handing it to Steph.

'What's her name?'

'Irrelevant just now.'

Steph smirked. 'Coy. I get it. Don't want me searching your socials for her.' She thought, her head tilted to the ceiling. 'Right, you don't want to go in too strong. Did you see her recently?'

'Yeah.'

'Cool. So,' Steph typed as she spoke, Gemma watching over her shoulder. 'Hey, really enjoyed hanging out with you the other day. Do you fancy coming round to mine to watch a film or something? Like, on a date? Not just as friends?'

Gemma recoiled, her chin nearly touching her neck. 'I can't just say that out of nowhere,' she sniggered.

'Sure you can, why not?'

'Like on a date?' she repeated. 'What if she says no?'

'Then she's an idiot.' Shit, was that too much? 'I mea—' Steph's phone vibrated, the word OFFICE illuminating her screen. She narrowed her eyes. 'Work's phoning me.'

Gemma used Steph's knee for leverage, craning to see the phone. 'Just ignore it.'

She did and guilt gripped her stomach as soon as it rang out. 'What if something bad's happened?'

'Like what? And what are you going to do about it? They can call the police or the fire brigade if it's that bad.'

Steph wasn't convinced. She stared at her phone, still clutching Gemma's, waiting for a text to ping through.

'They know I'm off. Why else would they call?'

'It's probably just Donnie being an arse.'

Now that she could believe. She pushed her hair back behind her ear and tried to regroup her mind. 'Okay, so, you don't want to go too subtle. But—' Her phone vibrated again. 'I need to see what they want.' She passed Gemma her phone before answering her own. 'Hello?'

~

GEMMA HAD TRIED in vain to get her to stay, but there was no option really: Donnie had arsed up the rota and Kara couldn't stay on. It was either come into work or have Stevie staff the cocktail lounge on her own.

It might be a Sunday but it was still too busy for the young woman to cope by herself. You needed two: one to take orders, one to make the cocktails. Steph couldn't ignore her. And she could make cocktails in her sleep; this wouldn't be stressful.

'Sorry again,' Stevie said, passing Steph another order slip. More mojitos. Did no one ever get sick of them?

'Not your fault. How's the week been?'

Stevie shrugged. 'Hellish, if I'm honest. You back soon?'

'Doctor gave me four weeks but I'm going to talk to Cal next week, see if he can shuffle the rotas, get me back. I'm bored out my mind.'

Stevie grinned. 'Feeling better, though?'

'A bit. I guess.'

Stevie patted the bar and left her to it. This was an easy shift: a few hours and she could head home, eat the food Gemma brought round. She felt bad bailing on her when they'd hardly seen each other, but Gemma had this new chick on the go. If she was lucky maybe she could text her and salvage the evening, hang out with her crush.

Steph's phone vibrated in her back pocket and she stole a look as she grabbed for the fresh mint.

'Another round of French martinis for table two,' Stevie said, putting another order slip on the bar.

It was good to see the place was still busy in her absence.

She pulled up Gemma's message as she gathered the ingredients for her next round of drinks. A new version of the text she'd drafted for her. Seemed simple enough: the girl should get the hint.

She fired off a quick reply: *Looks good. Let me know what she says x*

'Old-fashioned,' Stevie said with a forced smile, adding to Steph's ever-growing list of cocktails.

Typical that everyone would order at once.

She placed the finished mojitos on the bar. 'Order up, Stevie.'

At least she would always have work to fall back into when Gemma met her match.

24

Gemma growled, and resisted the urge to throw her phone at the wall.

Was Steph really that ignorant? Or just blissfully unaware? Maybe she did know and this was her way of letting Gemma down gently without losing their friendship.

She'd wanted to address things right after the wedding, but it wasn't the right conversation for a taxi and the week had gotten away from her with work. She'd thought today was the perfect opportunity to bring it up, but Steph had run off to bloody Cal's.

Maybe it was best she hadn't texted her while she was sitting beside her anyway. That would have been bloody awful.

Steph's dedication to Cal's had saved her colossal embarrassment. She could style this out: if Steph was going to act like the text wasn't for her, then so could Gemma. No biggie.

She grabbed her phone and texted Steph. If she didn't do it now she'd turn it over in her head, round and round like a tombola, for the entire evening. Better to do it now and get it done.

I got it wrong, she's not interested x

Done. She was stupid to think Steph was interested anyway. If she was there'd been ample opportunity to act on it from day one.

But. Gemma had made it abundantly clear what her type was, so Steph might have good reason to think otherwise.

She threw a cushion at thin air and it sailed across her living room. It did nothing to her mood but did relieve a little of the pent-up tension in her shoulders.

Yes, on paper, pretty feminine women were lovely, but none had made her feel like Steph did. How was she supposed to know she was swiping on the wrong women? So, she didn't know her type? She didn't know she was gay for most of her life; she was hardly a reliable source.

Part of her wanted to go down the cocktail bar and chill with Steph for the evening, like she usually would, but what if she did know the text was for her? Lordy, this was going in circles.

She needed to hit reset.

Some time away from Steph would be good. The cottage couldn't come soon enough.

She'd spent most nights imagining Steph at the cottage. Steph in the hot tub. Steph in the cottage's bed. Steph on the balcony. Steph on any available surface, really. Gemma shook her thoughts free. It had to stop.

They were friends. Nothing more.

Gemma let out a huff. She messaged Julie, hoping for conversation. Anything to distract her from climbing up the walls. She wanted to scream and shout, her emotions a coiled spring inside her.

She stared at the ceiling, hugging a fresh cushion close to her chest.

It was like her emotions were running at hyper speed. She'd hadn't even known Steph last month, but now she was all she thought about. Her chest twinged, embarrassment clawing at her insides.

Her phone vibrated and Gemma resisted the urge to check it straight away. A deep breath and she looked at her lock screen, disappointed at the way her stomach dropped when she saw it was Julie, not Steph replying.

Oh my God! I was just contemplating texting you. We're in a bar near you. Joanne lives nearby, she recommended it. With Logan and J though, maybe a bit weird for you to pop by? Xx

Great.

Absolutely, flipping, great.

Of all the places in Glasgow, she chooses the Southside? Sometimes Glasgow was smaller than a village. There were no such thing as coincidences here, just life in one another's pockets, existing in ever-decreasing circles.

She was in a foul mood: this wasn't the time for meeting Joanne. Plus, if they wanted to move on and ended up at Steph's work, it would look suspect. Not to mention she'd have to introduce her to Julie et al.

Gemma held the phone above her head, using both hands so as not to drop it and cause an injury.

No worries, was just wondering what you were up to. Actually out myself, have fun x

It was an obvious lie but Gemma was past caring.

Everything was falling apart.

Sometimes she wondered if it would have been easier to stick things out with Logan. Maybe things would have been different once they'd had kids. She could have focused on them instead of the misery that was slowly consuming her.

Lordy. How depressing was that?

Gemma grabbed the pillow and slammed it back into position on the sofa. She couldn't lie here and let her thoughts spiral. She was already down a dark hole.

She plodded through to the kitchen and poured herself a wine. She hadn't wanted to drink but it would take the edge off her bad mood, numb her frustration a little.

She took a seat at her dining table, taking a long sip as she pulled up Tinder on her phone.

A few new messages.

It was all so monotonous, though.

She scolded herself. There was no point being so negative – it would get her nowhere.

She scrolled through, hoping one would catch her attention.

Nothing clicked. She sipped her wine, her mood mellowing.

This didn't need to be the romance of the century. She just needed a distraction, to feel wanted. It was no good being jilted by the person you liked *and* your best friend. It was no wonder she felt crap.

She looked at the smiling profile pictures, guilt twisting her stomach. These were people, looking for real connections. Was she being an arsehole to use them for amusement, not actually wanting more?

She put her phone on the table, screen down. This was fast becoming a frenzy. Knee-jerk reactions were no use.

So Steph didn't feel the same way? She might be the first woman she'd had proper feelings for, but it didn't mean she'd be the last.

She'd been saved embarrassment. Time to count her blessings, create a little space, and move on.

25

Steph pressed the brass buzzer for Gemma's office on West Nile Street. She had to lean close to the console to hear the receptionist over the traffic.

'Hey, it's Steph Campbell, I'm here to see Gemma Anderson.'

'Do you have an appointment?'

'I'm a friend, just dropping something off.'

It wasn't a lie. She'd been to see Daniel and got Gemma a coffee. It was well on its way to getting cold, but it was the thought that counted.

Cal wasn't up for Steph returning. Quite the opposite, in fact. She was slowly losing her mind to boredom.

A shrill bell cut through the air and the door unlocked with a loud clunk.

The sterile stairs were pristine. Steph wished she could get her own flat this clean.

Heavy bass filled the stairway as someone exited the talent agency opposite Gemma's office, and a snippy-looking woman in a sharp suit gave her the once-over on the way past. It didn't look like she approved. Whatever. Steph was here to see Gemma and only Gemma.

Steph took a deep breath and pushed open the door to the office.

She'd felt beyond out of place last week when she'd turned up in her usual shorts-and-hoodie combo so she'd toned things down today and gone for a jumper and jeans. Classic. Maybe not the Hobbs or Joules ensemble this office was used to, but pleasant nonetheless.

The receptionist, a nice lady in her sixties with a corkscrew perm and cardigan buttoned to the top, greeted Steph with a smile. 'Was it Ms Anderson you were after?'

'Yes, please,' Steph replied, suddenly worried she was interrupting.

'She's just in a meeting, but she'll be done in five minutes if you want to say hello.'

Steph eyed the coffees in her hands. Did she want to wait five minutes? This was a silly idea; she was getting in the way. Would look daft to just leave a latte and dash, though.

'Yeah, I'll wait,' Steph said and took a seat. The receptionist smiled without another word.

She knew. She totally knew.

The truth was, Steph missed Gemma. She'd barely spoken to her since taking Steph's stupid advice and texting her crush. So it wasn't her fault she'd rejected Gemma, but it could have been avoided. Who texts, anyway? Was Steph twelve? It was no wonder Gemma was mad.

Steph sipped her coffee. She'd already had one with Daniel. She'd be up all night.

The minutes ticked by and Steph jumped when Gemma's door finally opened. A guy with a forgettable face and a black suit wandered out, briefcase swinging from one hand. 'Schedule me in for the same time in two weeks, yeah?'

'Of course,' Gemma replied, lingering in her doorway. 'Sheila will sort that before you go.'

Steph gulped. Gemma looked amazing. Her loose chiffon shirt accentuated all the right places and Steph's eyes trailed down her navy tailored trousers, all the way to her high-heeled shoes. Good God.

If Maisie and Shannon had another shindig, could she cajole Gemma into being her girlfriend again? It might be worth a shot.

Gemma did a double take and Steph snapped her thoughts back to reality.

'Steph, what are you doing here?' Her face was a mixture of confusion and surprise.

Steph hopped to her feet, extending the now-cold latte. 'I thought you might need this. Long hours and all.'

Gemma's brow furrowed as she took the drink. 'Thank you.' She took a sip and the cup hid a smile. 'It's cold. You been here long?' she asked with a laugh.

'Sorry.'

'No, no,' Gemma said, flapping a hand between them. 'I really appreciate it. Just worried you've been here for a while. That meeting lasted ages.'

'You're busy. I'll go,' Steph said with a shrug, very aware Sheila was privy to this awkward encounter.

Gemma gently grabbed Steph's elbow. 'Eh, excuse me. You can't just deliver a lady a latte and run off. I'm due a break and I'd love some fresh air. Fancy getting a warm coffee with me?'

∼

'I really did appreciate the coffee,' Gemma said as they walked round the corner to Gordon Street.

The sun was making her squint after a day inside and Steph felt her breath falter. She looked cute, eyes all scrunched up as she tried to make eye contact.

'Sorry again that it was cold.'

'Stop apologising. No one's ever brought me coffee before and now you've done it twice. Hot or cold, I'll take what I get, cause I'm just happy to get it at all.'

Steph smiled. 'You're busy. It's the only way I could think of helping.'

'Thank you. Will we go in here? I've never been,' Gemma asked, standing outside a donut shop. Steph had heard good things, but she was rarely in town. It was a new one for her too.

'Let's do it. Seems quiet enough.'

A glass counter greeted them on entry and Steph pursed her lips in wonder. She'd never seen so many different types of donuts. It was going to be a hard choice.

'Last meeting of the day is scheduled to last two hours. I think a little sugar is in order,' Gemma said, rubbing her hands together with glee.

They ordered coffees and Steph plumped for a double berry and white chocolate donut, while Gemma settled on a chocolate millionaire.

They grabbed a seat by the window and Gemma let out a long sigh, rolling her shoulders as she sat down.

'Long day?' Steph asked, eying her donut and wondering where to begin. The purple ring was bigger than her hand and drizzled with shiny white chocolate.

'Long week. Still, will be worth it. Holiday starts tomorrow.'

'Oh God, yeah. Excited?' She'd forgotten Gemma was

away this weekend. She'd been hoping for a movie night. Being off work was the worst. There was no routine, no clear days: everything was one big boring timeline.

'Of course. Three nights away with a hot tub all to myself – what's not to love?'

'I'd be lying if I said I wasn't jealous. I'm going out of my mind with boredom.'

'Still not enjoying being off work then?' Gemma took a bite of her donut, the chocolate cream that decorated the top oozing everywhere. A blob stayed on her nose.

Steph snorted. 'Got a bit on your nose.'

Gemma grabbed her napkin, pawing at the chocolate smudge. She got most of it but a streak remained.

'Gone?'

'Not quite.' Steph took the napkin from her and ignored the shiver that travelled the length of her spine as their fingers grazed.

Her hand stilled, her muscles suddenly incapable, as she hovered her palm by Gemma's jaw. The last time she'd done this they were kissing. A flush of desire burst in her core, extinguished by a wave of sadness.

She took a breath and placed her hand against Gemma's face, steadying her as she wiped.

Her palm burned hot at the contact. Even more so when she realised Gemma was staring straight at her. Those blue eyes could cut diamonds.

'Got it?' Gemma asked with a quiet chuckle.

'It's not budging. Do you mind if I . . .?' Steph asked, dropping the napkin and licking the tip of her thumb.

'No, no, lick away. I can't have a meeting looking like a clown.'

Gemma's cheeks blushed and Steph could feel the heat against her skin.

Chocolate gone, her muscles were useless again, refusing to remove her hand from Gemma's face.

They held eye contact for a beat and Steph wanted nothing more than to lean forward and kiss her. Did Gemma ever think about it? Or was it just a drunken snog, easily forgotten?

Chatter in the café brought Steph back to the moment and she dropped her hand. 'Erm, yeah, hating it.'

'Hmm?' Gemma looked confused.

'You asked if I was enjoying being off work.'

'Oh, yeah,' Gemma replied, faffing with her chocolate-covered napkin, her cheeks still flushed. 'You're not then?"

'I've made a few new beers, but other than that I'm bored out of my mind.'

'Cal doesn't want you back?'

Steph shook her head. 'He said my health had to come first, plus he wanted to see how the place ran without my input. Which I guess is good.'

'But?'

'But?'

'I can feel a but,' Gemma said, biting the corner of her lip.

'Well, I guess I'm happy he might finally catch Donnie out, *but* it means landing the team in the shit and I hate it.'

'It's not your fault, though.'

'I know, but if I can relieve their problems, why wouldn't I? Seems unfair to ignore things I can fix.'

Gemma blew her cheeks out. 'Sometimes the best thing you can do is let the bad play out. If you keep picking up the pieces, Cal will never see how terrible Donnie truly is. So the team has a few horrible days. If it means a Donnie-free future that's not a bad swap.'

Steph nodded gently. 'I guess when you put it like that, it makes sense.'

'Promise no more sneaking into work?'

'Promise,' Steph repeated with a smirk.

'Now. Don't you be making me mad. I need you to mean it,' Gemma said, a cheeky glint in her eye.

'I promise I won't go into work.' Steph took a deep breath, wondering if she should say what had been playing on her mind. *Screw it.* 'Although, I thought you were mad at me anyway.'

'Me? Why?'

Steph shrugged and played with her coffee cup, twisting it in its saucer. 'You've been super quiet, and I know you're busy with work. But it was more than that: it was because of the whole text thing, wasn't it?' Gemma looked like a gasping fish, so Steph saved her the trouble. 'I'm sorry she didn't like you back. Is there any way I can make it up to you? Like, who is she? Want me to go rough her up? Persuade her to go on a date? Give you a chance?' She was joking, but whatever Gemma wanted, she would do. She had to make this right.

Gemma took a moment, getting her thoughts in order. 'You have nothing to be sorry about with the text thing. I took a chance and it didn't land. That's life.'

'Still. I want you to be happy. You've been wanting to date someone since we first met and now I've ballsed things up with one person you liked.'

Gemma put a hand on Steph's and she flinched. 'You've. Done. Nothing. Wrong.' Her sky-blue eyes told Steph she meant it.

'I think what we've learned is: I'm the worst wingman ever. You can't call me Cupid any more, that's for sure.'

'I dunno. Still plenty time for you to redeem yourself.

And speaking of time, I really need to get back to work. Sorry.'

'Will you let me know you get to the cottage safe?'

'Nah,' she said, shaking her head with a smile.

'Gemma!' Steph whined.

'Nope. No need if you come with me.'

26

'You ready?' Gemma asked with a wink as Steph loaded her last bag into the boot.

'As I'll ever be.'

Gemma chanced a final look at Steph as she rounded the car to the passenger door. She had on her signature combo: shorts and a hoodie. Gemma was going to spend most of the next three hours reminding herself to watch the road, not Steph's gorgeous bare legs.

The idea to invite Steph had been pure impulse, but she was glad she had. The notion that Steph might like her still sat in her heart; she needed to know for certain one way or another. And what better way to find out than taking the girl you're madly crushing on to a remote cabin and having nowhere to go if things all went south?

It didn't take long to leave the city behind and soon they were surrounded by greenery and skirting the edge of Loch Lomond.

Steph had been quiet for a while, staring out at the water with a misty look in her eyes.

'You take the high road, and I'll take the low road,'

Gemma sang quietly, checking Steph's face for a reaction. A smile flickered on her lips. She ramped up the volume. 'And I'll be in Scotland afore you!' She couldn't contain the giggles anymore. 'I have no idea what the next words are.'

'Does anyone?' Steph said with a chuckle, her eyes still fixed on the water.

'You okay?'

'Yeah. Just thinking.'

'Want to share?'

Silence hung in the car, the quiet pop music spilling from the radio the only thing bridging the gap.

'It's just seeing water. It makes me think about stuff. You should see what happens if I spy the sea.'

Gemma wasn't sure if it was a joke or not. 'Good or bad?'

'Bad, I guess. But also good. I have lots of happy memories by the sea. When I was a kid me and my pals pretty much spent every spare hour on the beach.'

'You miss it?'

'Yeah. I miss the sea. None of the rest.'

She never knew if it was okay to push these things; how much Steph actually wanted to share, or if she was coming across as nosey. She left it, sure Steph would say more if she wanted to. 'There's something magic about being by a loch. I think it must be in our blood. If you close your eyes you can almost hear the bagpipes.'

'Please don't close your eyes,' Steph joked.

'I'll try not to.' Gemma looked at her passenger again. She seemed a little brighter. 'So, I was thinking we'd make a pit stop in Glencoe. It'll probably be busy but you've got to appreciate the view, eh? Be rude to pass through and not pay our respects.'

'I've never been. Looking forward to it.'

'You've never been?! You're in for a treat.'

By the look on Steph's face, Glencoe had lived up to Gemma's hype.

When she thought of the Highlands, Glencoe was never far behind. There was something about coming off the busy dual carriageway and driving on its slim one-track road, having to use the passing places peppered along its way, that thrust you into rural life. *Boom*, suddenly you felt you were on a different planet. Gemma's heart swelled with pride: she'd never take being Scottish for granted. How could you, with scenery like this on your doorstep?

They were lucky to get a parking spot at the viewing point: it was busy. Always was. Gemma stretched her legs, welcoming the rest, as Steph wandered to the edge of the gravelled area.

She turned back, her face etched with wonder, and Gemma wished she could have captured it on camera. She'd hold it in her heart instead.

Gemma walked level with her, rolling her neck and shoulders in the process. 'Not bad, is it?'

'It's beautiful.'

They were at the Three Sisters viewpoint. So called because it gave you the perfect vantage point of three Scottish mountains: Aonach Dubh, Beinn Fhada, and Gearr Aonach. (So the visitor board had told Gemma: she'd have no clue of their names otherwise.)

They rose to meet the sky with majestic wonder, the greenest grass Gemma had ever seen crowding their bases. They'd picked a good day for it. She'd been here before on a less sunny day and it had been quite bleak, truth be told. Steph didn't need to know that, though. Gemma wanted her to think it was always sunny in Glencoe. A little slice of perfection in a dreich world.

'Can you walk up them?' Steph asked.

'Probably. You'd need the proper equipment, though. Do you like walking?'

'Never done it. I could be tempted, though. Do you?'

Gemma shrugged. 'I'd give it a bash if the company was right.' She looked at Steph, hoping to catch the glimmer of something between them, but her eyes were fixed dead ahead. She followed her line of vision and spotted a large bird soaring overhead.

'Is that an eagle?' Steph asked, her mouth hanging open.

'Hmm. Probably not. Although you do get them here. Maybe a kestrel or something?'

'Amazing, whatever it is.'

Gemma's hand twitched, desperate to take hold of Steph's and bask in the moment. She stuffed it in her trouser pocket instead and studied Steph's profile. 'Yeah, it is.'

'Hello,' a German-sounding man with walking sticks said on his way past.

'Hi,' they chorused.

Steph looked at her white trainers. 'If I'd known I would invested in some boots.'

'Next time.'

~

Soon they were in Fort William and just a hop, skip, and jump from the cottage. Time to get some supplies.

Steph had nipped to the toilet, leaving Gemma to wander the aisles alone and fill their trolley with reckless abandon. This all felt very homely. She used to enjoy the Sunday shop with Logan. It was stupid, but she'd often fantasised about sharing it with someone again. There was a solidness to the triviality of it.

A finger poked into either side of her waist made her jump and Steph cackled with laughter. 'Sorry, couldn't resist. What have you got so far?'

'Erm, plenty of stuff for our barbeque, some breakfasty stuff; that's about it really.'

'So a trolley full of meat, pretty much.'

Gemma looked at the trolley's contents. 'Pretty much.'

'For two lesbians that's a heck of a lot of sausage.'

Gemma snorted. 'Still quite new to all this. Thank God I have you to keep me right.' She grabbed at Steph's side, intent on tickling her, but she escaped with a side-step.

'You hang here: I'll double back and grab some veg, even things out.'

'Just no aubergines, please.'

Steph threw a coy smile over her shoulder and Gemma couldn't help but shake her head.

It didn't take long to reach the booze aisle after that. 'Are you sticking to beer or do you want wine too?' Gemma asked, loading the trolley up with some Sauvignon Blanc.

'Maybe a bit of both. My home-made wine is finally ready, so I've brought that along for us.'

'Really? I can't wait.'

'Don't get too excited. It might be pish.' Steph led them to the beer aisle, expertly avoiding meandering tourists along the way. The place was stiff with lost-looking folk with paisley bandanas around their necks. 'I wonder what the local brew is?'

Gemma battled a smile.

'What's that look for?' Steph asked as she picked up a bottle.

'Do you want to know now or keep it as a surprise? I'd need to tell you tonight anyway, I suppose.'

Steph narrowed her eyes with blissful confusion. 'Tell me now.'

Gemma pointed to a can with *Fort William Brewing Co.* emblazoned on the front. 'These guys are local and I've booked us on a tour tomorrow.'

Steph's eyes grew wide. 'A tour? Really?' She popped the bottle she was holding back on the shelf and threw her arms around Gemma's neck, squeezing her tight. She'd not been expecting such a good reaction. 'Thank you. That's so thoughtful.'

She kissed her cheek and the heat from her lips remained on Gemma's skin, like she'd been branded.

'I know you like beer, so I figured why not?' she replied, playing it down.

'This is shaping up to be the best holiday ever and we've not even reached the cottage yet.'

Gemma beamed. 'Just wait until you see the hot tub.'

'I know, I can't wait. Is it near anyone or do we have the place to ourselves?'

'Middle of nowhere as far as I know. Why? Forgotten your cozzie?' *Please say yes.* Steph naked in the hot tub had passed through her mind more than once in the last twenty-four hours.

'Just getting a feel for the place. So, BARBECUE tonight. Cook a meal together tomorrow? Or see how the weather is again?'

'I'd say we've got enough meat to feed us a while.'

'You obviously take after your granny.'

'Speaking of which, let's get some gin too.' If she was going to tell Steph how she felt, she needed alcohol and plenty of it.

27

'This place is amazing,' Steph mouthed at Gemma as they reached the tasting room of the brewery.

It was an impressive set-up, way bigger than any of the microbreweries she'd visited near Cal's. They even grew their own barley and reared their own sheep for biodiversity.

She was looking forward to tasting their produce.

She'd caught Gemma looking at her a few times during the tour. In fact, she'd caught her doing it a few times last night as well. And there was a strange moment just before they went to sleep. It was like something was on the tip of her tongue but she couldn't quite bring herself to say it. Maybe she was still annoyed about the whole texting thing. Or feeling weird about sharing a bed after they kissed.

She would find out tonight. If something was annoying Gemma she had to bring it to the surface: left to fester it could grow arms and legs, and losing their friendship wasn't an option.

A few glasses of wine back at the rental would sort everything out.

The cottage was lovely and just what Steph needed. When her doctor had prescribed time off this was surely what he was meaning, not time spent in her dark and boring flat.

It was a gorgeous wooden building right on the edge of Loch Lochy, with a balcony perfect for watching the water. She'd enjoyed the seating area with a coffee this morning and she'd enjoy the hot tub with a wine this evening.

The place was idyllic.

Inside was basic but homely and the double bed certainly made things cosy, but they were adults. No need to make things awkward when they didn't need to be.

'Okay,' their guide Stuart said as the small group of six crowded round a barrel adorned with bottles and small plastic glasses. 'Finally, the bit of the tour you've all been waiting for.' He picked up the nearest bottle. 'This is our best seller, The Blondie.' He cracked open the bottle with a satisfying hiss. 'So who wants to try the lager?' A few hands went up, Steph's included.

He poured the pale yellow liquid into the cups, each one with a satisfying head of foam. He passed one to Steph and she took a sip. God, it was good.

Stuart made eye contact with Steph. 'Do you want to have a go at the flavour notes?'

Her heart raced. It was like being back at school. 'I'll give it a bash.' She took another sip, letting the liquid settle on her tongue. 'I'm getting biscuits, herbal notes, and—' words failed her. 'Something else. Sorry.'

Stuart grinned. 'No, no, that was brilliant. Spot on. So, I would say it's crisp. It's a nice lager, this one. Real palate pleaser.'

Thankfully he didn't pick on Steph with the next one, a dark porter, or she might have got a complex.

He did however, saunter over as she debated beers in the gift shop.

'Sorry to pick on you during the tasting,' he said with a sheepish smile. 'It's just you asked some brilliant questions during the tour so I figured you must be in the industry.'

Steph's cheeks grew hot. 'Not quite. I mean, I'd love to be, but I just make stuff at home for now.'

'Got any jobs going?' Gemma joked and soon found Steph's elbow in her ribs.

Stuart chuckled. 'I'm guessing it would be one heck of a commute if we did. Where you from?'

'Glasgow.'

'Ah, nice. So, you'll be familiar with Boss Brewery?'

Steph shook her head.

'No way – you need to check them out. They're completely women-owned and to say they're shaking up the industry would be an understatement. They're in the process of expanding: you should totally send them your CV if you're serious about getting a job. Tell Fi that Stuart sent you. We're good pals.'

'Thank you,' Steph said, not really sure what else to say.

'No probs. Enjoy your beer.' He was off.

Gemma's eyes were like saucers. 'Bloody hell, that's exciting. I'm going to Google them right now.'

∼

Steph hoped Gemma couldn't see her hands shaking as she tried to undo the cap on her home-made wine. She was trying in earnest to focus on the bottle and not the gorgeous woman in a bikini getting into the hot tub beside her. She was thankful she'd got in first or it would have been a wonder her legs could hold her.

Gemma was beyond perfection. If she thought she knew what a perfect woman's body looked like, she needed to scrap it. Nothing could beat Gemma.

She swallowed and finally the cap unscrewed.

'You ready for this?' she asked, not surprised there was a slight shake to her voice.

'I've been looking forward to it since you first mentioned it.'

Don't look at her boobs. Don't look at her boobs. How could she not, with them right there, though?! They sat right on the water line, begging for attention.

Steph twisted to face the glasses instead and poured two generous measures. She passed one to Gemma before raising her own in a toast. 'To Loch Lochy Locherson.'

Gemma laughed. 'You still don't really believe me, do you?'

'Nope,' Steph said, taking a sip of wine. It wasn't bad. Definitely potent, but she'd tasted worse.

The loch looked beautiful this evening. The nights still battled to stay light but the sun's mellow rays were slowly fading now, highlighting the water where the breeze gently ruffled it. It wasn't quite the sea, but it was comforting enough.

'That's not bad,' Gemma said, tasting the wine.

'You doubted me?'

'A little,' she said with a snigger. 'You know me, if it's not an Aussie Savvy B I'm not having it. This gets a pass, though.'

'High praise indeed.'

Steph sighed, enjoying the peace. Only the sound of the hot tub's jets broke the air.

'This is brilliant, isn't it?'

'It certainly is. I could live here.'

'If only.' Steph sipped her wine again. This was dangerous stuff; far too easy to drink. 'You feeling better about Julie?'

She'd put a photo dump on Facebook earlier, their first day in the cottage. Far too many willies and other typical hen-do shite for Steph's liking.

'How could I not, when we're enjoying this and they're probably hungover to hell and doing more drinking games this very moment? I'd much rather be with you.'

'I think the view is the main attraction but I'm glad I'm keeping you company.'

There was that look again. She didn't have near enough wine in her to broach the subject.

A comfortable silence wrapped around them.

'I looked at that brewery while you were getting the barbecue going earlier. It seems good.'

'Yeah?'

'You should totally apply for the job.'

Steph swooshed her free hand through the water, watching shimmering reflections become fragments. 'I could write my CV on the back of a stamp. I don't think there's much point. But thank you for the confidence. That means a lot.'

Gemma shuffled closer and Steph's grip on her glass tightened.

'Do you really think they're going to look at your lack of school grades and think *oh shit, she's not got a standard grade in Geography. Screw all the amazing life experience she has*?'

Steph forced a smile and shrugged. 'Just seems a bit far-fetched. Why would they ever pick someone like me over other candidates?'

'Eh, because you're amazing.' Gemma bumped her arm against Steph's and her heart sung. 'As soon as we get back, let's type a CV together. Then even if you don't apply this time, you have it for the future.'

∼

'Are you not wrinkly yet?' Steph asked, taking Gemma's hand in hers and tipping it over to inspect her digits. Surprisingly, she wasn't.

'Wouldn't matter; I'll stay here all night if I can. It's too nice to move.'

They'd polished off the first bottle of wine with ease and were now onto the second. During the course of the drinking they'd somehow lost the gap between them and were now thigh to thigh, enjoying the view.

'Thanks again for bringing me,' Steph said, feeling reflective.

Gemma shrugged and Steph relished the feeling of her arm brushing hers. 'Like I said, I'd much rather be here with you than Julie and her stupid hen weekend.'

Steph smiled, a pop of pure bliss settling in her chest.

'What was that look for?' Gemma asked with a smile.

'I just had one of those little shots of happiness? Do you ever get them? It's been a while.' She paused, thinking. 'Do you ever,' she gathered her thoughts and tried again. 'Do you ever wonder if you're on the wrong timeline?'

'Huh?'

'I used to. It really got to me sometimes. Like, I was a straight A student. My teachers really thought I was going somewhere: they had my Highers all picked out. I wasn't quite settled on a job but I knew it would be in the sciences. Something to do with chemistry, probably. I thought it would be cool to research drugs and stuff, potentially cure something.' She shook her head. 'Seems silly now.'

'It's not silly. You wish you'd stayed in school, then?'

'Of course. I was a total goof in class but I got my head down when it mattered.'

'Do you not like what you do now?' Gemma finished her wine and reached for the bottle, her breast pushing into Steph's shoulder. For a brief second she forgot how to form words.

'I do, but I guess I always wondered what would have happened if my parents weren't dicks. Like I said: silly. No point wishing for something that doesn't exist.'

'No harm in wondering.' Gemma held the bottle aloft. 'Top up?'

'Yeah, why not.'

'I wouldn't be here, though. So, I guess this path is alright.'

Gemma paused, her blue eyes fixed on Steph's. 'For what it's worth, I'm glad you're here. It would have been shit without you. In fact, I'm glad you work in Cal's because I don't know what I would have done without you the last two months.'

'Even though I mucked things up with your bird?'

Gemma laughed under her breath. 'Do you really still feel bad about that?'

'Of course. I thought you were mad at me too. That was horrible.'

'Who do you think it was?'

'Who do you like? I dunno, I don't know any of your friends. Is she on the hen do? Will I have seen her picture?'

Gemma tipped her head back, a quiet laugh lost to the sound of the hot tub.

'What?' Steph asked, confused.

'Nothing. It's just . . . so, feeling better about being off? You must be if you're happy.'

'You're changing the subject. But, not really. Hard not to be happy here though. Especially with you for company. I always feel better when you're around.' The strong wine was making her brave.

'Now I feel bad for avoiding you the last week,' Gemma said with a smirk.

Steph swivelled, the water in the tub sloshing side to side. 'So you were mad.'

'Not mad. Just confused. Embarrassed. Lots of things. But not mad.' She placed her wine glass on the wooden edging of the hot tub.

'But you *were* avoiding me?'

Gemma nodded. 'Yeah.'

Steph groaned, sinking into the tub. 'I'm an idiot.'

'Yeah you are.' Gemma slapped the water, splashing Steph.

'Oi,' she retorted with a wicked grin, splashing Gemma back as Steph put her glass on the side.

Gemma didn't hesitate to retaliate and before Steph knew it, in a haze of water and giggles they were standing face to face, the choppy water of the tub slowly settling.

'You just have no clue, do you?' Gemma asked, her voice low. She was so close Steph could feel the heave of her chest as she breathed.

'About what?'

Gemma's eyes flicked from Steph's eyes to her lips and back again. She ran a hand over her sodden hair: if it hadn't been tied up it would have been a tangled mess around her face. She closed the tiny gap between them, her hand finding Steph's and lacing their fingers together. 'That text was meant for you. I thought you were fobbing me off to save face. But you weren't, were you?'

'Huh?'

Water ran down Steph's nose but she ignored it, scared to move and break the connection.

Steph didn't know what was louder: the hot tub or her heart. Blood pumped in her ears as she held Gemma's gaze.

She dipped level with Steph, her lips finding hers with ease.

It took a hot second for her brain to catch up, Gemma was kissing her. Actually kissing her.

She pulled away. 'Wait, this isn't some weird only-when-we're-drunk thing, is it?'

Gemma pulled her closer, speaking into her lips. 'Definitely not.'

'You like me?'

It was Gemma's turn to pull back, stifling a laugh. 'Do you always talk this much when someone's trying to kiss you?'

'No, it's just—'

'Shush.'

There was no option to talk now, Gemma put her hands on either side of Steph's face and pulled her closer, their lips crashing together like the water at the loch's edge.

Fuck, she was a good kisser. Steph guided them back to sitting, scared her legs would turn to jelly at any moment.

This wasn't how she'd seen tonight ending.

Gemma straddled her, Steph's hands on her bum, keeping her in place.

She wanted to talk, gush about how pretty she was, how crazy this was, but she kept quiet, choosing instead to find Gemma's tongue with her own.

Gemma moaned. 'I wanted to do this at the wedding.'

This was news. 'Yeah?' Steph asked, moving her mouth to find the sweet spot on Gemma's neck, just below her ear. She gently sucked and a fresh moan escaped.

'Yeah. I wanted you to fuck me.'

Okay. She'd one hundred per cent misread that situation. Note to self: do not trust intuition.

Steph's core throbbed, her pulse thundering in her clit as Gemma pushed down on her thighs.

Gemma took her hands from the side of the tub and unclasped her bikini top, freeing her breasts. Steph watched in awe as they slipped into the evening air with a gentle bob.

This wasn't real life. It couldn't be.

Fuck. They were perfect. No surprise, given the rest of Gemma, but Jesus. She took the closest taut bud in her mouth and sucked, gently at first, then a little nibble for good measure.

Not to let the other feel left out, she brought up a hand, circling her thumb over Gemma's stiff nipple.

Even in the tub, Steph knew she was wetter than she'd ever been before.

She looked up at Gemma and couldn't stop the grin splitting her face. 'You're perfect.' It didn't seem enough. Nothing was enough.

'So are you.'

She daren't protest. 'Good thing we don't have any neighbours.'

'I wouldn't care, to be honest. I waited long enough: let them watch if they want. I'm not stopping for anyone.' She traced a finger from Steph's lips, down her neck and her chest, before settling between her breasts, on her bikini top. 'Can this come off?'

'Of course,' Steph said, leaning forward and kissing Gemma as she unclasped the fastening on her top. Without breaking their connection she slid it over her arms before chucking it to the floor.

Gemma leaned closer, Steph's breasts now pressed into

her stomach. She ran a hand up the inside of Gemma's thigh and felt her muscles stiffen.

'Can we go inside?' Steph asked, breathless. 'I want to feel you and the water's ruining my fun.'

'Sure,' Gemma said and lifted herself off Steph without another word.

Was she as nervous as Steph? It was a tug of war between nerves and adrenaline in her veins right now; the sooner she was on solid ground the better.

Gemma undid her ponytail, her wet hair spilling around her head like a halo before she took a towel to it and ruffled it drier.

Steph grabbed the other towel from the side as she stepped onto the wooden decking. It was like using her legs for the first time in years: they felt foreign and weak. She ran the towel over her hair and face then draped it over her shoulders, stepping close to Gemma. She was so much taller that Steph had to go on the balls of her feet to reach her. Thankfully Gemma was willing to meet her halfway.

Steph pulled her towel around them, creating a cocoon for just the two of them. Gemma's hands trailed her waist as they kissed, finally settling on her hips, her fingers pulling at her bikini pants as if asking for permission to shed them.

'They'll need to come off at some point,' Steph mumbled into Gemma's mouth.

She smiled in return, her fingers hooking under the sodden fabric and easing them off.

Steph stepped out of them, wishing her hands were free to return the favour. 'Yours now,' she encouraged.

Gemma didn't need asked twice. A quick shimmy and their naked bodies were pressed hard against each other, only a towel protecting them from the outside world.

They kissed lazily, Steph wanting to enjoy every second of this, just in case she woke up and it was all a dream.

The way Gemma's hands skirted over the curve of her waist told her it was real.

'You've got goosebumps,' Gemma said, almost whispering. 'Will we go inside?'

28

She'd felt brave before but without a glass of wine in her hand, Gemma's nerves were starting to get to her. This was Steph, though. There was no one she felt safer with.

Gemma led them to the bedroom, hopeful she wasn't using the last of her boldness.

'You okay?' Steph asked, her hands snaking under Gemma's towel to find her hips. Her own towel lay open, draped over her shoulders, only gravity keeping it on. Gemma let her eyes wander the length of her and a new surge of courage coursed through her veins.

'Yeah,' she said, surprised at how low her voice was.

With a gentle flick of her shoulders, Steph's towel fell from her shoulders and she climbed into bed.

She was an absolute marvel. Gemma had never been more thankful to be off work: she'd need days to explore Steph's body in the ways she wanted. She'd treat every inch as a mile, plotting and enjoying with careful precision. The question was – where to begin?

A final deep breath and she lost her own towel before

falling into bed, tangling her limbs with Steph's underneath the covers.

She kissed her and Gemma felt like she was falling in the best possible way. She was lost in herself, in the moment, with only Steph's capable hands to keep her safe.

It had never felt like this with Logan. She scolded herself for thinking of him at such an intimate moment, but decided to lean into the thought and be grateful for it. They'd only just begun and already Steph was making her feel things she'd never felt before. All those sleepless nights of agonising, worrying she'd made the right choice, and if she'd only had a crystal ball to see this moment, she'd know they were all unfounded.

Steph moved her knee, pushing her weight into Gemma's core, and she saw stars.

She was so wet, she could feel every beat of her heart between her legs.

Steph pushed herself up, leaning on her forearm as she slotted between Gemma's legs, her thigh not moving.

How could a thigh feel so good?

For years she thought sex was something to be endured, something she just didn't enjoy, and all this time thighs were providing this much pleasure?!

Steph moved her attention to Gemma's nipple as she ground her leg against Gemma's slick core.

She let out a groan, followed by a ragged breath.

At this rate, she wouldn't last long.

Were all lesbians like this or was Steph just particularly skilled? She'd hit the jackpot either way.

Steph parted her lips, releasing Gemma's nipple, and brought her head level with Gemma's ear. Her breath was hot. Gemma's skin cried out with desire.

'Can I touch you?' Steph asked.

'Please.'

If she didn't, Gemma would probably die.

She swallowed hard as Steph traced a finger down her shoulder and between her breasts, following an imaginary line to her navel. Gemma couldn't take her eyes off her, watching in awe as Steph's brown eyes kept pace with her finger, a smile lingering, like she was seeing a naked woman for the first time and completely smitten.

Gemma knew how she felt.

She brought a hand up and grabbed the pillow case as Steph dipped her hand between her legs.

She stopped, teasing her.

Gemma chuckled. 'Don't.'

Steph was still smiling as she kissed her.

Just like that, her fingers slid between Gemma's wet folds and stole her breath.

'Fuck,' she moaned, her head swimming with pleasure.

Steph moved her attention to Gemma's neck again, sucking and biting as her fingers traced her core, circling where she really wanted her, delaying entry, leaving Gemma right on the edge.

She arched her hips, inviting Steph inside.

It didn't long for her to oblige and soon her two fingers were in Gemma, thrusting gently, hitting her right where it mattered.

Desire was already building, steadily growing with each drive of her digits.

Gemma tried to focus on her breathing, scared she was going to come too quickly.

'You feel so good,' Steph groaned into her neck.

That nearly pushed her over the edge but she held,

fingers pressed tight into Steph's hip to help steady her, the other hand still gripping the pillow.

Steph changed her rhythm, bringing her thumb into play, gliding it over Gemma's clit as she thrust.

It was almost too much.

Steph had been hiding her fingers in plain sight but they should come with a warning: they were little more than supercharged weapons, capable of making a woman come in record time.

Gemma could hold off no more and let herself come undone. Steph continued to thrust as Gemma's inner walls clamped around her fingers, bringing her back to the edge before shoving her over once more.

She clamped her thighs around Steph's hand, bringing her to a stop. Her clit was still throbbing, the high of the orgasms refusing to leave.

'Wow,' she huffed.

Steph collapsed in a heap beside her. 'You're amazing.'

'Me?' Words were too much to ask for.

Steph used her last ounce of energy to sit up and kiss Gemma before flopping back into the pillow.

Gemma could do nothing but stare at the ceiling, trying to wrap her head around the joy buzzing through her veins. This was new. So sex *was* fun.

Finally, she was compos mentis enough to lean on one elbow, her other arm draped over Steph's torso.

She took her in, her eyes not truly believing she could be so lucky.

Gemma could wait no longer.

Without another word she ducked her head to Steph's breast, sucking the nipple into her mouth.

Steph moaned and it lit a new fire in Gemma's chest.

She raised her head, her face breaking into a smile as her hand trailed south. Steph snagged her gaze.

She paused when her fingers brushed hair.

'You don't have to if you're not ready,' Steph said, her voice gentle.

Gemma eased forward, her lips grazing Steph's as she spoke. 'Just savouring the moment.'

And she was. Something told her nothing would be the same after this.

They kissed, Gemma's tongue quickly finding Steph's as she opened her legs, making room for Gemma's hand.

Her breathing quickened; she hadn't expected to be so turned on at the thought of touching Steph. She could already feel how wet she was and, in turn, Gemma's core was coming to life again too.

She ran the back of fingers down Steph as they kissed, before tracing a single digit along the line of her centre. She was so neat, so tucked away, so different to Gemma's own core.

She was perfect.

Gemma moaned as her fingers slipped into Steph.

She'd touched herself a lot recently but nothing could have prepared her for how wonderful another woman would feel.

The heat, the slickness, the way Steph responded to her touch: the slight stiffening of her muscles, the shift of her hips. It was ecstasy.

Gemma moved her fingers north, finding Steph's hard clit.

Steph stilled, then arched her hips. 'Just down a bit, there, yes.'

Her breathing told Gemma she'd found the right spot.

She took Steph's nipple in her mouth again, mimicking her finger's circles with her tongue.

'That feels so good,' Steph groaned.

Gemma varied her pace and movement, paying close attention to Steph's response.

'Oh God,' Steph moaned, gripping the pillow with both hands. 'That's so good.'

Something told Gemma Steph wasn't usually so vocal, but the encouragement was appreciated.

'Don't stop,' she panted.

Gemma couldn't if she wanted to.

A few more circles and she felt Steph's muscles tense, her back arching as she came.

She placed a hand over Gemma's, holding it tight against her core. 'Fuck,' she gasped.

She held them in place for a moment before using both her hands to pull Gemma close.

They lay in silence, only their ragged breathing filing the room.

~

It was too early to sleep so they ventured back outside, a blanket of stars waiting to greet them.

Steph kissed Gemma's shoulder as they huddled on the outdoor sofa, a throw wrapped around them, Gemma's legs flung over Steph's. Any more twisted and they'd be in a knot.

'I thought earlier was perfect, but I was wrong. Now is perfect,' Steph mumbled in Gemma's skin.

'It is.'

'This doesn't feel real.' She took Gemma's hand in hers and skirted a thumb across her palm. Gemma's skin tingled at the touch.

'I promise you it is.' She looked at the sky, a shooting star making a brief appearance before it fizzled out. 'What do you want to do tomorrow?'

'Dunno. Bed all day?'

Gemma snorted. 'Tempting. But it's our last day here: we can have the morning in bed. We should do something in the afternoon.'

'Then bed?'

Gemma felt Steph's smile against her skin and nearly melted.

'If you behave in the afternoon I'm sure you could twist my arm into a pre-dinner bedroom excursion.'

'Fancy.'

'Always.' Gemma leaned back and fished her phone out from between the cushions. 'We could go for a walk?' she said, intent on Googling what was close. Her lock screen was filled with messages from Julie. 'Urgh,' she groaned, facing the screen towards Steph.

'Is she wasted?'

'Must be.'

'What does she want?'

Gemma skimmed the partial messages filling her screen, along with a peppering of missed calls.

'She misses me. She's sorry. Must be feeling the guilt big time tonight.'

'You going to call her back?' Steph asked, kissing a line along Gemma's shoulder, settling on her neck.

'Not if you keep doing that. I can't think straight.'

'Is that not the point?'

Gemma sniggered, gently elbowing Steph in the tummy. 'I can't be bothered talking to her if she's hammered. I'll just text her. She can call tomorrow if she's that fussed.'

'You're very busy now, anyway.'

'I am?'

'Yes,' Steph said, nibbling on the dip between Gemma's neck and shoulder.

'Yes, very busy, you're right,' she replied, twisting round and pulling Steph in for a kiss.

29

This had felt like a good idea at the time, but now she was here, Steph was having second thoughts.

Back home in Glasgow she was going out of her mind being off work, and Gemma was legitimately busy.

One evening, in a haze of post-orgasm fog, she'd agreed to help Gemma's granny in the garden. 'She's desperate and Archie is being a dick,' Gemma had said.

Seemed simple enough. But on the long drive over to Bearsden, it dawned on Steph: she didn't know this woman at all.

Too late. She'd knocked on the door now.

It was a nice little whitewashed bungalow with a terracotta roof. The front garden looked pristine. Surely no one too scary could live in its walls?

'Steph! Hello!' Gemma's granny said, wrapping her arms around her. They were nearly the same height.

Shit. What was her name again?

'Hey.' She released Granny from her grip. Steph scratched the back of her neck. 'I'm so sorry,' she said, cringing. 'Can you remind me what you'd like me to call you?'

'Margaret, my dear, and no need to look so worried. I forget names all the time. In you come.'

Her house was beautiful. Family portraits lined the walls and what seemed like every available surface. It was a real family home and love filled its rooms. It was a wonder the roof didn't pop off with it all.

Steph paused, her attention stolen by a bespectacled little girl with bunches in a frilly pink dress. She tilted her head to the side, studying the photo. Was that the Easter bunny in the background?

'Yes, that's Gemma. Early nineties. That's her Uncle Harris in the rabbit suit. We still get it out at Easter, for the little ones.'

Steph smiled. 'Looks like fun.'

'Never a dull moment with the Andersons and MacDonalds.'

Steph guessed that was Gemma's mum's maiden name. She rounded the corner to be greeted with a wall of certificates. Margaret was a proud granny personified.

'Just through the back,' Margaret said, ushering Steph along. It was a good thing, too: she was in danger of lingering.

'Do you have more photos of Gemma when she was little?' Steph asked as she followed Margaret to the kitchen.

She stopped at the patio doors. 'Oh, aye. Loads. I'll look them out and we can have a gander over a cup of tea later. Gemma will be here by then as well. Now, come out the back. Let me show you the shed and what I need you to do.'

She turned the key in the lock but the heavy patio door wouldn't budge. Either it was stiff or Margaret's arms weren't as strong as they used to be. It didn't matter. Steph said,

'Here, let me,' and yanked it open. The cold air made her shiver, despite only being inside for all of two minutes. Winter wasn't far off.

'Thank you,' Margaret said, doing the two steps out of the door at an angle, her leg looking stiff. 'Got a new hip not long ago. It doesn't like the cold much.'

'I know how it feels,' Steph assured, pulling her borg-collared jacket tight.

'Not far now,' Margaret said, leading them along a gravel path towards the shed. Steph felt bad having her out in the cold. Couldn't she point out of the window, or something?

Soon they were at the small wooden shed. Steph took a deep breath as Margaret opened the door. It had been a long time since she was last in a shed and the smell brought back an ocean of memories. God, it smelled good.

'So, the materials are all there,' Margaret said, pointing towards a stack of packages and string on a rickety wooden table. 'Gemma said she showed you a video of what to do?'

She had. Although, she'd done it in bed last night and Steph had paid more attention to Gemma's boobs than the video. She'd soon pick it up.

'Gloves are here,' she said, patting the well-loved grey mitts. 'Now, follow me and I'll show you where the plants are.'

Steph stood aside and let Margaret lead the way again. She pointed to a spindly plant by the path. '*Euphorbia wulfenii*. You'll need to bag them. There's another over there,' she said, pointing a shaky finger towards the back of the house.

Step nodded: there was no point in even trying to repeat the name of that one. It was gone already. Sticky thing. That would do.

'Red hot poker,' Margaret continued, walking Steph to

another area of the garden. This one looked like thick sheaves of grass. 'You'll need to tie these up for me.'

'Red hot poker. Got it.'

They wandered further down the path, towards what Steph presumed was a pond.

'Forget the ornamental rhubarb, Rupert will sort that,' Margaret said, gesturing to a leafy giant of a plant to her right. She stopped by a paved area with seats. 'And these are my pots: they'll need to go in the greenhouse. It's just behind the bamboo.'

Steph craned her neck. Sure enough, the roof of the greenhouse just about poked out above the leafy bamboo swaying in the wind.

She clapped her hands together. 'Brilliant. I'll get started and if you can think of anything else, just bark out the back door.'

Margaret smiled, gripping Steph's arm and giving it a squeeze. 'You're a gem. Rupert, my usual gardener, he's running behind, and with the October frost coming soon I don't want to take my chances. Archie's so busy with work . . .' She trailed off, rolling her eyes.

'I'm here now. It'll be done in no time.'

She paused, as if she wanted to add something but had second thoughts. Steph recognised the look from Gemma.

'Cup of tea when you're done,' she finally said before pottering off.

Steph stood, hands on hips, and debated where to start. Probably the pots. Moving things from one place to another: couldn't go far wrong with that.

Jeez, they were heavier than they looked. She waddled along, carrying the bulbous pot like an oversized cannonball.

She positioned it in the greenhouse. One done, erm, a dozen or so to go.

The whole thing was surreal.

This time last week she'd thought Gemma was mad at her: next thing, they were having sex in a remote cottage, and somehow she was now in Bearsden having been stood in a tiny shed with Gemma's granny, talking about potted plants.

Had she died in the last week and somehow ended up in some strange heavenly limbo?

That almost made more sense.

Steph walked back to the patio area, going for a smaller pot.

The cottage had been great. Just what Steph needed to relax. And that was without the unexpected sex.

They'd enjoyed a peaceful walk through Killiechonate Forest on their final day, and the fresh air and pleasant views had done wonders for Steph's mental health. Gemma had even talked her into agreeing a CV might actually be a good idea.

The thought of going back to work and suffering Donnie made her insides twist and nausea shake her bones.

She'd be sad to leave Cal's: it was the closest thing to family she had, but it was for the best. She couldn't carry on like this.

Steph stopped for a breather, the chilly cold a thing of the past as sweat bloomed on the back of her neck, and looked back at Margaret's house.

She'd sworn off families after the heartbreak of losing Maisie's, but Gemma was special. Every rule had its exception.

Steph counted to three before tackling a large pot. A leafy purple thing sprouted in the middle.

Her knowledge of plants was miniscule. She'd helped Dad mow the lawn a few times, but Mum was the gardener. Did she still plant her flowers in neat little rows? The front garden was always immaculate. No wonder: she used a ruler to space them out. Wouldn't do to have the neighbours thinking there was disorder in the Campbell household.

The pot slipped and she only just caught the bastarding thing. She placed it on the ground, letting out a wavering sigh.

Sometimes she wondered what lie they'd spun to cover her disappearance. Who did Portsoy think she was? A doctor without borders, an astronaut, or maybe just plain old dead?

She'd looked up a few folks from school and thought about adding them on Facebook but ultimately decided that wasn't a can of worms she wanted to open.

Unlike the worm on her glove – he must have been hiding under the pot. She shook him free into the nearby shrubbery before picking the pot back up.

Soon the pots were moved, the poker tied and the whatever-the-diddly-do the sticky thing was covered in horticultural fleece.

Maybe she could train as a landscaper. Nah. Working outside in Scotland really didn't appeal.

On their first night back from the cottage, Gemma had cast another trademark spell and before Steph knew it she'd emailed the Boss Brewery. Nothing yet, but it was early days. Just doing it was a milestone.

There was something about Gemma. She got Steph pepped up, made her believe things that were once impossible were suddenly within reach.

Steph stood, hands on hips again, and surveyed the garden. Everything she'd been tasked with was done.

Margaret would be happy.

She stomped her boots, lifting each one up to check for mud. Nothing. She was safe to go indoors.

She was surprised to find Gemma at the kitchen table when she walked through the patio doors.

A smile instantly appeared, warmth flushing her cheeks.

'Nice to see you cosy inside,' Steph joked. She wanted to kiss her, on the cheek at least, but with Margaret sitting beside her granddaughter it felt inappropriate.

Gemma jumped to her feet. 'You looked like you knew what you were doing. I didn't want to interrupt. Want a cup of tea?'

'I'd love one, thanks,' Steph replied, peeling off her jacket and taking a seat. 'Is this a photo album I spy?'

Two thick albums sat on the table. The top one was opened to reveal baby pictures.

'Ask and you shall receive,' Margaret said. 'Wasn't she a cute baby?'

'Your eyes haven't changed a bit,' Steph said, leaning over the album.

'These old things,' Gemma said with a chuckle, pointing to her face as she put Steph's fresh mug of tea on the table. She turned the album to face her and Steph. 'I was a cute baby. No denying it.'

'And so modest, too.'

'Hoi.' Gemma sipped her tea. 'Shame there's no baby pics of you. I would have loved to have seen them.'

Steph wrapped her hands around the steaming mug, letting the warmth seep through her. 'Actually, well, it might not exist anymore, but if you put the right words in Google you can find a picture of teenage me in the Portsoy Journal's archives. That was the local paper,' she added for clarity.

'Shut up,' Gemma blurted. Grabbing her phone. 'What do I need to put in?'

Steph took the phone, figuring it would be quicker for her to just do it. A few clicks and there she was. 'There'd been a fundraiser for the church. That's me with some weather woman off STV or something. I don't really remember who she was. Some local celeb,' she said with a shrug.

Gemma held the phone like it was her most prized possession. A gooey smile curled her lips and added a sparkle to her eyes. 'Look at you. Apart from the brown hair you've hardly changed. How old were you?'

'Barely sixteen.'

A flicker of recognition flashed over Gemma's features. 'Fashion sense hasn't changed either,' she joked.

'Kappa sweatshirts are timeless.'

Gemma swapped the albums about, flicking the closed album to a page containing a spotty, moody teen. 'What do you think, Granny? Would we have been pals?' She showed her the photo on the phone.

Granny pondered. 'No. You were far too grumpy at that age. Still are sometimes.'

'Hey!' Gemma yelped with a pout.

Granny pulled a face at Steph as if to say *told you so*.

'You would have been twelve when that photo was taken. I would have been far too cool for you.' Steph joked.

Granny rose to her feet. 'I've just remembered where my other album is. Wait until you see her with braces.'

Gemma's face contorted into a grimace. 'I'd forgotten about them.'

Margaret was off before Gemma could talk her out of it.

She grabbed Steph by the jumper, pulling her into a kiss. 'I missed you,' she said, their noses touching.

'I missed you too.'

A gentle cough from the doorway stopped an encore. Gemma beamed bright red and focused on smoothing her shirt out; Steph chose to sip her tea.

'If you're done snogging will we get back to embarrassing Gemma? I've got photos of her dressed as Einstein. Steph, make me a fresh cuppa while I get these in order, please.'

Margaret gave Steph's shoulder a shaky squeeze as she dumped the albums on the table.

Steph couldn't believe she'd been nervous to visit. Margaret made her feel like she should already have a picture in the hallway. She couldn't help but grin.

30

'Are you sure about this?' Steph asked, walking level with Gemma after dodging commuters as they passed under Central Station's bridge.

'Definitely. I've had it booked for ages.'

Steph didn't look convinced.

'What?' Gemma asked with a nervous laugh. She skirted around two lost-looking tourists.

'You guys okay?' Steph asked on the way past.

'Central Station?' the man said, his European accent thick.

Steph pointed to the entrance not even a hundred feet away. Poor guy had his back to it. 'Just there.' He slapped a hand to his forehead as he grinned. She jogged level with Gemma again. 'It's a big step, y'know?'

Gemma shrugged. 'I've thought about it for ages. What's the harm? Only you and I will see it.'

She'd thought Steph of all people would be excited about this.

'Plus,' Gemma continued, coming to a halt at the crossing lights. 'I've seen your tattoos. You have similar.'

'Ish.'

'How ish?'

'They weren't my first,' she replied with a wink.

Gemma had settled on a crown to mark her foray into living her truth. It made sense: she was the queen of her own life, putting herself first, allowing herself to be free and finally living a life that made her happy. Plus, Steph had played a massive part in Gemma's journey: whatever happened between them, she would always be her first. Her name literally meant crown. It couldn't have been more perfect.

'Is it because of what it is?' she asked, crossing as the green man appeared.

'No. I happen to find that rather sexy.'

A man did a double take as he passed.

'So why are you worrying?' Another crossing to negotiate, then they'd be at the tattoo parlour.

'It's just, I dunno. A tattoo seems so un-you.'

Gemma pursed her lips. 'Well, a lot of things were un-me until a few years ago.'

'Promise you're not doing it to impress me or something?'

Gemma snorted. 'If you think that, you're kind of missing the point of me getting it.'

'No, I get that,' Steph said hurrying to Gemma's side as she strode across the road. 'Just making doubly sure this is what you want.'

'I've never been more sure.'

Steph grinned, apparently now okay with Gemma's decision. 'You nervous?'

'Shitting myself.'

'You'll be fine. Doesn't hurt a bit.'

'Is that a lie?'

'Completely.'

Gemma grabbed her side, making Steph fold over with giggles.

They were here. Gemma took a deep breath. It was now or never.

'It's small, it will be over before you know it,' Steph said, as if sensing her hesitation.

She'd purposely requested simple, nothing with too much shading or detail. It wasn't necessary. Plus, Steph had said some of her bigger pieces had taken a few sittings, never mind hours. Gemma wasn't sure she could take that kind of pain. This was a token reminder: it didn't need to be a work of art.

Gemma squeezed Steph's hand. 'Hopefully she's already here.'

'Who?'

'Just wait and see,' she replied with a twinkle in her eyes. She pushed open the door to the tattoo parlour, the distant noise of buzzing in the back room making her heart lurch. Her stomach flipped. This was really happening.

Thankfully, a familiar smiling face caught her attention from the saggy leather couch.

Granny looked very funny next to a gothic girl in fishnet tights and little else. She went to rise but Gemma batted the air, signalling for her to stay. She scooted to her side and gave her a hug.

'You're here,' Gemma gushed, relieved she'd actually come.

Steph took a seat on the armchair opposite. 'Margaret, don't tell me you're getting a tattoo as well.'

'I can't let you young 'uns have all the fun.'

'I can't tell if you're joking or not,' Steph replied with a quiet laugh.

She most certainly wasn't. When Gemma had mentioned her plans Granny had leapt at the chance, and luckily her tattoo artist, Harris, was over the moon to be tattooing an eighty-eight-year-old and had shoehorned her into his bookings.

Harris appeared from the back room—heavily tattooed with a bushy beard and inch-wide expanders in his ears—and greeted them with a smile. 'Ladies, you feeling good about today?'

'Most certainly,' Granny announced, sitting a little straighter.

'Good, because we've had a hellish day. I could do with a little laughter.' He ducked behind the desk and produced two clipboards, paperwork already prepared, a pen looped over each. 'If you could fill these out, I'll finish prepping my station. Who's going first?'

Gemma exchanged a look with Granny. 'I'll go first, or I might chicken out.' It was true. Her palms were already clammy.

Granny patted her leg. 'Sounds good to me. Steph can keep me company.'

'Are you really getting a tattoo or are you having me on?' Steph asked again.

'Of course I am,' Granny replied, her attention fixed on the clipboard as she filled her details out. 'You think I'm too old?'

'What? No, no, no,' Steph rambled. 'Just—'

'I'm winding you up,' Granny said with a rueful smile. 'I *am* old. Which is why I want it. If you can't live a little at my age, when can you?'

'What are you getting?'

Gemma sucked on her lips. She'd already gotten

emotional when Granny had declared her intentions the first time around.

'Right here,' Granny replied, tapping her forearm just below the elbow. 'Five hearts, with an initial underneath, one for each grandchild.'

'That's lovely,' Steph said, her eyes tinged with emotion.

Granny shrugged it off. 'I'm very proud of them all.' She gave Gemma's knee another shoogle. 'I would have got one for everybody but I don't know if the old ticker could take that much work. We'll start with this, and if I don't cark it I might add more in the future.'

'Granny,' Gemma scolded, knowing it would do nothing to hold her back.

'What? Always good to have an ambition.'

Steph hid a smile behind her clenched hand.

'Five grandchildren,' Granny said to no one in particular as she returned her attention to the form. 'You know, I nearly ran away and joined a nunnery. I'm quite glad I didn't now.'

Gemma paused her writing. This was news. 'No you did not,' she joked.

'I most certainly did. Was fed up with men. I only stayed because my friend Tina asked me to the dancing. Sometimes life spins on a penny.'

Gemma tilted her head, processing Granny's words.

Harris saved her the bother. 'Right, Gemma, in you come.'

~

'I CAN'T BELIEVE you just got a tattoo on the spot, after moaning at me,' Gemma jibed as she and Steph lay on the sofa that evening.

'What? They had a cancellation, so why not? Hardly the most complex thing I've ever had done.' Steph said, admiring the new line art on the back of her left hand, just below her thumb.

Gemma took hold of her wrist, twisting her arm to get a proper look. A diamond, or as Steph had explained, a gemstone. A tattoo just for her. It made her feel better about the pearl in a shell Steph had on her inner arm, presumably for Maisie.

'Let's see yours again,' Steph said, reaching for the hem of Gemma's joggers.

She lifted her top up and pulled the jogger low. A simple crown, just north of her hip.

'Do you feel like a badass?' Steph asked, kissing the side of Gemma's head.

'A bit, yeah.' She studied the plastic-covered ink. 'I want to look at it in sixty years' time and be proud of how far I've come.'

'Tell the grandkids about the time Granny got a tattoo?'

'Exactly. Although they probably won't be impressed, given how many Other Granny has.'

'Planning on keeping me, then?'

'It's definitely on the cards. Plus, my granny is totally smitten with you, so if I don't keep you, she will.'

'Is she really?'

'Yep, she wants you round for Sunday lunch ASAP. And trust me, she doesn't just ask anyone. Rumour has it my dad nearly didn't get invited at all.' Gemma shifted position, nuzzling closer to Steph. 'Will you come this Sunday? She's going to announce her tattoo to everyone then. If she doesn't accidentally post it online first.'

'I don't want to miss that. Plus, this Sunday might be the only one I have free if I'm going back to work.'

'Still nothing from Boss Brewery?' Gemma felt Steph shift. 'Steph,' she said, drawing her name out. 'Anything from Boss Brewery?'

'I didn't want to steal your thunder with the whole tattoo thing, but yeah. They want me to pop in for a chat next week.'

Gemma twisted and instantly regretted the move as her joggers pushed into her tattoo, sending a jolt of pain through her. Didn't matter though. This was mega. 'Steph! This is so exciting!'

She didn't match Gemma's enthusiasm. 'It's just a chat. Probably won't come to anything.'

'But they're calling you in, that's worth celebrating in itself.'

'Will you get a tattoo of a beer if I get the job?'

Gemma turned further round, looping Steph's arm over her. 'I think I'm going to leave the tats to you from now on. I've got what I needed.'

'Shame. I think you'd look good with a face tattoo,' she joked, poking Gemma in cheek.

'Oh, really?' she replied, laughing as she wrestled her way on top of Steph, a thigh either side of her hips, Gemma's hands on her ribs.

'You'd certainly not be forgotten at all your solicitors' parties.'

'Solicitors' parties?' she repeated, pushing her bum against Steph's thighs as she pretended to wriggle free. 'You really have no idea what I do, do you?'

'Drink coffee and eat donuts. That's about right, is it not?'

'You're for it now!' Gemma yelped as she ducked for Steph's neck, biting and sucking below her ear. She didn't want her to go back to Cal's. Right now, everything was perfectly balanced: if Steph went back her hours meant they'd barely see each other.

Gemma had come back from the cottage a different person. Her brain was brand new. She needed to eat, sleep, and breathe Steph. She'd never experienced this with boyfriends. It was an obsession and one that made her deliriously happy.

If she wasn't with Steph she was thinking about her, finding reasons to text her, to pop round. The only thing tearing them apart was Gemma's job. If she'd known, she would have taken more than a few days off. Surely this feeling couldn't last? Or was this what love felt like?

The tattoo was a big step, but it was always on the cards: connections had just fallen into place. However, she could already sense her heart getting carried away. This was like nothing she'd known before. It was like she'd been asleep her whole life and suddenly she was awake –every sense was tenfold, heightened, like she was feeling it for the first time.

And the sex. Bloody hell. It was a wonder more women weren't lesbians: the amount of orgasms she'd had in the last week was phenomenal. The only thing slowing them down was Steph's period, which had terrible timing. She used to love the excuses her own period brought when it came to the bedroom, but now it was nothing short of a chuffing big inconvenience.

Gemma paused her attack on Steph's neck. 'Are you still bleeding?'

Steph laughed. 'It's been two days, so yes, very much so.'

Gemma groaned. 'It feels like it's been longer.'

'Bad timing, eh?' Steph replied, her hands gripping Gemma's bum.

'I'll say.'

'Shouldn't stop you having fun, though,' Steph said, her voice low as she captured Gemma's lips with her own.

There was no arguing with that.

31

Steph looked down the Clyde as they passed over the expressway, en route to Bearsden for Sunday dinner.

'You okay?' Gemma asked, eyes fixed on the road.

'Yeah, just thinking.' Steph didn't take her eyes off the river below. She was almost bursting with her news but was waiting for the right time. She knew it had to be in person, but now she was face to face with Gemma she wasn't quite sure where to start. Was it that big a deal or had she inflated it in her mind?

Her meeting with Fi had gone fantastically. It was a cracking little set-up, too.

Boss Brewery's unit was in Dennistoun, or as Steph liked to think of it, the Shawlands of the East. The commute would take getting used to – right now she could practically roll out of bed and into work – but it would be worth it. A job in a brewery. Monday to Friday. Normal hours. In a company that didn't take her for granted.

She had a bottle of fizz in the fridge, intent on celebrating with Gemma as soon as she could get the blasted words out her mouth.

'Good thinking or bad thinking?' Gemma asked. Steph didn't need to look at her to know she was smiling.

She couldn't help but reciprocate and bit down on the corner of her lip, scared of the manic grin that was threatening to break free. It was now or never.

She turned to Gemma who eyed her suspiciously. 'I have to tell you something.'

'Uh-huh?'

Was now the right time? In the car, stuck at the traffic lights before the Clyde Tunnel? She'd opened her big mouth; there was no going back. Gemma's brow was creasing more with every passing second.

She'd imagined telling her a thousand different ways since Fi called yesterday evening to confirm everything. Despite their top-notch meeting Steph hadn't wanted to believe it until it was set in stone. And now the contract was sitting in her inbox, it was really happening. Her tummy did a flip at the thought.

Maisie was going to lose it, too.

She'd not actually told her about Gemma. She and Shannon were currently on honeymoon in San Francisco. It felt kind of odd to be messaging her when she was away with her new wife. Steph would need to do a news dump when she got back. She was going to think she'd returned to an alternate universe.

'Steph?'

'Yeah?'

'What's up?' The lights turned green and they entered the tunnel, the passing lights casting flickering shadows over them.

Steph had wanted to play it cool, ham things up a little, but now the time had come she couldn't stop the smile taking over her face. 'I had my interview with Boss Brewery yesterday.'

Gemma's muscles stiffened, a look of amusement clouding her features, her mouth now locked in a stunned smile. 'Oh, really? You kept that quiet. I was starting to wonder when it would be. So?'

She'd felt bad keeping it from Gemma, but nerves were close to getting the better of her. If Steph had had to talk about the impending meeting she would have lost her cool. Much better to deal with it on her own and let Gemma know the good news after the fact.

'It was amazing. Really nice bunch, great set-up, love their ethos, seems like a good place to work. Fi and I just clicked – we basically chatted the whole time. It didn't feel like an interview at all.'

'So?' Gemma asked again, sounding hopeful.

Steph bit her bottom lip, failing to keep her composure. 'She offered me a job!'

They squealed in unison, Gemma drumming her hands against the steering wheel.

'It still doesn't feel real,' Steph chuckled before her eyes turned serious. 'Thank you. I couldn't have done this without you.'

Gemma shrugged. 'It was all you. I just helped write stuff down.'

'Nah. This was all you. If you hadn't taken me to the cottage this wouldn't have happened.'

'I hardly planned that. Pure luck.'

Steph wished she hadn't done it in the car now. All she wanted to do was pull Gemma in for a kiss. And then some.

She studied her profile as Gemma watched the road ahead. She was gorgeous. Sometimes just looking at

Gemma was enough to make her chest tight and desire pop in her belly.

Speaking of tight chests: she'd not had a panic attack since being signed off. A few moments when her heart had done a little freestyling, but nothing that didn't sort itself out. It was a relief. Left alone to amuse herself in the flat, Steph had made the mistake of looking her symptoms up online. She didn't want a lifetime of medication. Chances were they could come back, and maybe they would, but she had high hopes they would never be like what she'd endured recently.

'Anything else you want to share?' Gemma asked with a light laugh. 'You looked like you were in a wee dream there.'

Steph was starting to think she was living in one permanently.

'No more news,' Steph replied, shifting in her seat so she was sitting straighter. 'Just excited for what the future holds.'

Gemma stole a quick look at her. 'Me too.' They exited the tunnel, Glasgow's lead-grey sky visible once more. 'Are you nervous about today?'

Sometimes, Steph wondered if Gemma could actually read her like a book. 'Nah, I've already met your granny. It'll be fine.' A lie: she was nervous as hell to meet the whole family, but Gemma didn't need to know that.

'It will. And thank you again for agreeing to come.'

'Why wouldn't I?'

Gemma shrugged. 'No reason. It's just it means a lot. Especially going early with me. Logan never wanted to do that.'

'What do you mean?'

'I like to see my granny for a bit before everyone else, catch up. Logan didn't want to do that, said it made him uncomfortable. And that he got bored.' Gemma squirmed, like she didn't like talking about him.

Steph nodded. 'Well, I've no problem with it. It's just the gin I'm not keen on.' She placed a hand on Gemma's thigh, giving in a reassuring squeeze.

'Granny always has a well-stocked fridge, I'm sure we'll find something for you.'

∼

'Hello,' Gemma shouted as she let them inside.

'In the kitchen, darling,' Margaret shouted, her voice carrying through the house.

Gemma gave Steph a supportive smile as Steph closed the door. She reached out and took Steph's hand in her own. 'Shoes off and we'll put them at the back door, if that's okay?'

Steph nodded and was about to bend down to undo her laces when Gemma stepped closer, ducking in for a quick kiss.

'It's great having you here,' she said, taking off her shoes.

'Looking forward to lunch. It already smells amazing.'

'Always is with Granny.'

Finally they ventured to the kitchen and Steph dumped their shoes at the back door while Gemma gave her granny a side-on cuddle. She had barely moved from her position at the table, her iPad set out in front of her.

'You okay?' Gemma asked, uncertainty coating her words.

Margaret pulled a face like she was sucking on a lemon. 'I've done something silly.'

Gemma's features turned serious as she pulled a seat out. Steph followed suit.

'How silly?'

Margaret stabbed at the iPad, bringing it to life. 'Bit silly.'

Gemma rolled her eyes. 'Granny, what have you done?' A smile now skirted her lips, severity established.

A few clicks and Steph could see a Tinder profile. Margaret's picture was front and centre.

'Granny!' Gemma yelped. 'What have you done?'

Margaret threw her hands up in mock surrender before waving them in front of the tablet, as if the gesture might make it vanish. 'It was before, when you were having trouble with your dates. I thought I was helping but I couldn't get it to work, so I forgot about it. Well, I went to delete it now you have Steph, and . . .' She trailed off, bringing a hand to her mouth and looking sheepish.

'Granny, this is a profile for you. Look at these pictures,' Gemma said, her mouth agape as she pulled the iPad closer and swiped through the photos.

Steph held her hands over her mouth to contain a snort of laughter at the last photo: a picture of a half-eaten shepherd's pie.

'I didn't put that there. I don't know whose that is.' Granny sulked.

'It's literally this tablecloth.'

It was. No denying it.

Margaret shrugged. 'Can you get rid of it? I don't want this on my tablet. Men are messaging me.'

Gemma's eyes just about left her head. 'What?'

Steph composed herself. 'Does that not mean you matched with them?'

Gemma did a double take. 'Granny! What have you been up to?'

'Match? What does match mean? Like a card game? I did nothing of the sort.'

'Match means you swiped on their profile to say you liked them.'

'I should think not. I don't even know how to swipe, swap, whatever,' Margaret replied, defiance clear.

Gemma brought up potential suitors and swiped through a few. 'It means you did this.'

Margaret's face twitched, realisation hitting. No way was she owning up, though. 'Never in a million years. Look, will you just get rid of them? They want me to be a sugar mummy, or something.'

That did it. Steph's shoulder's shook with silent laughter. Gemma's look of abject horror only made it worse.

'Granny!' She sucked on her lips, hiding a grin as she turned to Steph. 'You see what I have to put up with?'

'Shhh, now. Steph. Grab us all a gin, will you?'

'How's your tattoo, Margaret?' Steph asked, getting three glasses. They were easy to find since that particular cupboard was glass-fronted.

'Very well, thank you. Been using the cream you suggested.'

'Granny! You've replied to this man!' Gemma screeched. Steph leaned over her shoulder, and sure enough she had. Telling him to get off her iPad and that she was only after lesbians. Steph stifled a laugh.

'Where's the gin?'

Margaret pointed towards a cupboard in the corner. 'I didn't want him on my iPad. Can you get rid of him, please?'

Gemma rolled her eyes, still intent on looking at what Granny had been up to. 'I just want to check you've not broken anyone's hearts. Or caused World War three.' She tipped back in her seat, snagging Steph's gaze with her own. 'Can we tell Granny your news?'

Would be a bit hard not to now, but why not? It wasn't like Margaret would be that fussed anyway.

'What's happened?' Margaret asked, looking relieved that the attention had shifted from her.

Steph fixed her eyes on the gin bottle as she poured. 'I, erm, I've got a new job.'

Margaret squeaked. 'At the girl brewery?'

'Boss Brewery,' Gemma corrected with a smile.

'That's the one,' Steph said, still looking at the half-finished drinks in front of her.

Margaret got to her feet as quickly as possible, the chair screeching on the tiled floor. Before Steph knew it she was in a tight hug.

'This is amazing news!' She pulled back, taking Steph in fully. 'You should have said earlier – we could have had the Bollinger chilling.'

Champagne? As if. Margaret was just being sweet.

'Gemma, quick. Go out to the garage and grab a bottle, will you? If we pop it in the fridge we can toast after lunch.'

Gemma didn't need to be told twice.

'Champagne? For me?' Steph asked, still in Margaret's grip.

'Of course! It's tradition when someone in this family does something wonderful. I'm so proud of you,' she gushed, squeezing Steph's biceps.

Steph swallowed hard, happy Gemma wasn't in the room to see the tears rimming her eyes.

32

'Back to work tomorrow then?' Gemma said, taking a seat in Shawlands' hottest brunch spot, Cafella.

'I know. I can't believe it.'

The last week had passed in a flash. Steph hadn't told Cal about her new job, either, thinking it was the kind of thing that should be done in the flesh.

She felt guilty to have sat on the news for the last seven days, but if she told people there was a chance it could get back to Cal's. So for now, only Gemma knew.

The trendy café was hoaching and after a twenty-minute wait for a table Gemma was ravenous. Thankfully, they didn't have to stand about because of Cafella's text-to-table system, so the time had passed in a flash as they wandered around neighbouring shops.

She settled on avocado on toast with poached eggs and ham hock. Cafella's brunch was like no other. Her mouth watered at the thought.

'You nervous to tell Cal?' Gemma asked once the waitress had left them.

'A little. It's for the best, though.'

Gemma smiled. 'I can't wait. Everything is falling into place.'

'All thanks to you.'

'And Lovefest.'

'Hardly.'

'Eh, completely,' Gemma sniggered. 'If I hadn't gone to the matchmaking event this wouldn't have happened.'

'Suppose you're right.'

'Always.'

Two coffees appeared as the table next to them filled.

As good as Cafella's food was, you couldn't be a massive fan of personal space. The marble-topped tables with hairpin legs were packed together, the mismatch of old metal school chairs positioned to maximise covers. The turnover was fast, too: this wasn't a place for lingering. It was all part of the charm, though. Beth was the Queen of Brunch for good reason: the decor and speed was as much of the experience as the food.

'Oh my God, Gemma,' a voice boomed from the freshly filled table.

Shawlands was tiny sometimes. Was no café safe from unexpected acquaintances?

Gemma's face drained of colour, her coffee paused on the journey to her mouth. The smile that had left sparks in her eyes was long gone.

Shit.

'Julie,' she said, placing the cup down. Her eyes assessed the other members of the party. 'Logan.'

Her heart boomed, each beat reverberating in her chest.

Julie. Paul. Logan and Joanne. Wow. The universe had really done her a dirty. She glanced at Logan. He looked as awkward as she felt.

Steph shifted in her seat.

The waitress appeared at their table for a drinks order and it felt like the world let out a collective breath.

'How are you?' Julie asked, her tone far too friendly to be genuine.

'Yeah, good. Just out for some brunch,' Gemma replied, her words timid. Could she conjure an excuse to leave?

'Can you believe the wedding is in a week? Madness.'

'Yeah, gone quick, hasn't it?'

She could feel Steph's eyes boring a hole in her skull. She hadn't introduced them. *Shit, shit, shit.*

Julie saved her the bother. 'Julie, by the way,' she said with a meek wave at Steph.

'Steph,' she replied with a thin-lipped smile.

Silence descended, heavy, thick, and smothering.

They could hardly just go back to their own little world, ignoring the party beside them.

Gemma wanted the ground to swallow her.

'Have we interrupted something?' Julie asked, leaning an arm on the back of her chair as she turned to Gemma.

Gemma furrowed her brow. 'Like what?' she asked with a nervous chuckle.

Julie had one of those faces that pulled taut in all the wrong places: smugness ruled her features. 'I dunno, you just seem a bit,' she paused, not to search for a word, more to pack a punch. 'Weird. Are you on a date?'

Gemma blushed, her heart missing a few beats before stumbling in double-quick time to catch up. The quick glance she gave Steph didn't go unnoticed. 'No,' she replied, shaking her head. 'We're just friends.'

This wasn't the place or the time for judgement, questions, and condescending looks.

Her gaze caught Steph's and an unidentifiable emotion

bridged the gap. She couldn't tell if she was mad or confused.

She'd justify her actions later. Steph would understand. Hopefully.

Julie's coffee arrived but it didn't stop her trying to make conversation. 'Good, because I'd hate to interrupt anything romantic,' she said with a wink. 'Are you seeing anyone yet? Or still coming solo to the wedding?' She sipped her coffee, batting her eyelashes like she was made of sweetness and light.

The flicker of a brain malfunction flashed in Gemma's eyes. She took a draw of her coffee, buying time. Steph did the same, her eyes trained on Gemma. She'd mentioned Julie's wedding plenty of times but she'd never hinted at having a plus one. The idea of taking Steph brought her out in nervous hives.

She wasn't ready. Not yet.

'I'm not bringing anyone, no.' Gemma said, his voice not quite sounding like her own. She avoided Steph's gaze.

Julie narrowed her eyes. 'Something feels off. Are you seeing someone? Why do you not want to say? Logan, cover your ears,' she joked, playfully batting at Gemma's ex.

Gemma put her cup down, feigning an unphased smile. 'It's nothing like that. I'm just tired. A little hungover, if I'm honest.' Lies. They hadn't drank at all last night.

'It's fine if you're seeing someone,' Logan interjected. 'It's not like I haven't moved on.'

This was like watching a car crash, but worse than that: Steph was in the passenger seat, Gemma at the wheel.

'I know. I'd tell you if I was seeing someone. We're adults.'

Steph tried and failed to meet Gemma's eyes. She'd fucked this, but there was no going back now.

'Look, I'll leave the option open. If you find a date then bring her,' Julie said, giving Gemma's knee a patronising tap.

'Better get back on Tinder,' Steph sniped.

Finally, Gemma looked at her, hoping she would see there was more to this than met the eye.

Still, she didn't reply. Instead she shot Steph a stupid, weak smile.

The waitress brought their food but Gemma wasn't hungry. Quite the opposite. Panic and embarrassment sat heavy in her stomach.

The café was tiny, suffocating.

Steph bobbed her head, as if making an internal decision, and stood abruptly.

'I need to go,' she said, getting to her feet. There was no time for awkward goodbyes or pleasantries: she was off.

She slid between the tables and out the door, not a word from Gemma.

'She okay?' Julie said, her face contorted with amused confusion.

'I, erm, I'd better go check.' Gemma fumbled in her handbag and slapped thirty quid on the table, tucking the notes under her cup. That should cover it.

'You not coming back?' Logan asked.

'Probably not.' Gemma grabbed her coat, putting it on as she walked.

The cold air was like a slap in the face. She hugged herself tight, striding down the pavement, towards the fast-moving shape of Steph.

Only the traffic lights halted her escape.

She looked surprised when Gemma appeared at her side.

'Steph, please, let me explain,' she said, her trench coat and hair blowing in the wind.

'Are you ashamed of me?' Steph asked, choosing not to look at Gemma.

'It's not like that, it's just—' The green man interrupted her flow and Steph didn't want to hang around. 'It's a lot to explain.'

'Come on then.'

'What?'

'Explain.' Steph urged, her eyes wide.

It was a struggle to keep up. 'It's just, they're different.'

'Different? To who? Me?' Steph asked, stabbing a finger to her chest.

A lady with a pram gave them a look on the way past. Gemma ignored it. 'Yeah, it's a lot to explain. I'm not ready for them to know about us yet.'

Steph walked in silence for a few metres. 'So you'd rather go alone to a wedding you're dreading, than take me?'

'It's not like that.'

'Really? Because it seems that way.'

Gemma sucked on her top lip, willing herself not to cry.

Steph stopped. They were away from shoppers and prying eyes, up near the houses on Pollokshaws Road. They were nearly at Steph's flat: a chat back there and all this could be cleared up.

'Say it. Say you're not ashamed of me,' Steph demanded, her arms crossed.

The words caught in Gemma's throat. It should have been an easy sentence but she couldn't bring herself to say it.

Steph waited, her eyes unblinking.

Gemma opened her mouth, intent on repeating what Steph wanted to hear, but her brain had other ideas. 'Ashamed isn't the right word.'

'Wow,' Steph groaned, dropping her hands to her side as

she power walked across the road. Safely on the other side she stopped. 'Fuck you, Gemma.'

'Steph, wait,' Gemma shouted, trying to keep pace.

'Just don't, okay? You've done enough. Leave me alone.'

What was she meant to do? Grovel all the way to Steph's flat? Get down on her knees and ask for a second chance? Something told Gemma anything she said now would only make things worse.

She watched Steph disappear round the corner.

33

First day back and it felt like she'd never been away.
Probably didn't help that she was in an absolutely stinking mood from her fight with Gemma.

She'd barely slept last night, flip-flopping between anger, dread, and sadness.

How could Gemma be so callous?

The last few weeks had been amazing, but obviously it meant nothing. Steph wouldn't be someone's dirty little secret.

Gemma had texted plenty of times; phoned a few, too. She'd ignored them all. The damage was done.

Did Gemma think she was better than her, or was she just ashamed to be seen in public with someone like Steph?'

She obviously didn't think her friends would rate her.

If she looked like Izzy no doubt Gemma would be shouting from the rooftops about her new squeeze.

'Good to be back?' Stevie asked with a grin. She'd rushed over to Steph when she arrived earlier, enveloping her in a bear hug.

'Something like that. I'm going to the toilet. Tell Cal I'll not be long if he turns up.'

It was now or never. Better to get this out the way and close one of the tabs open in her head.

She took her time in the toilet, studying herself in the mirror. Guilt twisted in her stomach. She couldn't help but feel she was letting Cal down. But he'd let her down by prioritising Donnie.

The fact he was still here told her everything she needed to know.

This was the right decision.

Cal was waiting for her in a booth when she came downstairs.

She took a seat opposite him. He greeted her with a grin. She could almost believe he'd missed her.

'Cal.'

'Steph. You feeling better?'

'Much.'

His eyes grew sympathetic. 'You don't sound happy.'

'Personal stuff. So, how have things been while I was off?'

Cal nodded, bobbing his head like one of those silly toys people put on their car's dash. 'Good. Interesting. Eye-opening.'

'Not the adjectives I was expecting.'

'I don't think I realised how much you did.'

Wow. Miracles did happen. 'I've been telling you for years.' She kept her voice level, not wanting to gloat.

Cal tensed his jaw. 'I've spoken to Donnie and we've already implemented changes.'

'He's staying?'

'Of course.'

Why did that surprise her?

Cal took Steph's silence to heart.

'Is that a problem?'

'I'm just wondering how anything will be fixed if he's still here? Especially now you know how bad the problem is.'

'I've taken measures. I'm hoping it will put a stop to the bad habits Donnie has developed.'

'Bad habits?' Steph snorted, unable to contain her laughter.

'He got lax, cut corners he shouldn't have, took liberties that weren't his to take.'

'And what about all the pieces I picked up? I don't have to fix his problems now?'

'You're still expected to do your job.'

'Obviously. But you've already admitted you didn't realise how much I did. What about all that?' Her palms were soaked.

Cal laced his fingers together, placing his clasped hands on the table. 'I've hired someone to unpick the accounts and I'll be overseeing rotas, keeping a closer eye on final stock checks. I think that should put a stop to the worst of it.'

'So, more work for you and another body on the payroll. Why's he so special? Why are you desperate to keep him?'

Cal squirmed a little. 'The decision to keep Donnie is mine and you have to respect it, but I'm doing what I can to help you, too.'

She'd come in today almost wanting Cal to convince her to stay. Yes, she was excited about Boss Brewery, but Cal's was home. It would always have a place in her heart. Nothing was changing, though. It was time to let it go. She pulled the envelope from her back pocket and put it on the table, sliding it towards Cal. 'That's my official notice. One month from today I'm leaving.'

Cal's eyes misted. 'Leaving?'

'Yeah. Got a job in a brewery.'

'Wow. I can't lie and say this isn't a shock.'

'I can't go on like we were. You saw how my health suffered. I need to look out for myself for once.'

Cal nodded gently. 'Okay. Well. Nothing I can do to change your mind?'

She shook her head. 'I'm actually really looking forward to my new job. Sorry.'

He pursed his lips, making his beard bush out. 'I think I'm the one who should be sorry.'

∽

Now Lovefest was over, the pub was quiet. The afternoon had dragged by, despite Stevie's best efforts to keep Steph entertained. She wasn't in the mood for jokes and chatter. A black cloud was anchored overhead, threatening to rain on anyone who got too close.

She'd been braced for two things today: her conversation with Cal and Gemma turning up.

Despite knowing what was inevitably coming, her heart still went into overdrive when Gemma turned up later that evening.

She took a seat at the bar.

Steph carried on stacking the replen glasses. Task done, she walked over.

'What do you want?'

Gemma looked like she was ready to cry and Steph felt a stab of guilt in her chest. She wasn't the one in the wrong, though.

'A Savvy B? And in return I can offer you a grovelling apology?'

Looking her in the eye made this so much more difficult. On the one hand, she hadn't changed from the woman Steph was falling head over heels for. On the other, she was now someone completely different, a shallow narcissist only concerned with a selfish, superficial checklist.

'I'm not serving you and I'm not having this conversation with you in work.'

Gemma's face fell further. 'Okay. Well, can we talk after work?'

'I won't be home until one.'

'I can wait up.'

'I'll be tired.'

'Steph.' Her name came out as a squeak.

She steadied herself, swallowing to tamp the emotion swelling in her chest. 'This won't work; there's no point dragging it out.'

'What do you mean it won't work? Us? Do you mean us?'

Stevie glanced from the other side of the bar before busying herself with cleaning. This wasn't the time or the place for a scene.

'Gemma, just drop it. We're done.'

'But,' she said, sliding off her stool and going to the end of the bar. 'It was a silly mistake.'

'A mistake?' Steph hissed, joining her at the end of the bar. An imaginary dividing line kept Gemma on the customer side. 'A mistake is counting something wrong or picking up the wrong spirit when you're making a cocktail. What you did was far beyond a mistake.'

'Can you just give me a chance to redeem myself?'

'There's nothing to redeem. You are who you are.'

'You're really not going to give me a second chance, are you?'

A guy stood at the bar, wanting to be served. Stevie was nowhere to be seen.

'I need to work. Bye, Gemma.' She walked down the bar and Gemma skirted down her side. This was getting embarrassing.

'Steph. One conversation, that's all I want.'

'Bye, Gemma,' Steph said, force behind her words. She fixed her attention on the customer and Gemma took the hint. Steph watched her leave out the corner of her eye as she spoke. 'What can I get for you?'

She barely heard his order: every fibre of her being was focused on not crying. She was so close to the edge, the slightest nudge would tip her over.

She poured what she presumed was the correct beer. He didn't complain.

'I need to go to the office,' she mumbled to Stevie when she reappeared.

Steph jumped when she found Cal in the tatty swivel chair. The office door was open and she turned on her heel to go upstairs. She just wanted two minutes' peace to compose herself.

'Hoi, hold on,' Cal called. She stopped. 'You okay?'

'Yep, fine.'

'That didn't sound fine.'

She took a long, wavering breath before turning to face him. 'You heard that. Sorry. She won't come to work again.'

'Come in, close the door.'

Steph chewed on her cheek as she kicked the door stop away. Cal waited until the door was closed to speak.

'You want to chat?'

'Huh?'

'About your girlfriend?'

The heat on her cheeks was instant. 'She's not my girlfriend.'

'Well, about your break-up, whatever.'

They really didn't have that kind of relationship. It was sweet of him to ask, though. 'It's fine. It's fresh: she's not taking it well.'

'And you? You taking it okay?'

Steph shrugged. 'Is what it is.' She was crushed. She wanted nothing more than to go home and cry.

Cal nodded. 'I'm sorry about us, too.'

'You are?' Despite what had happened, she still had a soft spot for Cal. She didn't think it was reciprocated, though.

'Of course. We've known each other years. You're good at what you do, if I could convince you to stay I would. You'll be happier at your new job though. I know that. They're lucky to have you.' His cheeks blushed. In all the time she'd known Cal he'd never been so honest. It was usually all business with him.

'Thank you. Just my time to go, I guess. It might have been different if Donnie wasn't here, but . . .' She trailed off, deciding instead to end the sentence on a shrug.

Cal pursed his lips, swivelling the chair slightly, as if were a pendulum marking the seconds of silence. 'He's my wife's cousin.'

'Ah.'

Well, fucking hell. That made sense.

'Puts me in a tight spot.'

'I'll say.'

'So in any other circumstances you can probably guess how I would have liked things to turn out.'

'If it helps, I don't have any hard feelings towards you.'

'That's good to hear. And you know you're welcome back

here any time you want. Or if you just fancy a pint, pop in. Staff discount still stands.'

Her emotions wobbled on their knife's edge. Cal being so nice was almost too much.

'I, er, I need to use the loo.'

If only Gemma hadn't been so shit, everything could have been perfect.

34

The taxi stopped outside the church.

Gemma was tempted to tell him to turn around and take her straight back to her flat.

It was too late now. Lottie had already seen her. Hanging out with a bunch of people she'd barely spoken to since she and Logan broke up. Fantastic.

It wasn't that they'd taken his side, so to speak, but Logan didn't exactly take things well. Gemma had found solace in distancing herself and focusing on finding who she really was. Logan had taken solace in beer and bitching about her at parties.

They'd fixed things now. They weren't friends, by any means, but at least they were civil.

'Hey,' Gemma said, joining the huddle in the carpark. She had on the same dress she'd worn to Maisie's wedding but she didn't feel half as confident. At Maisie's she'd felt a million dollars: here, she wished she could keep her coat on and hide away.

Joanne gave her a little smile. She was nice but Gemma couldn't help but feel like a spare part in her presence.

The group echoed their *hellos*.

'How have you been?' Johnny asked.

'Good, busy, the usual. You?'

'Yeah, the same really.'

That about summed it up. She braced herself for a day of staccato conversation.

'Just Gavin to go,' Lottie said, filling the gap.

'Lovely church,' Gemma offered. God, this was tedious.

She'd texted Steph this morning in a last ditch attempt. She'd had nothing but radio silence all week.

She deserved it.

No denying that.

But she also deserved a second chance.

Standing here now, she believed it more than ever. She was a square peg being forced into a round hole. Why the hell had she put these people ahead of the woman she was falling in love with? Who cared what these people thought?

The voice in her head was screaming at her to leave.

'There's Gavin; will we head in?' Johnny asked.

Gemma considered her options. It would be so easy to leave now. But her legs wouldn't comply. Instead, she put on a brave face and walked inside the church.

~

THE CEREMONY WAS bearable but now the awkward bit between that and reception was dragging on forever. They'd been syphoned off to the hotel bar. If only she could close her eyes and be teleported to Cal's.

She downed her glass of champagne.

Logan was best man, so Joanne had been with the group all day. It would seem Julie wasn't the only one hanging out with her regularly. Which was fair enough, but being the outsider with a group you were once front and centre of was a strange feeling.

She looked at her phone again. Nothing.

What was she expecting, though? Steph to magically come around? What Gemma really wanted was for her to be here.

'Are you okay?' Joanne asked when the lads had gone off to find more booze.

'Yeah, fine,' Gemma said, not believing a word herself.

'You weren't right in the café either.' She turned to Lottie. 'We bumped into each other in a Southside café.' Lottie simply nodded, having nothing to add. Gemma's eating habits obviously weren't interesting.

'Just a lot on my mind.'

'Is it to do with your friend? She seemed upset.' Since when was Joanne an expert on her life? She'd barely met the woman.

She should just be honest, but damn, did it feel hard. Was Steph right? If Izzy was the one she'd been spotted with would she feel the same? The thought of laying anyone bare for their scrutiny was terrifying. Was she due a lifetime of this? You didn't come out just once. It was daily. It was like being under a microscope, constantly justifying your actions.

'We were dating. Not any more,' Gemma finally managed. Not too painful.

'Ah,' Joanne replied. No sympathy. Nothing. There were a hundred questions that could have filtered off that. Lottie was silent too. What was the deal?

Talk about a conversation killer.

The trio stood in awkward silence.

She could imagine Steph here, the two of them versus

everyone else. It would still be excruciating, but they could at least have had a laugh.

'I see Julie managed to sort the dress,' Lottie said to Joanne, raising her eyebrows conspiratorially. That was Gemma's love life done with, then.

'What happened to her dress?' Gemma asked, hoping to shoehorn her way into the conversation.

'She lost too much weight, so when she tried it on last night it was far too big,' Joanne replied, rolling her eyes as she rubbed her pregnant bump.

Gemma swallowed her initial reaction: Julie has a major issue and her first port of call is Joanne? And worse than that, Gemma wasn't even privy to the problem now.

'That sounds stressful,' she eventually managed, keeping her tone level. 'How did she fix it?'

Joanne took a deep breath, signalling this was a mammoth story. 'Well, of course, when she phoned me she was freaking out, so I went round, needle, thread, stapler, everything but the kitchen sink in hand, and—'

Logan's arms wrapped around Joanne's shoulders and he kissed her cheek. It was nice to see him so happy, and it certainly eased Gemma's conscience for how things had ended.

She shot him a half-smile.

'Gemma,' he said, standing straight behind his girlfriend. 'How are you?'

'I'm good.' It was all she could manage. She was in no mood for small talk today. Which was a shame. It was all the day had consisted of so far.

He turned to Joanne. 'Julie wants you for photos.'

Gemma's lip twitched. She kept shtum.

Julie's mum and dad had barely registered her either,

apart from an awkward exchange outside the church. It had felt like they couldn't get away from her fast enough.

Gemma searched the crowd for the lads, suddenly aware it would soon just be her and Lottie.

It said a lot that her stomach dropped at the thought of being left alone with someone she'd supposedly been friends with for the best part of a decade.

These people weren't her friends any more.

The biggest surprise was: Gemma didn't really care.

'I need to pop to the loo,' Gemma said, with no intention to return.

∼

HER UBER TOOK AN AGE, but finally she was at Cal's.

Gemma hugged her coat tight around her body as she entered. It wasn't too busy for a Saturday afternoon.

It took Steph an nano-second to spot her. Her face dropped as she mumbled something to Novak.

Unperturbed, Gemma took the only free stool at the bar, deciding to keep her coat on. It was one thing having the balls to come in here: it was another to be so dressed up. She stood out like a sore thumb.

Steph opened her mouth to speak but Gemma cut her off. 'Look,' she said, raising her palm. 'Just pour me a wine. You don't need to talk to me.'

She'd had oodles of courage in the journey over. Now she was here she needed a moment. Suddenly it felt like the world was collapsing around her.

If Steph didn't take her back she was well and truly solo.

How the fuck do you make friends as an adult?

Was there an app for that? Maybe she'd fare better on that than dating apps.

A Sauvignon Blanc appeared in front of her.

She downed half without a second thought. The warmth of the alcohol carried some of her fear away. Or at least boxed it up for later. Out of sight, out of mind.

There was no game plan. But if she could at least get Steph to talk, she was winning.

'Hard day?' the guy on the next bar stool asked.

'My best friend got married.' If you can't offload on a stranger, who can you spill your heart to? Gemma kept her eyes straight ahead, aware Steph was sneaking glances from the other end of the bar.

'Is that not a good thing?' he asked with a quiet laugh.

Gemma stole a look. He was okay. Early thirties. Clean-shaven. Glasses.

She shrugged. The thought of talking to a stranger wasn't appealing any more. She wanted to stomp her feet, make a scene, get Steph to notice her. If she got to her knees, would that be enough?

People must think she was mad. Sitting at the bar in Cal's, in a flipping gown. It was too much. She was mad. Must be to come here and think it would change anything.

The guy went back to nursing his pint.

Steph made eye contact and Gemma motioned her over. Her speed suggested she was walking through tar.

'I'm going to pay for this then go,' she said, fishing in her bag for her purse.

Steph stopped wiping the glass she was holding. 'Are you okay? You seem a little, erm, manic.'

The word froze Gemma's muscles. 'Just realised a few things.'

'Why aren't you at Julie's?'

'Like I said, I realised a few things.' She put a tenner on the bar. Steph ignored it.

'I'll take a break. Let's have a chat.'

Was she really coming across that badly? If it got Steph to chat it didn't matter.

Steph took the money and chatted to Stevie while she got Gemma's change from the till.

Her phone remained silent. Not a peep from her pals at the wedding. Did no one wonder where she'd gone? She shoved it back in her bag.

'Let's go to the office,' Steph said on her way past.

Nothing felt right today. Gemma wanted to blink and slip out of existence. Restart the day. The week. Everything.

Regardless, she followed Steph. She held the door open, closing it behind Gemma.

'Has Julie done something?' Steph asked, leaning against the office desk.

Gemma shook her head. 'No. Just being there, with them, it made me realise how unaligned I was. Everything's a mess.'

She was calm, though. Her heart rate was normal: she was centred, grounded.

'That doesn't sound good.' A nervous smile flickered on Steph's lips.

'Probably not, but I'll be okay once I get my head around things.' Gemma played with a button on her coat. 'Sorry for texting you so much. I'll leave you alone now.'

'Is that what you want?'

Gemma sucked on her top lip, her resolve faltering. 'Of course not, but you deserve better.' She stood, wanting this over with before the tears hit. 'Sorry again.'

The door weighed a tonne when she yanked it open, not bothering to hear what Steph had to say.

What a massive, stupid, mess.

35

For the second time in as many weeks, Steph found herself nervous to knock on a door.

She swallowed her fears and gave three hard raps. It was only on the final knock she noticed the doorbell. *Oops.* She pushed it for good measure.

Noise spilled out of the house, a tirade of children's voices and footsteps.

Two boys answered, their faces streaked with mischief. 'Steph!' they chorused. Gemma pushed her way between them, the twins now jumping and roughhousing in the hall.

'Can we chat?' Steph asked.

Gemma looked like she'd seen a ghost. 'Yeah, course. You'd better come in first.'

She stepped aside and the boys scarpered, tearing through to another room and yelling over each other as they updated the rest of the family on who was visiting.

'You okay?' Steph asked as Gemma closed the door.

'Yeah. Just confused.'

Steph hushed her voice. 'You didn't seem right yesterday.

I just wanted to see you were okay. I thought I'd find you here.'

'Good guess.'

'You wouldn't miss your granny's cooking for anything.'

Gemma led them to the living room.

'Steph's here,' she said, with a flap of her hand in Steph's direction and sounding flatter than ever. 'Will we go a walk?'

'Have you seen outside? It's minging. Cup of tea instead?' Steph asked. She was rooted to the spot, aware all eyes were on her. 'How are you today, Margaret?'

Gemma's granny perked up, shifting her attention from the boys to their visitor. 'Good thanks, Steph.'

'Come through the kitchen,' Gemma said, her voice still monotone.

They padded through, out of the watchful eye of Gemma's family.

Steph stuffed her hands in her pockets as Gemma filled the kettle. Should she sit? She opted to lean on against the unit.

'Nice lunch?' she asked, the smell of Sunday roast still lingering in the air.

Gemma didn't respond; she just nodded. It was like someone had done a hard reset on her but forgotten to load her back up.

'You really don't seem right.'

Gemma shrugged. 'Don't feel it, if I'm honest.' Gemma retrieved two mugs from the cupboard and popped a tea bag in each.

'Don't feel right? What's going on, then? Can I help?'

The kettle clicked off and Gemma filled the mugs with hot water.

'I don't get why you're here.'

'Because I care about you and yesterday it was like watching the start of a breakdown.'

'I wasn't that bad.'

'I know you and I could see the internal monologue playing out in your eyes.'

'Good thing you couldn't hear it.'

'What would I have heard?'

'A mess.' Finally a smile. It was fleeting. But it was there.

She might be mad at Gemma but she still cared. There was more to this than how Gemma had reacted in the café. Steph got that now.

'Why did you leave the wedding?'

Footsteps echoed in the hall and the twins tore into the room. Gemma stood straighter, and her face lifted.

'Auntie Gemma, Steph, we're going to watch a film. Will you come help pick?' one of the boys asked.

Gemma's brother was next to make an appearance. 'Sorry, Gem,' he said, already ushering the boys out. 'Like whippets, these two.'

The boys whined and protested while Archie explained they needed peace. After an age, they were alone again.

Gemma looked at the mugs of tea, then outside and the pouring rain battering off the window. She turned on her heel, grabbing her trainers from by the patio door. 'Let's go somewhere we can talk,' she said, taking a seat and pulling her trainers on.

'Out there?' Steph said, unable to mask the uncertainty of her tone. She'd get soaked in seconds.

'Just for a bit. Let's head to the shed,' Gemma replied, jumping to her feet. She pulled on a jacket from the hooks on the wall. It was slightly too small and looked like it belonged to Margaret. She yanked at the sleeves.

Steph shrugged, still not fully on board with the plan

but happy to go along with it anyway. They could at least talk properly if they were outside.

Gemma opened the patio door and an icy chill swirled into the room. Steph hugged her jacket tight.

It felt farther than the last time she'd been out here. Finally, they were at the shed. Gemma pulled the door closed behind them and flicked the latch: no one was coming in without knocking first.

'Much better,' she said, leaning against the potting table.

It was bloody freezing out here and the noise of the rain battering against the roof was like a ricochet of pellets. The tiny window near the top of the far wall didn't offer much light and she wished the bulb was brighter so she could at least read Gemma's face.

'So? Why did you leave the wedding?' she asked again.

Gemma screwed her face up, thinking. 'I had this moment of clarity. I don't think it's their fault, though. They're just them. They're happy. It's me that's different. They shouldn't have to change. No one should change.'

Steph ran that through her brain once more, tilting her head as she thought. 'It's clear to you that's what matters.' She punctuated her words with a laugh, not meaning for them to sound critical.

Being alone with Gemma was softening the edges of her anger, sanding them down, rounding it into empathy and pity.

'Tell me, straight up, why you didn't want me at the wedding, why you didn't introduce me,' Steph asked. She needed to know. If there was ever a hope in hell that she would forgive Gemma she needed to hear it from her own mouth.

The air was supercharged, the shed tiny.

'Ever since I've come out I've felt under all this pressure

to conform and meet other people's standards and expectations. Maybe it's all in my head,' she said, lightly kicking her trainer into a full bag of compost. 'But it was like . . . they'd already shunned me for not being with Logan. I didn't want any more surprises. If I turned up with someone who could just blend in, merge instantly with their look, et cetera, then I could have a quiet life. I know I'm an asshole, by the way. But you asked, so.' She shrugged again.

'It's okay to crave stability. A lot's changed for you recently. But I don't want to change to fit that.'

'I know.' Gemma stared at the ground and crossed her arms.

'I thought you liked me, so it hurt, you know?'

She nodded. 'I do like you. I don't want you to change. Never. Did you not read any of my texts? It was a moment of stupidity. I don't know what else you want me to say.'

The sound of the rain filled the shed. Steph had so many conflicting emotions flying around her head she was sure she'd rattle if shook.

'What if we bumped into someone next week? What would you say?' she asked.

'There's nothing to say. You hate me.'

Steph edged closer, sliding into position to lean against the table. 'I mean if we were dating again. Would you be comfortable enough to be honest?'

'Of course.'

She smiled, turning her head towards Gemma. 'You sound very sure.'

'Why's that funny?' Gemma asked with a chuckle.

'Just, having witnessed you in action, I'm not so convinced. What if Julie appeared at your granny's house right now?'

'I'd be like, yo, Julie. Why you stalking my granny? I didn't tell you where she lived.'

Steph snorted. 'Okay. Fair enough. And then?'

'Well, why's she here? I might have follow-up questions to that.'

'Gemma,' Steph squealed, playfully grabbing at her side. She'd missed this. She'd missed them. 'Seriously. Would you tell her we were dating?'

She swallowed, not sure she wanted to hear Gemma's answer. They couldn't continue without honest foundations, though.

Gemma pulled her phone out. 'Say the word and I'll make it Facebook official. Let everyone know. I'll put up that photo from the cottage.'

'What photo?' Steph said, her features creased with confusion.

'The one of you kissing my cheek on the bench, when I was on your lap. We were wrapped under the throw.'

Steph considered it. As mad as she'd been, her feelings for Gemma had never faltered. A second chance wouldn't be the worst thing she could do. That would be walking away and forever wondering *what if*. 'Go on then.'

'Now?'

'Second thoughts?'

'No, no. Just, okay, let me compose a caption.'

Steph watched her write and delete again and again, her face tensed with focus.

Was she really going to do it?

Steph leaned back, placing her hand on the table, closing their gap a few more inches. Being with Gemma was so natural. The last week had been torture. She wished she'd hurry up so she could kiss her, but it was cute seeing the concentration on her face as she chose her words. She resisted the urge to read what Gemma was working on.

Perfect caption seemingly decided on, Gemma turned the phone to Steph. 'Does that seem okay? I decided to go simple.'

Steph read the unposted photo: *Love you, @Steph Campbell.*

She wasn't lying when she said simple. Steph chose to ignore the revelation for now: they had other hurdles to negotiate before she could process anything close to the L word.

'It's perfect,' Steph said, grinning. 'But you don't need to post it. The thought's enough.'

Gemma snatched the phone back. 'No, no. I want to. And do that relationship request thingy,' she said, twirling a finger over her phone screen.

Steph gently placed her hand around Gemma's arm. 'You do what you feel comfortable with. But as it stands, I think we should give things another bash. Any more nonsense and I'm out, though.'

Gemma sucked on her lips, her eyes still on the phone cradled in her hands. 'You mean it?'

'Of course. Now you going to kiss me, or do I need to keep talking?'

'I thought that was what you did anyway?'

Steph cut their laughter short by putting a hand on Gemma's jawline and guiding her closer. God, she'd missed those lips.

The wind picked up, battering a fresh deluge of rain against the shed, and Steph felt goosebumps flush over her skin. The cold was a distant memory, though; only the heat of Gemma's lips and tongue registered.

She slid her hand under Steph's jacket and took a

handful of jumper in her grip, using it to pull her closer. Steph responded by using Gemma's thigh as a lever and angling herself to get as near as humanly possible. The table creaked below them.

'I missed you,' Gemma said, pulling back as she peeled the tight jacket off and placed it over the nearest spade handle.

'It's been a shit week, hasn't it?' Steph mumbled into Gemma's mouth as she found purchase again.

'Still time to turn it around,' she replied, standing up and slotting herself between Steph's legs. She leaned in, their faces millimetres apart. 'I promise I'll never take you for granted again. Now I want to show you just how I feel.'

36

Gemma cupped Steph's centre, heat obvious through her jeans, as she sat on the edge of the table.

She pulled back from their kiss, her face close enough for Gemma to feel her breath on her skin. 'Here?' Steph asked, the word almost lost to the howling rain.

'Why not?'

She smiled, her eyes shining. 'Because your family is in the house.'

'So? The door is on the latch. No one can come in.'

Gemma waited. If she looked hard enough she could probably see the scales of indecision teetering in Steph's eyes. Finally they tipped and she announced her choice with a chaste kiss, scooping Gemma closer.

The already-growing fire roared in Gemma's belly. She'd thought about this moment all week, played it out a thousand different ways in her head.

Had she foreseen it happening in her granny's shed? Definitely not. But beggars can't be choosers and she wasn't going to let this moment slip.

She pushed her thigh against Steph's centre, her jeans

preventing Gemma from getting as close as she wanted. But it was fine. She wanted to prolong things, gain the maximum amount of pleasure after imagining it for so long.

Gemma rocked, the squeak of the potting table marking her rhythm. Steph angled her hips, trying for better friction.

She could cry with happiness, but pushed the emotion as low as possible. She wanted to scream and shout and do a silly little dance: Steph was giving her a second chance. Gemma could do that later, though. Now, her sole focus was getting Steph's jeans off.

With a shaky hand she lifted Steph's jumper and found the top button of her jeans. She popped it open and stilled her hand on the zip.

Steph's lips pulled into a smile. Her breath quickened.

Gemma held, her own lips battling to grin, but she stayed in character, keeping her excitement under wraps.

Today she was cool, calm Gemma. Master of Steph's body.

When it seemed like Steph could take no more she slowly slid the zip down. The motion bought a little space and Steph responded by opening her legs wider, Gemma's thigh pushing harder against her centre.

'I'm allowed to touch you?' Gemma asked, punctuating the sentence with a light bite on Steph's bottom lip. She held it between her teeth, pulling gently before releasing her.

'Yes.' If Steph had said it any quicker Gemma might have doubted she'd heard it at all.

Gemma snaked her hand inside Steph's jeans, the scratchy zip catching on her skin. She skirted her fingers over the fabric of Steph's pants, relishing how wet they were.

The angle was all wrong but she wasn't willing to sacrifice the proximity.

'These jeans need to come off.'

Steph shimmied, the jeans falling to rest at her ankles. They were still restricted, but it was enough. Plus, where was the thrill without a little challenge?

She pushed Steph's pants to the side, her fingers easily finding her wetness. Gemma ran a finger up the centre of her core, teasing Steph closer to the edge.

Her own breath fractured as she dipped her fingers lower before driving them inside. Steph arched her hips, begging for Gemma to go deeper.

She quickly found a rhythm, her thigh helping to drive her fingers to exactly where Steph wanted them.

The moment was surreal, like she was watching herself from the outside. She'd helped her grandfather plant seeds at this table, now here she was, touching a beautiful woman as its legs threatened to fold beneath them.

'Fuck,' Steph moaned into Gemma's ear, urging her to continue.

She'd been so scared to first touch a woman, petrified of doing it wrong, like figuring things out later in life would put her at a disadvantage. But it would seem the skill came naturally to her.

Everything was easier with Steph, though. There was never any pressure.

Guilt twisted in Gemma's stomach, the realisation of how close she was to losing something so special hitting her between the eyes.

It only made her work harder; this was all about showing Steph how she felt. She hadn't recoiled when Gemma had said she loved her. She'd considered saying it all week but it wasn't the type of thing you blurted over text. Especially when there was radio silence on Steph's end.

Seeing her today though, it was the only option. Why

not be honest when she'd dug a hole anyway? The worst had already happened.

She dipped her head, finding Steph's neck, and kissed her below the ear. She smelled amazing. Hopefully they could spend tonight together too, make up for lost time.

Gemma shifted, moving her arm into a better position so she could bring her thumb into play. It swiped Steph's clit with purpose, matching each thrust of her fingers.

The old table creaked, banging against the side of the shed.

Gemma worried about her family for the first time.

Nah, no one would be out in this weather. Not when they knew they were having a chat. Besides, they'd not said they were coming here. They could be on a walk for all they knew.

'I'm so close,' Steph panted, snapping Gemma back to the moment.

She could feel it. Steph's clit was so hard Gemma could almost feel a pulse. She slowed her pace, savouring how Steph felt, the way her clit moved under her thumb, how her internal walls tightened the closer she got.

Three words lodged in Gemma's throat, growing bigger by the second, a fresh weight crushing her chest.

She had to say it.

Didn't matter if Steph didn't say it back.

'I love you,' Gemma whispered as Steph came.

Steph gripped her wrist, bringing Gemma's hand to a halt between her legs. The sound of their breathing merged with the rain, and they leaned against each other, safe in their own wee bubble, Gemma's heart thundering against her ribs, threatening to explode at any moment.

Steph moved first, giving Gemma a quick kiss. 'I love you

too.' Her eyes said she meant it: this wasn't some hazy, post-sex declaration.

Gemma swallowed, the emotion she'd dammed earlier looming closer to the surface.

She scooped Steph into an embrace and nestled into her neck.

They held each other, their breathing evening out, and Gemma's heart returning to a normal pace.

'Hold on,' Gemma said, bolting her head upright. 'I never posted our photo.' Steph chuckled as Gemma reached for her phone, still holding Steph tight with her other hand. A few clicks and it was done. She returned to Steph's shoulder, her hand now finding its way under Gemma's jumper and stroking her back.

'So that's us official, then?' Steph asked.

'It would seem so. That okay?'

'I'm just wondering where you're taking me for dinner. You know, to celebrate.'

Gemma stood straighter, her hands gripping the top of Steph's thighs. 'Oh, I'm taking you out, am I?'

'Erm, yes,' Steph said with a grin. 'You have a lot of making up to do. I'm going to be milking it for a while.'

Gemma nodded slowly, a smile twitching at the edge of her lips. 'Fair enough. Well, in that case, I think we should get a pizza or something delivered, repeat the performance I just gave a few times, and cement my intentions so you know I really mean it.'

'I could cope with that,' she replied, leaning forward for a quick kiss. 'Now, let's go in, before I get splinters in my bum.'

THREE MONTHS LATER

'Are you not totally stuffed?' Gemma asked, rubbing her belly.

'I am,' Steph replied, as she pulled her boots on. 'But I promised the boys, so there's no going back.'

'You're a better woman than me.' Steph couldn't contain the grin when she fully took Gemma in. She looked almost drunk with happiness, her half-closed eyes hinting sleep was threatening and her paper crown lopsided on her head.

It had been Steph's best Christmas in years.

'Will you not join us?' Steph asked, doing up her laces.

Truth be told, she was rather looking forward to building a snowman with the twins. Even the mountain of food they'd just consumed wouldn't put her off.

Gemma struggled to sit up straight. 'I'm worried I'll be sick,' she said with a chuckle.

'Nonsense. It'll burn it off quicker, make room for pudding.'

Gemma looked over her shoulder, in the direction of the kitchen, despite the walls between them. 'True.' She hauled herself up. 'Right, I'll get my boots.'

The low rumble of thundering trouble roared through the hall, eventually coming to a stop as two snowsuited boys tumbled into the living room. They could barely walk for the clothes they had on: sno suits topped with bobble hats, not to mention the full outfits underneath, Christmas jumpers and all.

'Auntie Steph, are you ready yet?' Noah asked, clapping his gloved hands together.

Steph grabbed her woolly hat off the radiator. 'The real question is: are you ready? This is going to be the tallest snowman there ever was.'

Leo thrust a carrot towards Steph. 'Daddy says we need this.'

She took it in her hand, pretending to examine it carefully. 'We certainly will. Will we give it to Auntie Gemma to look after?'

Noah scrunched his face up. 'Maybe. She's not even got her boots on.'

Steph watched as Gemma struggled to pull them on.

This was a job better done without an audience.

'Come on, boys. Let's go outside,' Steph said, ushering them from the room.

She stopped on the way past the living room, peeking around the door frame to the five adults scattered around the table.

'Are you sure you don't want me to help clear the table?' Steph asked Margaret.

She waved her away. 'Nonsense. You go play outside.'

'Better you entertain the troops and we let our food go down,' Gemma's dad said, patting his belly.

'Just call when you need us in,' Steph replied.

A small gloved hand yanked at hers. 'Come on, Auntie Steph, you're taking ages,' Noah whined.

Steph grabbed him under the arms and tickled as they ran through to the kitchen. 'Careful, mister. Or you'll be getting chucked in that snowdrift.'

The look in Noah's eyes said Steph had just given him a brilliant idea.

She was battling with the stiff patio door when Gemma entered the kitchen. Finally, it flew open and a blast of cold air tickled Steph's skin. The boys ran into the garden, only pausing to pick up snow to throw.

Gemma put her arms around Steph and rested her head on her shoulder. She squeezed tight, kissing her cheek. 'Had a good day?'

'The best. I think everyone else is happy too?'

'I'll say. I think you've got Archie drunk, though. Did you see how red his cheeks are?' Gemma replied with a mischievous giggle.

'Boss Brewery's not for the weak.' She turned, her nose now touching Gemma's. The boys were content enough to be playing on their own. Snow flew in the air as they dived around. 'And you've had a good day, yes?'

Gemma nibbled Steph's bottom lip before replying. 'It's been unforgettable. You've certainly set the bar high.'

They'd enjoyed a morning of sex and a flute or two of champagne as they opened presents before going to Gemma's granny's. If you can't go all out at Christmas, when can you?

'Not as high as your parents. I still can't believe all the presents they got me.'

Gemma squeezed her tight. 'It's because they love you.'

A lump formed in Steph's throat. 'The feeling's mutual,' was all she could manage before serious emotion threatened.

A snowball whacked off the window with a thud,

evaporating all sentimental thoughts and making them disappear like the powdery snow being lost to the air.

'Come on!' roared Noah, in a fit of giggles.

'Better hurry up or we'll stand no chance,' Gemma said, releasing Steph from her grip.

'Quickly though,' Steph urged, checking her phone before putting it back on the window sill. 'Daniel is dying to confirm you'll come early tomorrow.'

'Is he still freaking out?' Gemma pulled her woolly gloves on, clapping them together as if to better position them.

'Just a bit.' It was Aiden's fortieth and Daniel was intent on throwing the surprise party to end all parties, Boxing Day or not. He was currently having an eleventh-hour meltdown, his confidence wavering. Probably because he'd switched a fire dancer for a tin drum performance. The whole thing went over Steph's head, but Gemma took it all in her stride. She had a way with Daniel, and Steph was glad they'd become close friends over the last few months or he would be unbearable just now.

'If you're still fine to keep Aiden in the pub, I've got no issue spending the day with Daniel. Why didn't he text me?'

'He said he did. But you've not replied.'

Gemma checked her phone on the kitchen counter. 'He messaged ten minutes ago. He knows it's Christmas Day, yeah?' she asked with a chuckle.

'Let's leave him a while. Play with the boys. Otherwise you'll be getting frantic texts all evening.'

Gemma watched her nephews over Steph's shoulder, and content they were entertaining themselves, she pulled Steph in for another kiss. 'I don't mind. He's nervous, that's all.'

'I don't know what I did to deserve you.'

'I often think the same about you.'

LEAVE ME A REVIEW?

Will you leave me a review?

I hope you enjoyed Love Magnet. If you have a moment I would really appreciate an honest review on Amazon and / or Goodreads. Reviews help me grow as an author and help new readers know what to expect. The more people that take a chance on my books, the more books I can write. It doesn't need to be anything fancy, a few words will do. Thank you.

∽

Allie McDermid is a lesbian romance author. Her debut novel, Love Charade, was published in July 2022.

Born and raised in Perth, Allie now lives in Glasgow with her ever-growing gang of cats. She is partial to a good scone.

ALSO BY ALLIE MCDERMID

Want to know what happened at the first ever Lovefest?

LOVE CHARADE

Holly Taylor didn't expect to return to Glasgow. And she certainly didn't expect her parents to enter her into a dating competition on her first day home.

Jen Berkley is happily single. Having vowed to never date again after her horror ex broke her heart, no one is more surprised when her best friend convinces her to take part in a dating contest.

Jen wants to win the money. Holly wants to regain the trust of her parents. Will they get what their hearts desire or will the charade fool no one?

Set in Glasgow and full of Scottish charm as well as lashings of delicious desire, smouldering sexual tension and even a few laughs, buy Love Charade today and find out if some things just can't be faked...

ALSO BY ALLIE MCDERMID

Missed what happened at the second year of Lovefest?

LOVE DETOUR

Kirsty Hamilton would do anything for family, but when her mother insists she enters a dating contest to publicise her cafe, her commitment is put to the test.

Rhona Devi dreams of travelling the world. When she takes on a photography job to earn some cash, she never expects it to lead to her biggest adventure yet.

Rhona thinks she deserves a chance. Kirsty doesn't see the point. Will they be able to meet somewhere in the middle?

Book two in the Lovefest series features a love on a time limit romance oozing with sexual chemistry and flirtatious banter. Buy Love Detour today and see if love truly can defy the odds.

Printed in Great Britain
by Amazon